HIGHLANDER IN MUSCOVY

by

Janet MacLeod Trotter

a tale of treachery, secrets and undying love

(One of the Scottish Romance Collection)

Published by MacLeod Trotter Books

Paperback edition: 2019

ISBN 978-1-908359-58-2

www.janetmacleodtrotter.com

About the Author

Janet MacLeod Trotter was brought up in the North East of England with her four brothers, by Scottish parents. She is a bestselling author of 24 novels, including the hugely popular India Tea Series, and a childhood memoir, BEATLES & CHIEFS, which was featured on BBC Radio Four. Her novel, THE HUNGRY HILLS, gained her a place on the shortlist of The Sunday Times' Young Writers' Award, and the TEA PLANTER'S DAUGHTER was nominated for the RNA Romantic Novel Award and is an international bestseller. IN THE FAR PASHIMINA MOUNTAINS was shortlisted for the RNA Historical Romantic Novel of 2019. A graduate of Edinburgh University, she has been editor of the Clan MacLeod Magazine, a columnist on the Newcastle Journal and has had numerous short stories published in women's magazines. Find out more about Janet and her other popular novels at: www.janetmacleodtrotter.com

By Janet MacLeod Trotter
Historical:

In the Far Pashmina Mountains

The Jarrow Trilogy
The Jarrow Lass
Child of Jarrow
Return to Jarrow

The Durham Trilogy
The Hungry Hills
The Darkening Skies
Never Stand Alone

The Great War Sagas
No Greater Love (The Suffragette)
A Crimson Dawn

The Tyneside Sagas
A Handful of Stars
Chasing the Dream
For Love and Glory

The India Tea Series
The Tea Planter's Daughter
The Tea Planter's Bride
The Girl from the Tea Garden
The Secrets of the Tea Garden

Scottish Romance Collection
The Jacobite Lass
The Beltane Fires
Highlander in Muscovy

Mystery:
The Vanishing of Ruth
The Haunting of Kulah

Teenage:
Love Games

Non Fiction:
Beatles & Chiefs

Short Stories:
Ice Cream Summer

***

PROLOGUE

Moscow, May 1682

Dr Ewen Putulo gazed uneasily from the large first storey window of his home, across the deserted square and the elegant brick mansions of the Foreign Quarter.

The only noise in the deathly calm was the listless splash of the fountain. No children played, no merchants called to each other down the leafy avenues, no ladies took the air. All were barricaded behind locked doors, waiting and fearful.

At any moment the bloodbath gushing through the streets and palaces of the royal Kremlin fortress could boil over and swamp the fragile safety of Moscow's foreign enclave. Was it only two days ago that his beloved Sybil had given birth to their second daughter and they had rejoiced at the happy event? Away across to the west, the golden domes of the city flashed in the harsh fiery sunset, bold and ominous.

'Sir,' an urgent voice broke through the doctor's thoughts. He turned to see Fiona the housemaid hurriedly entering the drawing-room, her pale thin face anxious under the severe white cap. 'Sir, there is someone beating at the back entrance,' she gasped, 'I'm afraid to open up–'

'I'll go,' Ewen Putulo said at once, glad of the diversion from fearful imaginings. 'Does your mistress sleep?'

Fiona nodded. 'And the bairns too, the Lord be thanked.'

'Good,' he smiled tenderly as he thought of them. 'Now go upstairs and lock yourself in with them,' he ordered more briskly. 'I may be needed somewhere in the Quarter and I don't want you to move, do you hear?'

'But master,' Fiona protested, 'it's too dangerous–'

The doctor recognised the beginnings of a Presbyterian sermon and cut her short.

'Don't be afraid,' his deep set eyes filled with kindness in the tired lined face, 'I will be careful for all our sakes.'

The pounding grew louder as Ewen Putulo headed down the back stairs, anxiety gripping him once more. 'I'm coming,' he shouted and pulled back the iron bolts.

A tall peasant dressed in a rough cloth shirt tied at the waist with string and baggy trousers stuffed into cloth leggings, stood before him. The doctor stared in surprise; the man appeared to be alone, his bearded face shadowed by a worn fur cap in spite of the warm evening.

'Putulo, please in God's name let us in!' The man gripped the physician's arm with iron strength. This forceful man was no peasant; Ewen Putulo recognised his lilting voice and raised the lamp to search his face.

'James MacQueen!' he gasped in disbelief at his old friend. 'What is one of the Tsar's officers doing dressed like a Russian woodsman?' For a moment he wanted to laugh out loud at the comical appearance of this proud Highland chieftain, but the grim shocked face dispelled his mirth. Sweat ran down his dust-stained cheeks and brow. He seemed on the point of fainting; the doctor steered him onto a rough kitchen chair.

'Ewen, it is my wife,' James MacQueen fretted, eyes glazed with pain. 'You must help Katya. She's outside–'

Ewen Putulo turned and strode quickly back across the courtyard to a cart half hidden by overhanging trees heavy with blossom. A small delicate woman lay enveloped in a coarse loose gown and as he gently coaxed her down, he felt the largeness of her belly. The poor woman was heavy with her unborn child.

'Come my dear,' he spoke to her soothingly, concerned by the feverish flush of her dark handsome face and the huge slanting eyes filled with terror, 'you will be safe here with us, you and the child.'

She did not answer, staring fixedly ahead as he helped her indoors. The doctor remembered James MacQueen had caused a scandal in both the Russian and foreign communities by marrying a lower ranking Russian princess, but his military skills were so sought after that Tsar Fedor had smothered the criticism of his xenophobic Muscovite nobles. Ewen Putulo had often wondered what James' father, the old Chief of MacQueen had thought of the match. This was the first time he had ever set eyes on the beautiful princess, for she had remained a recluse in the Russian manner despite her marriage to an 'infidel'. He understood why the forthright James had ignored opposition to the match.

'She does not understand what you say,' MacQueen said wearily as the doctor helped her inside. 'And the sights of these past two days have left her speechless ...' His voice trailed off as the vivid nightmare of the carnage in the Kremlin squares and palaces overwhelmed him anew.

He had dragged Katya from the tiny windows of the *terem*, the women's quarter, as the rampaging Streltsy guards skewered her relations onto their pikes and trampled them underfoot in a hate-fuelled orgy of bloodletting. MacQueen retched now at the memory of the soldiers' blood-spattered green and blue coats, their yellow boots stained dark red as they guarded the piles of dismembered bodies in front of St Basil's Cathedral.

Ewen Putulo asked no questions, but called for Fiona and set about making them comfortable in an upstairs room, bidding his nervous maid boil water for washing and prepare glasses of vodka and a plate of smoked fish with which to revive them.

Later, while Katya slept fitfully upstairs the doctor joined the chieftain in the drawing-room. MacQueen sat in the shadows below a gilded mirror, the room lit pink by an eerie summer's night sky. Behind him a clock chimed prettily inside an inlaid cabinet and he found it unbelievable that so much horror could be going on so close to this quiet civilised home.

The doctor regarded his friend. It was some time since he had seen him, for MacQueen's profession as mercenary soldier kept him away from the Quarter for long periods. The aquiline nose and strong square face – bearded in the Russian fashion – was the same, proud and regal. But the grey eyes were dark-ringed and new lines around his mouth scored the handsome face and spoke of his harrowing escape. MacQueen threw back his vodka and began.

'It was terrible,' he whispered, 'even the Tartar hordes are not so barbarous. They could not hack the boyars and princes into small enough pieces, these devils that call themselves the Kremlin's guards! Even Tsar Peter is threatened and he a boy of ten. They think his family poisoned Tsar Fedor, but it is just an excuse to take revenge on some of the nobles.' MacQueen shook with anger and his friend filled up his glass and let him continue.

'I tell you none of us are safe Ewen; they are hounding out foreigners as well as the Naryshkin royals. They think we are about to take over the army,' he laughed harshly, his look bleak. 'Would that I had never set foot in this barbarous country.'

'You would never have met your beautiful wife then,' Ewen Putulo added gently. James MacQueen met his steady compassionate look, feeling unaccustomed tears of exhaustion and sadness sting his eyes.

'Oh, my dearest Katya,' he shuddered, 'she will never be the same after this insanity. She has not spoken one word since witnessing the murders from the Kremlin palace windows. I tried to cover her eyes as we escaped through the bloody streets, but I could not protect her from the screams and the murderous shouts of the crowd.' The chieftain grew agitated again and leaning forward, gripped the doctor's arm. 'You are a good physician, Ewen, tell me what you think. I fear she does not even recognise me anymore.'

For a moment Ewen Putulo hesitated, and then he gently removed his friend's hand and stood up, walking to the un-shuttered window. He thought of the silent woman upstairs, too deep in shock to respond to Fiona's kindly ministering. Such a traumatic episode might well bring on her labour and he feared she might not be strong enough to go through with it.

'She must stay here until she has had the child,' the doctor spoke matter-of-factly, 'for her to travel now in such a state of shock would be folly. She would almost undoubtedly lose the baby and her own life would be in danger too, James.'

'No!' the other man got to his feet and clattered his glass onto the delicate table. 'We have placed you in enough danger by coming here tonight, I must get Katya safely away from Moscow. We will find a passage back to Scotland with one of our merchants. Besides Katya is a strong woman–'

'I won't hear of her travelling in such a condition,' Ewen Putulo was firm. He turned to confront the black bearded chieftain and spoke more gently. 'Do you have any idea how long it might take you to reach Archangel? Weeks on those rough roads in the summer dust and heat would tire the fittest of women. Your wife is about to give birth and she has suffered too much already.'

The doctor's gaunt face and kind dark eyes shone in the glow of the lamplight. He pitied his friend and the decision he must make, but he was not going to risk the life of the woman upstairs whom Ewen Putulo now thought of as his patient.

'You must leave tomorrow alone,' he continued with quiet authority. 'If they want you as a scapegoat for the many foreigners who make their living here in Muscovy, then you only endanger all our lives by remaining here.'

'But how can I leave Katya?' James MacQueen almost sobbed in his frustration.

'Because it is the safest thing you can do,' the doctor steeled himself against his friend's obvious anguish. 'My wife Sybil has just given birth to our second daughter. If necessary we can pass Princess Katya off as her wet-nurse when her baby is born. It is unlikely that anyone will come asking questions and the blood-letting will stop like a staunched wound soon enough.'

James MacQueen bit on his knuckles but did not argue, so the doctor went on. 'You must make your own way to Archangel. Arrange a ship and wait until I get word to you that your wife and child are strong enough to travel,' Ewen Putulo instructed. 'If all goes well you should be able to leave Muscovy with your family before the port freezes over at the summer's end.'

James MacQueen sank back into his chair with sudden exhaustion. He did not have the will to fight his friend's logic although he was grief-stricken at the thought of leaving Katya so abruptly and in such a tortured state of mind. But perhaps if they could get back to Scotland safely, the wild beauty of his lochside fortress at Penstroun would be a place where she could heal her wounds. He tried to imagine his quiet, proud Russian wife running affairs in his ancestral home, yet the picture would not come. She had never been out of Moscow before, hardly out of the maze of palaces and churches of the Kremlin where he had first espied her and fallen in love. He hung his head in despair.

'Come James,' Ewen Putulo laid a hand on his shoulder and gently shook him, 'I will do my best for her.'

The chieftain looked up gratefully and determined to lift himself out of his self-pity. 'You are a good man,' he smiled, 'and a true friend. I could not leave Katya but for knowing that she is in the kindest of hands with you and Sybil.'

The doctor smiled back. 'You must get some rest now; you have a long journey ahead tomorrow.'

They regarded each other in silence, each plagued with unspoken doubt. Suddenly the tall Highland chieftain stood up and clasped the doctor in a firm embrace.

'So be it,' he said hoarsely.

Behind them, through the wide Western-style windows, the blood-red sunset seeped into the uneasy mauve of the short summer's night.

Scotland, 1689

The rain splashed down relentlessly on the captured remnant of Graham of Claverhouse, Viscount Dundee's Highland army, as they huddled for shelter under their sodden plaids. The groans of their wounded and dying comrades lying in the mud of the battlefield around Dunkeld Abbey were all but drowned out by the Presbyterian psalm singing of the victorious government troops.

Alexander Ballantyne closed the eyes of his dead father and pulled his plaid over his lifeless face. Angry tears swelled in the youth's throat as he watched the pious thanksgiving of the supporters of the usurping Dutchman, William of Orange, who now called himself King of the Scots. To him they were traitors to the rightful Stuart monarch, King James VII, who had been forced abroad, and the sight of their rejoicing around the warm fires sickened him.

For the first time Alexander realised how cold and hungry he was and he stood up and wrapped his plaid tighter about his tall frame.

'Which one of you is Ballantyne of Culduggan?' a soldier appeared out of the gloom. Alexander felt a bitter twisting of fresh grief inside.

'This is him,' he answered in English and stood protectively beside his father's body. 'But you are too late if you wish to execute a loyal subject of King James,' Alexander added disdainfully, 'my father is dead.'

'You'd do best to curb your savage Highland tongue,' the soldier snapped and swiped him in the ribs with the butt of his musket. The young Ballantyne doubled up with the sharp pain and the soldier laughed. 'Well if you're the brat of the dead savage, you're the one I'm looking for. Move in front of me,' he ordered and made to hit him again.

Alexander stiffened and raised his head proudly. 'What do you want with me?' he glared back.

'For some reason Sir Archibald Maitland wants to see you,' the soldier spat contemptuously on the ground. Alexander was surprised to hear of the noble's presence in Dunkeld; he was not one to put himself in danger or the forefront of action. Since he had married Christina MacQueen, sister of Alexander's own Chief James, Maitland had played a careful game of switching loyalty between Protestant Dictatorship and Stuart Kings.

Now, Alexander thought disgustedly, it would seem he was for the Revolution that had placed King William and Queen Mary on the thrones of England and Scotland. It was just like Maitland to wait and see the outcome of the battle before arriving to pick over the spoils.

'Personally I'd string the lot of you up and let you rot,' the soldier added and pushed Alexander forward.

He was led up the steps of a small house in the main street of Dunkeld, obviously commandeered by the military and from the pervading smell of sheep's fleeces, Alexander guessed it belonged to a wool merchant. The well-guarded door opened into a brightly lit furnished room, the merchant's best silverware gleaming in the candlelight.

At one end of the heavy oak table laden with bottles of claret, a man rose at his arrival. Young Ballantyne recognised the short stocky frame of Archibald Maitland, brother-in-law to Alexander's Chief, James MacQueen. He wore a heavy wig that fell either side of his thick jowl, but the focus of his face was the dark patch over his left eye that seemed to mask all expression. Some claimed he had received a glancing shot that should have taken his head off, while serving with the army under the Commonwealth. Others less kindly alleged he had his eye poked out in a brawl with a fellow Lowlander over money.

'Young Ballantyne,' he smiled and gestured for the rain-sodden Highlander to sit. Alexander stood his ground stubbornly. 'It is unfortunate we should meet under such unhappy circumstances,' Maitland continued, ignoring the slight. 'I had heard you were doing well in your studies at Aberdeen, is that not so?'

Alexander stared at him in silence. Maitland's pretence at friendliness evaporated and he sat down abruptly.

'It was foolish of you to join your headstrong father in this charade of Dundee's,' he said coldly. 'Dundee got his just deserts at Killikrankie; a pity you had not decided to end the childish game then and returned to your books.'

'King James's army was victorious at Killikrankie,' Alexander was stung out of his defiant muteness by his enemy's words. He remembered with pride for a fleeting moment, the thrill of the charge down the slopes of the Pass, scattering the regiments of General Mackay along the River Garry. 'We would have routed you here at Dunkeld if Claverhouse had lived!' He wanted to add that had their brave leader done so, Maitland himself would no doubt have joined their camp and be now drinking toasts to King James and not William of Orange.

'Brave words for a boy of fifteen,' Maitland sneered quietly, 'I hear you were quite the little soldier at Killikrankie.'

Alexander bit on his lip, realising this insufferable man was delighting in provoking him. It was better to remain silent.

Maitland eyed him with one watery brown eye. 'Anyway, what's done is done,' he spoke more brusquely. 'James Stuart will never return; the country has rejected his villainous rule and will profit under the leadership of Their Majesties King William and Queen Mary.'

He stood up and began to pace the cramped room. 'Your father as the head of the cadet branch of Clan MacQueen will doubtless lose his life over this treasonable affair,' Maitland seemed to speak his thoughts aloud, 'his Papist sympathies are well-known.'

He stopped and considered his captive. 'But you Alexander are more intelligent and a brave fighter in spite of your youthful foolishness and high spirits. My brother-in-law, James MacQueen speaks of you highly. He wished that you had stayed at home, as he did himself, instead of following your father. You realise you have put the lives of your mother and younger brother in jeopardy by your actions? The Chief of MacQueen set a wiser example by staying loyal to the Protestant King.'

Alexander remained stonily silent. Maitland took this for a sign of weakening and continued in a lighter vein. 'I am willing to plead your case and secure an indemnity because you are a close kinsman of my brother-in-law. If you agree to take the oath to King William, I have no doubt I could get you a commission in the King's army. It would probably be best if you served in England or abroad for a while and in time you might be able to return to your father's lands, on the guarantee of good behaviour, of course. Or I might have a good use for you in my own household, young Ballantyne,' he smiled. 'What do you say, eh?'

Alexander gave a mirthless laugh. 'You are right in one thing,' he spoke without a trace of fear, 'my father has indeed lost his life in this 'treasonable affair'. He lies dead outside the Abbey walls. But at least he did not stay at home and wait to see whose would be the winning army,' Alexander mocked, 'he died a loyal subject of King James.'

He knew he hung himself with every word, but he could not stem the anger he felt at this man's smugness. 'My Chief had his own reasons for remaining at Penstroun,' said Alexander, 'but I for one am proud of my part in Dundee's campaign. I will never take an oath to the Dutchman, as long as I live!'

Maitland shot a furious look at the tall, dark-haired lad who stood before him, his vivid blue eyes contemptuous and the strong chin jutting out stubbornly. He wanted to strike him for his impertinence. Well, let him hang for his stupid Highland pride and go to the Devil!

'Guards!' he snapped turning his back on the accusing eyes. 'Get him out of here.'

Alexander was thrown into a byre where dozens of other prisoners were already crammed. From their listless talk he gathered they were MacLeans from Mull and Skye men who had rallied under Sir Donald MacDonald of Sleat. He eventually found an exhausted sleep, huddled against the back of another man for warmth. The following day he was taken along with others of the Highland gentry to the cellars of a large house. The word was passed round that they were to be marched to Edinburgh for trial.

Alexander sat removed from the others in the darkness and escaped in his thoughts to the thickly wooded mountain slopes around Culduggan and the stark castle tower on its mossy mound protected on all sides by the rushing Duggan River. He pictured his mother tending to the herbs in the sheltered woodland garden on Culduggan Island, waiting for news of her husband and son, while his brother Hugh made boats from driftwood and threw them recklessly into the rushing torrents.

Alexander's heart ached with sadness for his gentle fair-haired mother and the sorrow that would soon envelope her, wishing he could be there to break the news of her husband's death and comfort her himself. How uncertain her life would be now, especially as a practising Catholic. Would their Chief be able to protect her from the vengeance of men like Maitland?

'He's over there I think,' a voice broke into his thoughts and a stab of light flickered round the pillar from a candle.

'Alexander?' a deep voice questioned in the dark.

'Yes?' the young Ballantyne of Culduggan half rose in curiosity, finding something familiar in the tall, thickset figure closing in on him. The candle flared up in his face and threw light on the greying beard and craggy features of James MacQueen.

'Sir!' Alexander exclaimed in amazement and grabbed his hand. 'How did–?'

'Maitland reluctantly allowed me to see you before you're taken to Edinburgh,' James MacQueen said gruffly, 'though you appear to have mightily upset him.'

Alexander pursed his lips stubbornly.

'I heard of your father's death,' the Chief went on quickly. 'It is a great sadness to me; he was a good man.'

There was silence between them, then MacQueen indicated for them to sit. He lowered his voice to a murmur. 'I told your father I would not bring out the Clan without a general rising; we lost too many men fighting for the Stuarts before King Charles was restored to the throne. I had no choice; you do see that?'

'Yes sir and my father understood,' Alexander whispered back, 'he did not blame you for your decision.'

The older man sighed as if reassured. 'It grieves me to see your life wasted too,' MacQueen continued, 'will you not reconsider your position Alexander?'

The youth heard the wistful pleading in his Chief's voice, but they both knew he was too much his father's son to retract. He shook his head.

'Then you must listen to me,' James MacQueen drew even closer, 'your only hope is to escape from here before they take you to Edinburgh. If you can make your way to Aberdeen by the end of the month I will arrange for a boat to take you abroad. Sweden or Poland are good places for soldiering and if you get as far as Muscovy, the opportunities for advancement in the Tsar's army are considerable. You must contact my old friend there, Dr Ewen Putulo, he will stand sponsor to you until you are established and I will reimburse any kindness done to you.'

He laid a hand on the youth's shoulder. 'When things have quietened down here, I will send word to you if it is possible to return, be assured of that.'

Alexander felt his throat squeeze tight at his kinsman's generosity. 'What do you propose?' he asked, feeling a small spark of hope and excitement flare inside.

'I have men outside who are going to cause a diversion by starting a drunken quarrel in Gaelic at the time when your gaolers bring the evening food. You will come out with me dressed as my servant,' MacQueen drew out a bundle of rough woollen clothes from under his plaid as he spoke. 'And just pray that they don't recognise you.'

'But you must not put yourself in such danger,' Alexander protested, astounded by the brazenness of the plan. 'Maitland will delight in punishing you if I escape him.'

'Let him try,' MacQueen grunted. 'Now put these on.'

It seemed an age before the door opened again, though it could only have been ten minutes or so. A dim light spilled in as the gaoler appeared with some hard bannocks and water. The sound of raised voices in the courtyard grew louder as MacQueen and his stooping servant moved towards the door.

'I have finished with the prisoner,' the Chief said brusquely, adding over his shoulder in a louder voice, 'you're a young fool and you'll regret spurning my offer, Ballantyne.'

The guard looked suspiciously into the dark recess and then caught sight of Alexander. 'I don't remember a servant–'

Someone shoved into him from behind as a brawl broke out in the darkness. The guard cursed and dropped the food, turning to defend himself. As other guards ran from all around to break up the fighting, several of the prisoners, realising MacQueen's intention, moved forward to protect Alexander from view.

The Chief, speaking in Gaelic told young Ballantyne to make for the courtyard arch. Immediately to their right they dived down a narrow alley as more men clattered into the courtyard and added to the confusion. A group of retainers with horses waited for them under a clump of trees, hardly visible in the twilight. Luckily they were given the most cursory of challenges at the town port, but did not stop until well clear of the town. At the top of the glen, MacQueen reined in his horse and turned to his young kinsman.

'This is where we must part,' he spoke breathlessly, 'your safest route is to follow the drovers' tracks north and then cut east through the high passes, avoiding the coastal burghs.' He swung his horse side-on to Alexander's and they briefly embraced.

'My mother?' the young Highlander spoke of what had been preoccupying him on the ride.

'I will do my best to protect her and young Hugh,' MacQueen smiled encouragingly. 'You must send word that you are safe when you can, Culduggan.' Alexander knew he used his father's title deliberately, a poignant reminder that he was now head of his household even in exile.

'Please give her my love,' Alexander said hoarsely. 'I cannot thank you enough, sir–' his voice cracked and he spurred his horse around before MacQueen could answer. Plunging down the hillside to avoid a ravine, Alexander turned his sure-footed beast back along the ridge.

***

For a long time MacQueen waited and watched Alexander's progress, though he could hardly detect the lone figure in the dark moonless night. He feared for the lad as if he were his own son and was full of apprehension for the dangerous journey that lay ahead. He sighed heavily. Deep in his heart James MacQueen doubted whether he would ever see the brave young Ballantyne on Scottish soil again.

CHAPTER 1

Moscow 1702

'It will be your turn next Katherine,' Rosa pinched her friend's arm teasingly and looked at the tall elegant figure in the profusion of peach satin and lace of her best dress. Katherine Putulo flashed a look from dark-lashed green eyes and tossed back her ringlets under the high lace headdress.

'I have no intention of marrying some rich German merchant just for his money, like my sister Elspeth,' she pouted, her straight nose and high cheek bones catching the light as she raised her chin.

Rosa giggled and nudged Katherine playfully, delighted to have provoked her friend out of her easy-going indifference to the wedding party.

'Oh no? If you turn down many more suitors you will be left an old maid. I would be happy to marry for money,' Rosa wrinkled her nose prettily. Katherine made an impatient noise but did not reply.

'What about that young Hector Maitland, your godfather's nephew?' Rosa leaned her dark head closer and whispered conspiratorially. 'He has been watching you all day, and I've seen the way he looks at you, big brown eyes like a love-sick puppy! An only son, is that not so? He will inherit a big Scottish estate from his rich father, Sir Archibald, so I have heard.'

Katherine glanced over her fan at the thick-set young man with a full face and florid complexion, weighed down by his enormous powdered periwig. He was elaborately dressed in blue velvet coat and breeches, bedecked in lace at the throat and cuffs, and ostentatiously taking snuff from a silver box. He stared at her and she quickly looked away.

'From what I've heard of him, he's a gossip and unkind with it, I don't know why my godfather has brought him to Moscow. Hector Maitland will give himself a headache with all that false hair,' she murmured to Rosa behind the fan. 'But you seem so interested in him that I must introduce you at once and I promise not to be jealous.' Katherine laid long tapering fingers on her friend's arm and pulled her forward.

'No!' Rosa squealed, 'let us forget about the puppy Maitland.'

The two young women dissolved into laughter.

'Daughter!' Ewen Putulo called across the room to Katherine. 'Come and greet your godfather.'

Katherine spun round in a swirl of lace to see her smiling father with his hand on the other man's arm. James MacQueen was still in his boots and fur-lined velvet coat, which like his white hair and unfashionable beard were sprinkled with a fine dusting of snow.

'Godfather,' Katherine picked up her dress and rustled across the room, 'where have you been?'

'Katherine,' he growled affectionately and kissed the top of her head in greeting, 'I hope you will not chide me too much for missing the ceremony, but I had business to attend to.'

'I knew you would come before Elspeth had to leave,' Katherine's broad lips curved into a smile, 'didn't I say so Papa?'

Ewen Putulo laughed and nodded. 'Uncle James has promised to stay for the rest of the evening and not to disappear off on any more mysterious jaunts; we see too little of him as it is.'

The two men held each other's look, the deep bonds of friendship which bound them, unspoken but acknowledged.

'I shall enjoy this great celebration, Ewen, as much as Moscow appears to be enjoying the defeat of the Swedes in Livonia. The city is wild with the news,' James MacQueen grinned.

'Then that is why the bells have been making such a din,' Katherine smiled, 'it was not just for Elspeth.'

Her godfather threw back his head and laughed in the way she remembered him doing on his rare trips to Muscovy on business. She knew vaguely that it was something to do with selling grain and buying furs. But they were magical visits, a part of her happy childhood when he would appear unannounced in the Foreign Quarter with gifts for her and Elspeth, recounting vivid tales of adventure across the seas and of his rugged Highland homeland and the people of Penstroun.

Her father had told her that the Chief of MacQueen enjoyed their company the more because he had lost his only wife and child in the early days of turmoil in Tsar Peter's reign. She knew her father felt very deeply about it because the Princess Katya had been left in his care. Now this was the first time they had seen the Chief since Katherine's own mother had died, just two years ago from summer fever. It was the only shadow that lay over this happy occasion and she strove to smother her sadness.

'Uncle James, this is my dear friend Rosa Panini. Her father is one of the Tsar's architects from Rome.'

James MacQueen bent his head of wiry white hair over the young Italian girl's hand and kissed it. Rosa curtsied before the ageing Chief.

'Katherine has told me much about you sir, we are the best of friends,' she smiled.

'A delightful chaperone for my goddaughter,' MacQueen's face creased with a rare flash of boyish humour, 'the young men of the Quarter are slow indeed to appreciate such beauty; we would not have been so backward eh, Ewen?'

Katherine threw her tortoise-shell fan in front of her face at this second allusion to marriage and caught her father's eye.

Ewen felt a stab of pain at the memory of his own Sybil. He studied Katherine, noticing the tell-tale tinge of colour heightening her cheeks and the creamy skin of her neck below her fan.

It was becoming an increasing worry that his second daughter appeared to spurn all offers of marriage. He was growing old and retiring to Scotland occupied his thoughts more and more. Although the death of Sybil had brought him and Katherine even closer, he was not so selfish that he could allow his daughter to be tied to nursing him in his old age. Perhaps his friend James could make her see sense.

Katherine's amused eyes shone back at him beneath thick lashes and he could not remain glum in her presence.

'Katherine and Rosa will choose in their own good time, I hope,' Ewen Putulo said affectionately. 'And now, James, you must come and share the wedding feast and watch the dancing.'

The Chief discarded his heavy cloak and followed his host, the two men chatting animatedly. Katherine saw her older sister Elspeth hanging on the arm of her new husband, Frederick Sholt, conversing politely as they moved among their guests. She was smaller than Katherine, a doll-like figure with quick lively brown eyes and naturally curly dark brown hair.

For all her bossy sisterly manner and sensible advice, Katherine knew she would miss her only sibling dearly, soon to leave Moscow for good and take up residence in Konigsberg, the Prussian port. They had been happy as girls, romping through the gardens and parks of the Foreign Quarter and as young ladies, joining in the picnics and theatrical entertainments of the lively foreign community that their mother had so enjoyed, but of which their housekeeper Fiona was still disapproving.

No doubt since their mother's death they had been indulged by their widower father, yet the Scots doctor's daughters were well liked by the mix of European fortune-seekers and émigrés who made up the cosmopolitan society on the edge of Moscow. Now Elspeth would soon be gone and she would be left to run the household for her hard-working father. It seemed to Katherine that this wedding finally marked the end of her girlhood.

'They say Tsar Peter and some of his Jolly Company will be calling to toast your sister and her husband,' Rosa's gossiping brought Katherine's mind back to the present. 'There will be much revelry tonight Katherine!'

Katherine felt a spark of excitement watching her friend's animated face. Outside in the gathering dark, thousands of church bells rang and boomed their approval at the Russian victory. It would be just like the Tsar to appear at the Scottish Hostelry, here in his own capital, to celebrate the nuptials of the daughter of one of his foreign friends. She had seen him before at weddings and christenings, a tall energetic figure surrounded by fellow revellers.

Then she had no more time to dwell on the thought as Hector Maitland came to claim her for a dance. Katherine took his hand with a cool look, trying to avoid Rosa's wicked smirking.

'You are quite the prettiest thing in the room,' he squeezed her hand tightly and regarded her with prominent brown eyes. 'I have called at your father's house on several occasions Miss Putulo, but have not succeeded in finding you there.'

'Oh?' Katherine tried to sound surprised. She had bidden a reluctant Fiona to make excuses on her behalf to avoid his visits.

'Perhaps as the snows begin to thaw we could arrange an outing, Miss Putulo?' Hector Maitland persisted, beginning to perspire from their exertions. Katherine thought he would burst out of his heavily brocaded coat.

'How long are you to be in Moscow, sir?' Katherine parried as they met again in the dance.

'We shall not sail until early summer,' he smiled, his heavy jowl creasing, 'there is plenty of time for amusement before we return to Scotland.'

At that moment the far door was flung open and in burst a noisy troupe in a flurry of snow. As Katherine moved among the dancers she was aware of a commotion as people moved aside for the Tsar. Not one for ceremony, he strode forward in his German green coat, fur cloak and high boots, seized a tankard of beer and made for the newly wedded couple.

The music, laughter and Hector Maitland's bumptious comments made it impossible for Katherine to hear the monarch's words, but she saw the delighted embarrassment on her sister's face. Of the Tsar's company of followers she recognised the French officer, De Maton, the Danish Ambassador Paterson and some of the actors who had stayed over the winter in Moscow. The rest she assumed to be Russian.

At the finish of the dance she disengaged herself quickly from the affronted young Maitland and joined Rosa on the fringe of the admiring crowd.

'... and at a Russian wedding we view the consummation before we eat,' Tsar Peter's cheerful voice bellowed and he wiped his mouth and moustache across his sleeve. 'Young Sholt has the Devil's own patience!'

Katherine saw Elspeth redden, uncharacteristically lost for words by the sovereign's bluntness. But his laughter and merriment was infectious and no one took offence.

'We are honoured that you attend,' Frederick Sholt acknowledged quietly, hanging onto Elspeth, 'especially on this day of celebration for your own army.'

'We have all night to honour our returning heroes,' Tsar Peter joked, raising his tankard to them. 'Now please accept these gifts and continue with the dancing.'

Two of the party staggered forward with a wooden chest. Elspeth gasped in amazement at the beautiful cloths and brocades displayed inside. Nestling among them was a miniature jewel-studded portrait of the Tsar himself.

Katherine suddenly grabbed Rosa's arm. 'Let's follow them into the streets,' she whispered, 'I want to see the bonfires and the fireworks. It is so seldom we see Moscow at celebration.'

Rosa's dark brown eyes widened in astonishment. 'In our best gowns Katherine and among the Muscovites? You must be mad. What would our parents say?'

'Just for a short while Rosa,' Katherine's eyes flashed with daring, shaken out of her sadness at her sister's leaving by the Tsar's presence. 'We can borrow skirts from the Hostelry maids and go in disguise. With all this noise and dancing no one will think us missing for an hour or so. We shall be back before Elspeth and Frederick leave. Oh do say yes, Rosa!'

The young architect's daughter looked at her friend's face, suffused with excitement, a mad-cap streak spurring her into this devilment.

Rosa wondered how Katherine could at times be so calm – almost detached – and at others alive with a recklessness that swept all along like a spring river in flood. She knew Katherine would go with or without her and she hated to be left out of anything.

'An hour only,' she frowned and then smothered a giggle. The two young women slipped from the banqueting hall unnoticed.

***

On Sparrow Hills, a soldier in the red uniform of the foreign officer corps reined in his snorting black horse and gazed across at the blue and gold domes of Moscow. Crosses gleamed in the dying afternoon sun, the walls of the Kremlin glistening as white as the packed snow that covered the surrounding gardens and trees.

His breath froze like a cloud, the clear azure sky fading and darkening by the minute. From here, all was an eerie silence. The triumphal entry of the victorious troops, leading their half frozen prisoners into the wooden city to the blast of cannon volley, was over.

Major Alexander Ballantyne should have been a part of it, but had chosen instead to make a detour to one of the pleasant country mansions lying by the Moscow River. He scratched the dark stubble of his square jaw, feeling the cold biting into his cheeks and nose, and clinging to the thickness of his eyebrows. Smiling to himself at the recent pleasure of being reacquainted with the widow Countess Natalya Alexeevna Matrapov, he twisted round at the impatient stamping of his companion's stead.

'Sir, do you wish to freeze into a monument on Sparrow Hills or enjoy a night of drinking?' a deep voice reproached from under a hairy cloak of goatskin.

'Baturin,' Alexander chuckled indulgently, 'you have shown the patience of a saint while I quenched my thirst at Countess Matrapov's. Now you shall have your fill.'

The servant grunted, the icicles already forming on his bushy moustaches. In spite of the tired smudges beneath his master's eyes, their blue sharpness danced with liveliness, his broad frame showing nothing of the fatigue of weeks of winter campaigning. That is the tonic of a Russian woman, Baturin thought wryly. At least for the moment his Scots master appeared to have stopped fretting over his encounter with the white-haired foreign chief that had so put him out of sorts on their return march.

'Come!' Major Ballantyne spurred his twitching horse into a canter and they ploughed towards the city in a flurry of snow.

***

Two servant girls wrapped in rough woollen capes and linen skirts, their dark ringlets hidden under kerchiefs, joined the mêlée of revellers through the street. The wooden pavements were icy and the early evening air bitterly cold, but the mood in the city was merry. The usually darkened and deserted streets were lit with cheery bonfires; vendors sold small meat pies known as *pirozhki*, acrobats and musicians entertained while the peel of silver bells and the clanging of iron drowned all.

Katherine breathed in the sweet acrid smoke of burning logs, exhilarated to be out of the stuffy atmosphere of the wedding banquet hall and the endless formal conversing. Her father and Uncle James had been deep in conversation and wine when she and Rosa had slipped out; she would not be missed for a while.

'Look, there they go!' Katherine grabbed Rosa's arm and propelled her forward, determined not to lose sight of the Tsar and his Jolly Company.

'Wait for me,' Rosa complained as Katherine's longer legs covered the ground more quickly, suddenly nervous to be out on the Moscow streets, with their dark shadows and raucous noises.

The large party stopped outside a mansion house, its wooden frame intricately carved. Someone fired off a musket, while another started beating a drum. The door was thrown open and a plump attractive woman, with fair hair uncovered, shouted something which evoked a barrage of ribald replies. The Tsar took her by the waist and swept her inside.

'That's Anna Mons, his mistress,' Rosa said breathlessly, her unease forgotten at the sniff of scandal, 'I've seen her at court balls. Rumour has it, the Tsar tires of her.'

'Well he doesn't appear jaded to me,' Katherine answered dryly. 'Let's stick close.'

'Katherine!' Rosa protested, but her friend was already slipping into the crowd of servants who followed the band, conversing in Russian with those around her.

'They say there is dancing in the kitchens for the servants,' Katherine whispered excitedly to Rosa, who understood little of the Russian tongue. Katherine on the other hand had picked it up easily by talking uninhibitedly to the kitchen servants and later with her father's cultured Russian friends.

'We will be found out,' Rosa quailed at the thought, 'this is madness Katherine.'

'Call me Katya,' her friend gave a wicked grin, 'and you shall be Sophia. And stop worrying, everyone is too happy or drunk to notice a couple of dancing maids.'

After the bitter night air, the kitchen quarters were a cosy fug of spluttering candles, roaring fire and rosy faces. Above the chanting and the music of the dance, already in full swing, was the thudding of the Tsar's booted followers in the rooms upstairs.

Both men and women downed cups of *kvass*, the heady Russian brew made from fermented bread, drinking toasts to the daring winter victory over the Swedes. The two girls stood in the shadows wide-eyed at the scene, the merrymaking beyond anything they had witnessed even among their own servants. Katherine felt a deep inner stirring at the primitive weaving dance, the stamping and singing which made their own rollicking country dances seem almost tame.

Just then the door from the courtyard was flung open and a cold blast of air whistled into the cosy warmth. Katherine turned to see two figures muffled in heavy coats, one tall and military; the other like a lumbering bear in his animal skins.

She watched the first man remove his bonnet and shake the snow from his thick cloak and red coat. This must be one of the Tsar's returning campaigners, for he still wore the travel-stained military uniform and riding boots of an officer, and a foreign officer at that. One of her own kind perhaps?

In the flickering light she could make out the strong outline of his unshaven jaw, the long straight nose and dark eyebrows. He did not wear a wig in the fashion of the European community though; his own dark unkempt hair was tied back behind his head like the Tsar's.

For a moment he took in the scene, an amused tired smile pulling at one side of his mouth. His rough moustachioed companion thrust a mug of *kvass* in his hand and the officer took a long swig, draining it in one. Wiping his mouth on the back of his hand like a common soldier, he called to his servant in Russian for a refill. Katherine decided that in spite of the bonnet and the uniform he must be a Russian officer, perhaps training with a foreign regiment.

‘And who do you think the handsome fighter is, Katya?’ Rosa looked archly at her friend, over-stressing the fictitious name.

‘Just some officer come to join the Tsar in the celebrations,’ Katherine answered, feigning indifference, ‘how should I know?’

‘Well now we’re dressed up like sacks of flour, he’s not going to notice of couple of drab maids is he?’ Rosa pulled a face. ‘More’s the pity.’

Katherine saw the officer glance around, surprised that he had not already made for the bright company upstairs. On a whim, she moved forward into the light of the fire and caught his wandering gaze. She felt as if the cold of a Moscow winter had seized her chest and frozen her breath, as the blue sharpness of his eyes held hers. She could neither breathe nor look away. They were the intense blue of the winter sky that dazzles and pains the traveller who looks into its brightness.

Then the officer looked away. Katherine felt the constriction in her chest ease as the air gushed into her lungs again. Rosa noticed her breathlessness.

‘What’s wrong Katherine, are you feeling faint from the heat?’ she asked in concern. ‘Let’s sit down.’

‘N-no, I’m fine, thank you, it’s nothing,’ she gulped, not quite sure what had come over her. She had imagined the moment, of course; the officer had not even noticed her. Her mind was too fanciful after the excitement of the day. And yet she knew something strange, even frightening had happened in those brief seconds, a response in her that she had never before felt for any man.

Now he had turned to speak to the coarse looking companion who still wore his goatskins and fur hat despite the intense heat. It irked Katherine that the tall soldier had not noticed her standing by the fire and that he was oblivious to the effect he had had on her.

Then she laughed at herself; Rosa was right. In their simple rough clothes and headscarves, their faces smutty from the flying ashes, they would be indistinguishable among the other servants. Why should an officer of the Tsar give them a second glance?

Katherine noticed that the dancers were forming themselves into a large circle, pulling everyone into a giant embrace. This must be the great Russian peasant dance, the *Khorovod*, that their cook Anna had talked about and demonstrated to the captivated young Katherine as a child.

Swallowing her disappointment at the officer’s indifference, she grabbed Rosa’s hand and tugged her into the circle. They began to move and sway, a vast human chain, chanting around a young man who strutted in the middle. As the ring turned faster and faster, Katherine threw back her head in delight, feeling a response deep within at the movement and the song as if she were made for this very dance.

The circle slowed and demanded that the young man kiss one of the girls. His eyes alighted on Katherine's flushed and beautiful upturned face, her large green eyes wide with pleasure, black curls escaping from under her cap, her red lips parted in a welcoming smile. He would have no other. Stepping towards her, the servant planted a robust kiss on her mouth and pulled her into the middle of the chain.

Katherine laughed as she caught sight of Rosa's scandalised face before the circle once again sped around, this time encircling her.

Although she had never before performed this dance, she remembered Anna's sensuous movements and found they came to her naturally. Katherine glided alone, tilting her head and flicking her wrists to the rhythm. She had never felt so alive. The dancers called in admiration and she obeyed their commands, touching the floor with the tips of her fingers, bowing and turning. The heaving mass of bodies slowed to give the final order, to choose the one she desired with a kiss, to perpetuate the dance.

Suddenly she was aware of the dark officer in the circle stripped of his red coat, standing in shirtsleeves and breeches, eyeing her intently. His cravat was loosened; auburn strands in his dark hair glinted in the firelight and the ghost of a smile twitched at his firm mouth.

Katherine had not seen him join the dance, so totally absorbed in its movement herself. She was sure he had still been watching when it first began. Now his bold blue stare seemed to challenge her, defying her to choose any other man. The dancers clapped and stamped for her to make a choice. Almost trance-like in her response, Katherine moved towards the officer – their eyes still fixed on each other – leaned on tip-toe and lightly kissed his lips.

A delicious shiver went through her as she did so, her heart jerking. Attempting to step back, she was pinned by strong arms, as her chosen man pressed his mouth firmly against hers, not satisfied with the tempting brush she had given him.

Katherine was completely taken unawares; if he had not held her so tightly she would have given way at the knees. Through her giddiness she heard the raucous cheers of the other dancers. It made her realise how undignified was her behaviour, carried away by the intoxication of the dance and this man's closeness. How quickly he had taken advantage of it!

If Elspeth could see her now, brazenly embracing a Russian soldier in front of a host of kitchen servants, her sister would give her the scolding of her life. Katherine tensed against the man's hold and pushed at his shirt, disconcerted by the warmth she felt beneath it. He held her for a moment longer and then released Katherine breathlessly and with a grin, pinched her cheek.

She was speechless and shaking from his touch, furious that he had somehow got the better of her. How dare he treat her like some common serving girl? She glared at him, the annoyance flushing her high-boned cheeks crimson, her eyes flashing with contempt. He would take no further advantage of her; she was a Putulo and a lady of breeding.

Biting her lip, Katherine realised how ridiculous was her pique. How could she reveal her true identity without causing a scandal or even endangering her friend and herself? Foreigners might be tolerated by the Muscovite nobility, but they were viewed with deep suspicion and mistrust by the ordinary people. What was a rowdy merry dance could turn in an instant to an ugly scene with the amount of drink this crowd had consumed. She must give no reason for suspicion.

Katherine recovered herself and smiled as the officer took to the middle. He threw her a quizzical look as he went.

'Katherine you go too far!' Rosa hissed under cover of the singing. 'It's time we went back to the wedding.'

'Hush,' Katherine gave a warning look, 'don't speak here. We'll leave soon.'

She did not like to admit that she did not wish to go while this big powerful Russian with the hypnotic eyes remained at the dance. Her lips still stung with the imprint of his kiss and her cheek from the scrape of his bristled chin. Katherine watched him kicking out vigorously, his arms crossed over his chest, his face glistening with energy in the warm light despite the dark shadows below his eyes. What was it about him that was familiar, she puzzled? Had she perhaps seen him before at a ball in the Foreign Quarter? The occasion eluded her and yet he did not seem a total stranger to her.

Katherine held her breath as his turn to choose a partner came, glancing at the floor with sudden shyness. Then her head shot up as the clapping began and she saw him planting a firm kiss on a fair-haired girl with a rose pink face. She was laughing back at him, obviously pleased with the conquest. Katherine felt a ridiculous stab of jealousy. Her face burned at her own stupidity in desiring his attention again.

'Let's go now,' she whispered to Rosa, without another glance at the officer. Her friend followed with relief as they fell out of the chain. Katherine slipped over to the far corner to collect her woollen cloak and wrapped it around her bare neck and shoulders. Pushing through the throng to the door she found the tall soldier blocking their retreat.

'Going so soon?' he asked in Russian with a strange rolling accent. 'I hoped you would dance some more.'

Katherine gulped, trying to avoid the searching eyes, her pulse beginning to race. 'You appeared to be enjoying it very well without us,' she could not resist the barb, 'please don't let us keep you, sir.'

She saw his jaw tighten and then he gave a sudden laugh. 'You are outspoken for a serf. I like it and would have you stay.'

Katherine inwardly cursed herself for her folly. Panic began to rise. 'I – we must get back to our master,' she stammered, looking at a point beyond his shoulder.

'And who would that be?' he laid a hand on her arm as she made to move.

'Oh, our master is a merchant, he is not from Moscow, so it is doubtful you would know him – we're from the south,' she answered evasively, knowing that she could not stand up to too much questioning.

'I have campaigned much in the south against the Tartars and know it well,' his look swept her and his grip tightened. 'Perhaps I do know your master after all. What is he called?' he persisted.

'Count Alexis Stromsky,' Katherine replied wildly.

'And your name?' her questioner probed, in no hurry to let her go. Katherine wondered with alarm if he was in the Tsar's intelligence service.

'Katya.' She dropped her voice, 'please sir, we must go now.'

'Come, stay and have a drink with me Katya,' he smiled and linked her arm through his, 'you and your friend. I would like to hear news of the south – and so would my servant – he's a Cossack like you.'

Katherine caught Rosa's frozen appalled look. If they did not go soon, they would be missed at the Scottish Hostelry and then there would be searches and reprimands. He must have seen the alarm on their faces, for he added amusedly, 'don't be afraid, I will see you safely home. Allow me to introduce myself, Major Alexander Ballantyne, a Scottish soldier of fortune in the Tsar's service – and now at yours,' he bowed gallantly.

Katherine's mouth dropped open, her heavily-lidded eyes wide in shock. This was terrible; he was a fellow Scot who no doubt knew her father. It finally came to her, she had seen him before at her father's house many years ago when she was a child. Alexander Ballantyne had appeared destitute and thin with hunger, having escaped Scotland with nothing. He had seemed like a man to her then, although he must have been younger than she was now. Yet this was a hardened soldier who stood before her, compared to the young fugitive her father had helped, though the eyes and the proud chin were unmistakably the same. She could not remember having seen him again in the Quarter since that time.

He would have no recollection of her as a girl, but they must escape at once before the situation got completely out of hand. Now she longed for the safety and civility of the wedding feast, the familiar faces and the feel of soft lace against her skin rather than this man's iron grasp.

He read her expression and laughed with amusement, mistaking her horror for the peasant's fear of the foreigner. 'There's nothing to be alarmed about,' he loosened the cloak from her shoulders, 'I'm quite harmless Katya.'

Looking into his direct steely gaze, Katherine did not believe that for one moment. Her heart began to pound with a mixture of dread and attraction, aware of his unsubtle exploring look.

'Surely sir, you wish to join His Majesty, the Tsar and his friends upstairs? We are dull humble company for a victorious officer.' She gave him a demure look, hoping to divert him.

'On the contrary,' he smiled, 'peasant company is a welcome diversion. I am a man of simple tastes, used to the ways of raw country people in my native land. I will join the Tsar later.'

Katherine hid her vexation, allowing him to lead her back to the fire, aware of Rosa's silent pleas.

'Drink this,' Alexander pressed a cup of vodka to her lips that the burly servant had passed to him. Katherine gulped and spluttered as the fiery liquid burnt her throat. The two men laughed, knocking their glasses together and threw back their drinks in one. Rosa mutely refused to accept the toast.

'To continued victory in the Northern Wars,' Alexander raised another glass. Katherine watched him, a rosy warmth stealing up inside from the vodka. Begrudgingly she admitted his coarse handsomeness, though he was mightily short on decency and manners for a gentleman Scot and one her father had regarded as brave and principled; he was too much the mercenary.

It was strange that she had not seen him even fleetingly since his first arrival. Was it ten years ago? There were over three thousand Europeans living in the Quarter, but as a fellow countryman it was odd that they had never met at some ball or picnic, or that her father never referred to him.

As he turned to speak to his servant, she saw the dark slash of an old scar running from his left cheek, across his jaw where stubble did not grow. He had indeed seen action in the pay of the Tsar.

'Tell me Katya,' he suddenly caught her staring at him, 'how long does Count Stromsky intend to remain in Moscow?'

'Oh, we are soon to go sir,' she gushed, 'he only came to attend the wedding of a friend's daughter. That is why we must leave to help prepare for the return journey.' Katherine looked down at her lap in discomfort. Alexander considered her; he spoke low and deliberately.

'It still gives me enough time to negotiate a price. I would buy your freedom if you will join my household and look after me and my man Baturin.'

Katherine's head shot up with indignation. What impudence! She felt sure he was teasing her.

'No sir,' she tossed her head defiantly, her dark eyes flashing, 'I am sure our master would not want to part with us.'

'As a merchant, this Count of yours will know that everything has a price,' he murmured and held her look. Katherine gasped in outraged astonishment at the casualness of his comment. Rosa looked at her in bemusement, wondering what the officer was saying to provoke her so easily.

'I would never leave the Count's household for a course foreign soldier,' Katherine blurted out, stung from her caution by his deliberate taunting. His offhand manner and insulting look were loathsome and she chided herself for having so easily been taken in by his apparent friendliness.

Alexander raised his eyes in surprise at the spirited reply of this tall servant girl with the slim waist and the dark bewitching eyes. There was something not quite right but he was too exhausted to discover what. She pulled her cloak about her creamy shoulders and turned from him, her lips in a stubborn pout. If he had not been in the saddle for days, he would have put up more resistance to her going, but he let the maid and her friend hurry from the room, spurning his offer to escort them.

Baturin guffawed behind him and Alexander turned to see his servant's merry face. 'You do not know how to handle a simple peasant girl,' he crowed. 'That one got the better of you, for all your fancy uniform and you know it.'

Alexander shrugged, trying to hide his annoyance, but Baturin's ribald laughter was too much.

'I want you to follow them now,' he snapped at the grizzled Cossack, 'and see where they are staying. Then you can drink yourself under the table for all I care.'

Baturin snorted and downed his vodka, reluctant to go running into the snow after a young servant girl who was too arrogant for her own good. Better that the Major limit his interest to the Countess Matrapov where they could get good food and a warm sleep. Catching sight of his master's angry face he thought better of protesting and got up to do his bidding.

***

Alexander felt suddenly overwhelmingly weary. The challenge of the dance and the sight of the proud servant girl watching him boldly from the fireside had given him a last spurt of energy. Now that she was gone he longed for a dreamless sleep. He would find a chamber upstairs and barricade himself in so that midnight revellers could not pull him from his bed. He did not wait for Baturin to return but headed upstairs immediately.

Sleep, however, would not come. He could not rid his mind of the servant girl's green eyes or the way her raven black curls of hair crept below her veil to lie on the soft ivory forehead and plum-tinged cheeks. She was tall and strong-limbed, with the healthy full figure of a peasant and yet her slim hands and wrists, the smoothness of her neck and shoulders suggested someone of higher birth.

Those hands had not seen the rugged daily chores of the kitchen, he would warrant. Neither was Katya's defiance of him the mark of servility he had witnessed amongst serfs in the past. Yet there was a feshness about her, an open unguarded look, which appealed to him too...

It was ridiculous that he lay tossing and turning on her account! He was behaving like the fresh-faced youth he had been thirteen years ago when he had left his beloved Scotland and Culduggan behind. He had sworn then to harden his heart and to feed on the bitter memories of his slain father, to forget tender thoughts of his mother and family.

He had been too long away in Livonia, he grunted aloud to himself. More time in the company of the witty and sophisticated Countess Natalya would banish tiresome thoughts of the young Katya. Thinking of the comely widow with the white-blonde hair and the attractive Slavonic face just beginning to show the lines of ageing, Alexander began to relax at last.

They understood each other well. Neither asked for love, only physical proximity; both recognised ambition in the other and Natalya had given him a home while his career in the Tsar's army advanced. He may have been ostracised from polite society in the foreign enclave for living so openly with the Russian widow, but he did not care. He would take her to the Victory Ball and afterwards rest for a few weeks at the Matrapov mansion. Sleep came over him like a silent heavy snowfall.

***

'Quickly, help me tie up my hair,' Katherine urged Rosa, her fingers a nervous bundle that would not obey her thoughts.

'Yes Katya,' Rosa bobbed a mock curtsey and took over her friend's fumbling attempt. They both fell into helpless giggles, the relief of being back at the Hostelry unscathed and seemingly undetected, making them euphoric. 'I wonder how much you are worth,' Rosa continued as she bound the ribbons in Katherine's hair. 'I mean how much is Major Ballantyne going to pay for you, do you think?'

'Rosa!' Katherine tried to wheel around, regretting having told Rosa all that was spoken. Her friend told her to stay still.

'It does not seem such a bad fate,' Rosa went on merrily, 'I think he is quite the most handsome man in Moscow.'

'He's insufferable and arrogant,' Katherine replied shortly, 'and I hate him.'

'What a disappointment it will be for him to discover you are the respectable daughter of his former acquaintance, Dr Putulo.'

Katherine gave a low howl of embarrassment, her hands flying to her cheeks to hide their blushing. 'You don't think he will discover that do you? What if he tries to track down the make-believe Count Stromsky?'

Rosa felt sorry for her friend, even though it was her own impetuosity that had got her into such a mess. After all, she had kissed the Major first.

'Oh, do not worry;' she pulled the lace headdress into place over the rich curls, 'he will be off fighting another war soon. By morning the Major will have forgotten the incident altogether.'

As they returned to the hall, the scene was one of jaded jollity, the men red and glistening in their thick frock coats, cravats and heavy wigs, the ladies fanning themselves vigorously after the country dances. Katherine saw Elspeth across the room, now in her fur cape and gloves for travelling. She was speaking to their father and then the two of them were clasping each other in a tearful hug. Frederick Sholt shuffled his feet and looked stiffly embarrassed behind them.

Katherine felt her eyes water and, biting the inside of her mouth, she rushed over to them. Elspeth caught sight of her younger sister and looked on the point of letting fly a comment; her disappearance had not escaped her sharp-eyed attention. But at the sight of her sadness she held back the flow of questions, they must not part with harsh words.

'Katherine, you will remember to practise your spinet and try not to annoy Fiona with your noisiness; she's getting old and doesn't need excitement. And make sure Papa eats regular meals, you know what he's like–'

'I'll miss you Elspeth,' Katherine's throat hurt as she interrupted her sister's lecturing.

'Me too,' Elspeth whispered hoarsely, clinging to the taller sister. Katherine was a woman now and yet there was a touching vulnerability under the gregariousness that made Elspeth long to hug and protect her from the harsh world beyond their sheltered childhood home.

'Come and visit us won't you?' Sudden tears streamed down the face of the married sister. Katherine nodded; her heart too full to speak. Frederick steered his young wife gently away, telling her they must leave, the troika was waiting. In a few minutes they would be at the merchant's house where they would spend their wedding night. In the morning the Sholts would start the long trek to Prussia and Elspeth's new home, speeding across the frozen rivers before the spring thaw broke up the ice and turned the roads into rivers of mud.

From the top of the wooden steps, Ewen Putulo and his younger daughter watched the couple depart in the green and gold sled. Fires still burned around the city and the bells carried on their insistent clanging, though now they sounded hollow to Katherine. There would be further dancing and drinking into the night, but she had no desire for it to continue. She wondered with whom Major Ballantyne danced at this moment in another part of Moscow. The unexpected thought of this tall commanding officer with the dangerously mocking blue eyes made her stomach lurch.

'Miss Putulo,' she was stopped by Hector Maitland, 'come and have a seat with me, you look tired.' He steered her aside.

'That I am sir,' Katherine fanned herself and looked away, 'we shall be leaving shortly.'

'I believe I know quite how exhausted you must be,' he lowered his voice and laid a damp hand on her arm. Something in his tone made Katherine stop and look into his red fleshy face, the powder from his wig running in white rivulets down his forehead and cheeks.

'Sir?' Katherine disengaged her arm from his hold.

'I must say you make a very fetching serving wench,' he leaned close and gave her a leering smile. 'But I doubt if it is the sort of behaviour that the good Dr Putulo would condone.'

Katherine looked at him in horror; she was sure no one had seen them leave. How long had the insufferable Maitland followed them?

'Of course, Miss Putulo, your secret is quite safe with me – providing you do not look unkindly on a visit from me and a trip out in my carriage perhaps?' He gave her a smug satisfied smile.

Distaste churned her stomach at his odious attempt at blackmail. It was contemptible. Yet through her own high-spirits she had risked involving herself and her best friend in a stupid scandal. She must at least protect Rosa from that.

Smiling tight-lipped at the young Scots nobleman, Katherine nodded. 'You are welcome to call at my father's house, Mr Maitland. A carriage ride would be pleasant – once the spring is here.'

'Good,' he patted her hand and regarded her with triumph.

Katherine controlled her anger and curtly made excuses to get away from him. As she fled from him, she wondered with mounting dread whether one carriage ride would be enough to silence Hector Maitland's malicious gossiping?

CHAPTER 2

'Baturin, you lazy Cossack bear!' Alexander Ballantyne kicked his slumbering servant none too gently with a large black boot, where he lay under a kitchen bench. 'Up with you this instant.'

The recipient of this unwelcome attention, grunted but barely flinched, his moustache quivering as if bothered by a mere fly. Alexander grabbed a pail of ice-cold water from a startled passing kitchen boy and threw the contents at the drugged body. 'Do I have to flush you out like a stoat, you worthless Turk?' he bellowed.

The insult brought Baturin to consciousness quicker than any icy washing, as his master knew it would. The blustering horseman was proud of his Cossack blood and despised the Ottoman Turks for filling their slave markets with his countrymen. He growled and shook his sore head, the main of matted hair and beard throwing droplets onto the black boots that stood astride him.

'Must I serve my own breakfast now that the campaign is over?' Alexander could not resist a smile at the bleary-eyed Russian. 'I see you can't take your drink as you used to, old man. Perhaps I should hire myself a younger comrade in arms, eh?'

'In the name of St Vladimir, you won't,' Baturin grumbled and staggered to his feet. He must have slept long for there was bustle all about and little sign of the past night's celebrations. 'Though why there should be such hurry now we are back in Moscow–'

'I have things to do here, even if you choose to remain in a drunken stupor, Baturin.'

The servant gave him a knowing look, he could tell that the Major had not slept well, but held his tongue.

'I have decided to speak with James MacQueen,' Alexander said brusquely. 'In the meantime I'd like you to arrange for my things to be taken to the Countess Matrapov's. I dine there tonight.'

Baturin's bleary eyes widened in surprise. 'I thought you had parted with the Chief on bad terms yesterday?' he grunted, recalling the brief, terse meeting with the white-haired Scotsman.

'I was overwrought from the recent fighting,' Alexander conceded, 'and uncivil to my Chief. I wish to give him the chance to say what was in his mind.' He turned to go. 'He is lodging at the Scottish Hostelry; you can meet me there when you have seen to the other arrangements.'

'Ah!' Baturin growled and spat onto the ground, remembering his errand of last night. 'That reminds me; the two serving girls.'

Alexander stopped. 'What of them?' he asked offhandedly. In the cold light of morning he had felt foolish for his interest in the saucy dark maid and had determined not to ask Baturin more about her.

'They returned to the Scottish Hostelry last night,' the servant replied, 'that's where they were staying.'

'Nonsense,' Alexander retorted, 'a Russian count would not stay at such a place; you must have been too drunk and followed the wrong pair.'

Baturin was adamant, 'far from it; I was not drunk enough in the bitter night air. I saw them go into the place, believe it or not as you will.' With that he stretched and yawned and went off to find something to eat.

Alexander doubted the tale and decided to push all thoughts of Katya from his mind as he rode to keep his assignation with James MacQueen.

***

Alexander was shown into one of the Chief's rooms, its windows still tightly shuttered, although the winter was almost at an end. After the dazzling sunshine outside he could hardly make out the tall figure across the low ceilinged chamber.

'Alexander!' the Chief greeted him warmly, as if his young kinsman had not spoken ill words to him the day before. 'I am glad you decided to come; please, sit by the stove and take a glass of vodka with me.'

Alexander took the proffered cup and sat on a rough wooden chair. 'I wish to apologise for my hasty words,' he said sheepishly; 'you did not deserve them, sir. I should not blame you for the fact that Archibald Maitland holds Culduggan.'

MacQueen waved aside the apology. 'I was perhaps wrong to come chasing out to meet you on your victorious return, but I have been kicking my heels in Moscow all winter and have not had the chance to meet or talk with you.'

Alexander observed him as he ran a finger round the edge of the cup and waited. But his Chief did not seem in a hurry to come to the point.

'You have done well as a soldier in Tsar Peter's army, I hear. Rumour has it you will be made a Lieutenant-General for your action in Livonia.' Alexander was silent, though his mouth twitched in the beginnings of a smile. James MacQueen went on. 'I know from experience that the Tsars repay the foreigner with honours and praise, rather than lands and material rewards, is that not so?'

Alexander shrugged, feeling defensive. 'Perhaps, but I am content with life in Muscovy,' he said, rubbing the scar on his chin.

'And the Countess Natalya,' MacQueen mentioned quietly, 'you are happy to remain as part of her household? I know you have been with her for the five years I have not visited Russia.'

Alexander swallowed his vodka, barely containing his annoyance. 'I don't see what that has to do with you, or anyone else, for that matter.'

The Chief kept his voice level. 'I do not wish to pry, Ballantyne, or tell you how to live your life. I merely want to know if you are indeed settled for good in Muscovy.' He looked reflective for a moment. 'God knows if things had been different I would gladly have stayed myself and lived out my years on a Russian estate with my wife. I would not have thought of returning to Penstroun at your age.'

Alexander gave a bitter laugh. 'You, sir, had the choice; I did not. Culduggan was forfeit and I have no home to return to, except Natalya Matrapov's. And you saw fit to allow that cursed Maitland and his brats to have the lands of my ancestors.'

MacQueen gave him a sharp look, but kept his anger under control. 'I have explained before, it was the price I had to pay for getting you safely away from Scotland and for saving your mother and brother Hugh from imprisonment. It was their decision to go into voluntary exile at the Jacobite court in France, they could have remained with me at Penstroun, but your mother was too proud to renounce her Catholicism and her loyalty to King James.'

Alexander's eyes stung at the thought of his humiliated parent, journeying alone with her nine year old boy to the exiled court at Saint-Germain near Paris. If he had known they would end up there, he would have gladly made his way to France rather than Russia to serve as a mercenary. He thought bleakly how easy his own escape had been once they had got clear of Dunkeld; his Chief had already struck a bargain with Maitland to turn his blind eye to Alexander's disappearance in return for the strategic lands at Culduggan. It was well placed in its fortress glen for trading between the sea and the government garrison at Fort William. No doubt Maitland ran a profitable business supplying the needs of King William's troops.

The white-haired chief stood up and poured them both another drink.

'But I have good news for once,' he could not keep the excitement out of his voice. 'Your brother Hugh has returned from France and is living with me at Penstroun. I have left him helping run my estates while I am away.'

'Hugh,' Alexander exclaimed, 'at Penstroun? Impossible!'

MacQueen chuckled. 'Not so, he has been back in Scotland nigh on four years. He's as lively and wild as ever, a good hunter and swordsman too. It was judged he was too young to know his own mind when his mother took him to France, so the King has allowed him back with me as guarantor.'

'And my mother?' Alexander asked, holding his breath.

MacQueen shook his head. 'She decided to take holy orders and has gone into a convent.' He added gently, 'It is unlikely she will ever return to Scotland now.'

Alexander sighed then looked at his chief keenly. 'So why are you telling me this? Surely you did not risk frost-bite to bring news of my brother Hugh?'

The older man put his vodka down and turned triumphantly to face him. 'I have with me your pardon from King William's government allowing you to return home. You do not even have to take an oath of allegiance; they have accepted my thousand pounds as guarantee for your good behaviour.'

Alexander stood up and paced across the cramped room making the candles gutter. He had resigned himself to a lifetime of exile and thought he had been successful in smothering the lasts pangs of homesickness for the Highlands many years ago. But now, faced with this olive branch, it was possible to return.

'What would I do?' he rubbed his chin savagely, his blue eyes searching the face of the other. 'I still have no lands to call my own and I shall not serve in William's army,' he lifted his head proudly. 'Yet all I am good for is fighting.'

MacQueen felt the yearning in his kinsman and pressed with his idea. 'You could return with me to Penstroun and learn how to run the estate with Hugh. He for one could do with the disciplined guidance of an older brother and he wants to see you again. He is a good boy but even the pious strictness of the court at Saint-Germain has not tamed his wildness altogether.' He paused and looked directly back at the questioning eyes. 'More importantly, Scotland is in need of good men to govern it. I cannot pretend that these years under King William and Queen Mary have been good ones for our country. We have come to an uneasy truce in the Highlands, but our trade has suffered greatly these past few years. England guards jealously her overseas trade, and now she is spoiling for a war with France because they have recognised young James Francis Edward as the new Jacobite heir. If war goes ahead we shall be worse off than before.' James MacQueen looked at him hopefully.

'Surely you are not proposing to groom me as your heir at Penstroun?' Alexander's mouth curved in wry amusement. MacQueen took a swig of vodka.

'I am offering you a home and in return will have need of you Alexander,' he answered softly, 'that is all I can say.'

The exiled Ballantyne was intrigued. It was possible as the elder of the senior cadet branch of the clan MacQueen that he might inherit Penstroun. The Ballantynes had married into the MacQueens of Culduggan in his great-grandfather's time. After all, the widower Chief had no heirs. But then Maitland was married to his sister, Christina, and no doubt felt his own son Hector had an equal claim.

'And what of Archibald Maitland?' he asked.

'That is a further reason for wanting your return,' MacQueen grunted. 'I am well aware that he is a ruthless man who will always put his own interests before those of his tenants or neighbours. You could help me contain his influence in the area before he grows too powerful. Like it or not, I have to co-operate with him, for the sake of my sister if nothing else. As for his family,' MacQueen shrugged, 'his daughter Sybilla is quite charming, although young Hector is rather too pompous for his own good. That is why, when his father asked if Hector could accompany me to Moscow, I agreed. I thought that prizing him away from the safety of his mother's skirts might knock some of the hot air out of the young man.'

Alexander swirled round at this. 'You have brought him here?' he felt his temper begin to boil. 'Hector Maitland! Well I hope I don't have the misfortune of bumping into the son of that cowardly thief who stole my father's lands from me!'

The ageing chief thought it best to let the matter rest for the moment. Young Ballantyne, with his veneer as the hardened mercenary, was still the hot-headed proud Highlander he had watched ride off across the mountains all those years ago. He felt a twinge of affectionate regret that he had not had just such a son of his own.

'Let's not talk of the Maitlands now,' he took Alexander by the elbow. 'You will stay and eat with me?'

Alexander was about to refuse and then felt it would be churlish of him. He nodded. James MacQueen ordered some food and a servant brought in plates of salted fish, cucumber, egg pastries and mutton seasoned with garlic and saffron. The Chief produced a bottle of claret from his own supply and they sat in silence for a while thinking their own thoughts.

'Is there to be a Grand Ball in honour of the Victory?' MacQueen asked unexpectedly.

'Yes,' Alexander replied, 'it will be a vast affair if Tsar Peter has anything to do with it.'

The other smiled. 'I was wondering if as my kinsman you would do something for me,' he added mysteriously, 'a favour for a good friend of mine? I promise that it will be no hardship to yourself.' The young Major raised a dark eyebrow quizzically. 'It is for Dr Putulo, who I believe was a help to you when you first came here.'

'Indeed he was,' Alexander agreed with a smile. 'I would be glad of the opportunity of repaying his kindness, though I fear I have offended his Presbyterian sensibilities by my association with Natalya. Perhaps I can make amends?'

'His younger daughter Katherine is my goddaughter,' Chief James continued, 'a charming young lady. Her sister has just got married and she will be alone with her father now. I would like you to accompany her to the Ball. It is time she met an eligible nobleman and especially a Scot. Ewen Putulo complains she will consider none of the young men in the Quarter.'

Alexander groaned inwardly. He had no recollection of what Putulo's daughters were like, just a vague impression of two scampering, giggly girls. No doubt they were now prim upright Presbyterian ladies and dull company to escort to a grand ball. There was probably good reason why Katherine was the unmarried sister, he would warrant. Still he had a duty to his chief and he had liked the genial doctor too.

'As long as taking Miss Putulo to the Ball is my only obligation to her,' he laughed.

'Of course,' MacQueen smiled back at his tall kinsman.

'There is only one concern,' Alexander added rather awkwardly. 'Countess Natalya will be expecting to attend it with me.' With annoyance he felt himself blush like a boy.

'I would be delighted to accompany her myself if you will permit it,' James MacQueen said gallantly. 'I remember the Countess and her late husband from my early days in Muscovy. Perhaps she would make do with an old Highland chief?' his grey eyes twinkled.

'Undoubtedly,' Alexander raised his glass in reply, thinking ruefully how pleased Natalya would be to have attention paid her by a member of the Scottish nobility who also had land and money.

As they polished off the food, something occurred to Alexander. 'Was there a wedding here at the Hostelry yesterday, sir?'

'Yes,' the Chief told him, 'in fact it was Elspeth Putulo's marriage. I celebrated too well with her father,' he grimaced.

'Was there a Russian merchant there, a Count Stromsky?' Alexander asked lightly. 'He lives in the south, Cossack country, I believe.'

James MacQueen shook his head. 'I don't think so, I'm sure I knew all the Russians there. Why do you ask?'

Alexander wiped his mouth and got up, feeling himself go hot. 'No reason; he is just an acquaintance of mine who I'd heard was in Moscow for a wedding. It's of no importance,' he added quickly, trying to hide his annoyance.

James MacQueen rose too and put a hand on his shoulder. They were the same height and considered each other for a moment.

'You will think hard about my proposal, Ballantyne?' he urged. 'I have important plans which rest on your decision.'

Alexander wondered what these plans might be and was impatient to hear more. Yet he was unsettled at the thought of returning to Scotland; he would need time to mull it over. He nodded agreement as he left.

Outside, squinting in the brightness, he chided himself for having asked about the mysterious Stromsky. Like him, the bewitching Katya had vanished as if she had never existed and he found it infuriating that he had been outwitted by a mere serving maid, if that was indeed what she was.

***

Katherine and Rosa took a troika ride down to the Yauza River. Well wrapped in fur-lined cloaks and hoods, their hands buried deep into muffs, they walked ahead of their servants by the frozen expanse that would soon begin to shudder and move under the spring thaw.

Katherine was withdrawn after the anti-climax of the wedding several days ago and could not shake off her sad mood.

'Rumour has it, your Major Ballantyne will be awarded the Order of St Andrew by the Tsar for his gallantry in the field,' Rosa babbled excitedly out of earshot of their chaperones, giving Katherine a sly look.

'He's not my Major Ballantyne,' her friend sniffed, feeling a sudden warmth in the air.

'He would have it that way, *Katya*!' Rosa giggled. 'And you should be honoured; they say he's a close friend of Tsar Peter's as well as one of the best foreign officers since General Gordon passed away.'

Katherine lifted her chin impatiently, forcing her velvet and sable hood to fall from her pile of rich black curls. 'You talk such nonsense Rosa,' she pouted, her dark lashes fluttering over large green eyes. 'I have no intention of renewing my acquaintance with the Major. And as far as he's concerned, I'm just a serving girl whom he shamelessly flirted with for an evening; that is all.'

'The flirting did not seem altogether one-sided,' Rosa teased and nudged Katherine's arm.

Katherine's cheeks went pink above her warm fur tippet thrown around her shoulders. The memory of their kiss became increasingly uncomfortable and she could hardly recognise herself in the brazen peasant girl who had danced the *Khorovod* with such abandon. 'It was merely high spirits,' she pulled the hood back over her head. 'Anyway he would never recognise me as I am now, were we to meet socially.' Inwardly, her confidence did not match her breezy words.

'Well, that is unlikely to happen,' Rosa admitted, warming to the subject. 'People say he lives like a Russian and hardly sets foot in the Quarter. When he is not following the rough life of a soldier, he lives with his Russian mistress in her mansion outside Moscow.'

Katherine shot a scandalised look at her small friend and noticed the excited glow on her face from the gossip. For a moment she was lost for words.

'Of course it does not surprise me,' Katherine snorted, 'that such a man would have no scruples about breaking the conventions of society. No wonder my father does not refer to him anymore. And what must the Russians think?'

Rosa noticed the tight line of annoyance suppressing Katherine's full lips.

'Luckily for the Major, the Tsar condones his behaviour and protects him from the outrage of some powerful boyars who hate everything us foreigners do.' She hesitated, slipping the other woman a side-long look. 'They say the Tsar will make them marry though, if it continues much longer in so open a manner.'

Katherine stopped and gazed out over the glittering landscape that stretched into a white eternity. Why did this news make her insides twist with something akin to jealousy? She had no claim on him, or he on her, and yet she resented this rich widow without even having set eyes on her.

'Who is she – this Russian woman?' Katherine tried to sound disinterested.

'Countess Natalya Matrapov,' Rosa answered, pleased that she could be the first to relay the scandal to new ears. 'Her late husband was a rich landowner, which is just as well, because she apparently lives extravagantly. Alexander Ballantyne is not the first of her lovers either, so they say. The Danish diplomat, Captain Paterson says she clings to these young men so that her husband's greedy relations do not try to force her into a convent – the fate of so many highborn Russian widows. No doubt it would suit her to marry your Scots officer.'

Rosa saw with alarm that Katherine did not find this amusing or entertaining. She detected distress in the dark eyes. 'I'm sorry, I did not think you would mind so much.'

'Oh, it's not that,' Katherine gave the Italian girl an unhappy look, 'I've remembered something else from the other night.' She recounted the brush with Hector Maitland and his unwanted advances and the assignation she had been forced to promise.

'That's terrible,' Rosa was suddenly terrified. 'I cannot imagine what my Papa would say if he knew where we had been Katherine, the disgrace!' Katherine saw the fear in her friend's petite dark features and pulled herself together.

'Don't worry,' she smiled, linking arms, 'I will deal with the pompous Maitland. I'm sure he is quite harmless, if a little too full of his own self-importance.'

For a moment they stood in silence each in their own thoughts, then Katherine became aware of a new sound in the air. The river was groaning and creaking like some ancient Russian chant.

'Listen,' she whispered, excitement catching her breath.

'What is it?' Rosa sounded puzzled.

'The ice is starting to crack,' Katherine felt her usual optimism returning, 'spring is on the way.'

***

As the Panini troika drew up in the courtyard of the Putulo house, Katherine noticed the green canopy of her godfather's troika. 'Uncle James is here,' she cried, 'you must stay and meet him again.' Rosa needed little persuasion, the winter and the lack of social contact had seemed endless.

'Godfather,' Katherine beamed and crossed the drawing-room to greet the white bearded man, still bulkily dressed in his wool plaid and Russian felt boots.

'Katherine!' he enveloped her in a hug, admiring the healthy flush in her smooth cheeks, the broad lips red as summer cherries and the long feathery lashes sweeping up from the deep green eyes. 'And where have you been?'

James MacQueen delighted in their uninhibited chatter as they told about their ride and the ice breaking up across the Yauza River. He always found the Putulo house so refreshingly lively and homely after the starkness of the old castle at Penstroun which was seldom enlivened by the company of women.

'Are you going to the Grand Ball, Miss Panini?' the Chief asked Rosa.

'Captain Paterson has asked me to join his party,' she blushed prettily and the young women exchanged knowing looks. Rosa had talked of little else until the conversation had come round to Major Ballantyne. Katherine glanced at her father, 'and we shall be going too Papa, together?'

Ewen Putulo gave an awkward look. 'Your godfather comes bearing an invitation from a kinsman of his.'

Her eyes widened in surprise. 'This is most mysterious,' she laughed. 'Uncle James, do tell at once!'

'Your father has agreed to allow you to be escorted by one of the Tsar's own officers, one who will be honoured at the Ball. His father was a kinsman and loyal friend of mine. You may recall meeting him some years ago; Major Alexander Ballantyne. He wishes to take you to the celebrations.'

It felt like a mass of Moscow starlings had been released and were beating against Katherine's ribs trying to escape. She must have misheard; it was too awful to contemplate. But from Rosa's gasp she knew her godfather had spoken the dreaded name.

'Surely not,' she whispered, hardly able to breathe, 'how could this Major possibly know about me? It is a joke, Uncle James?'

For one appalling moment Katherine thought the officer must have discovered her true identity and done this to punish and embarrass her for her rudeness towards him. But that was not possible; he knew nothing about her and could not have traced her. It must be a ghastly coincidence that Ballantyne and the Chief were in some way related.

'No joke, my dear,' MacQueen laughed indulgently. 'I admit the idea was largely mine, but the Major was at once enthusiastic. You should not be missing out on gay assemblies because your sister is now married and away.'

'Papa,' she looked at him imploringly, 'surely you want me to go with you?'

He mistook her breathless look for coyness. At first he had been dubious at MacQueen's proposal, knowing of Alexander's liaison with the Russian widow, but had been persuaded that the officer would be a good match for Katherine.

He remembered having liked the penniless youth who had sought refuge with him when first he had arrived in Muscovy and he could hardly protest as Katherine had turned down all other suitors so far.

'You will go with this fine gentleman and enjoy yourself, daughter,' he insisted. 'As for myself, I would far rather sit at home by the fire with a good book and a dram.'

Katherine gulped, catching Rosa's look of alarm. 'If that's what you wish, Father.'

The two men laughed at her reluctance, taking it for girlish nerves.

'Katherine promised to show me some silks of hers,' Rosa said quickly, steering her stunned friend from the room before she gave herself away. Upstairs in her chamber, Katherine sat on a pink upholstered chair and hid her face in her hands.

'It can't be true,' she moaned, 'of all the bad luck–'

'Oh Katherine,' Rosa put a hand on her arm, 'he won't recognise you all dressed up in a fine gown and headdress.'

'But what if he does?' her friend's dark eyes looked forlorn. 'I can imagine the trouble he could make, would probably delight in making.'

'You will simply deny all knowledge of the other night,' Rosa replied firmly, 'and if he is a gentleman he will not press you further.'

'Oh, this is absurd,' Katherine got up and paced the room. 'I will pretend a headache and not go.'

'Katherine,' Rosa remonstrated, 'you know how much you love a ball. Besides you cannot decline the invitation. It would be a gross insult both to Major Ballantyne and to your godfather. They might suspect something; you must go!'

The tall girl gave a deep sigh. 'I suppose I must. I will just have to try and look as unlike Katya the peasant as possible. Papa cannot have heard of this Russian mistress, else I'm sure he would not be so keen on the idea.'

Rosa gave a nervous giggle. ‘At least you keep them apart for one evening; I wonder how annoyed the Countess will be?’

Katherine was about to protest then dissolved into reluctant laughter too.

***

Alexander Ballantyne sat beside the Countess Matrapov on a gilded couch in her tapestry-hung withdrawing-room. In the flickering candlelight she looked alluring in the gold brocade of her loose-fitting gown richly braded at the bosom and wrists, pearl buttons winking like eyes.

The chiselled, high-boned features of her once devastatingly handsome face were softened in the warm glow. Her pale blue gaze consumed him. Alexander, mellow from the intimate dinner and French wine, felt desire stir as the conversation lapsed. He leaned over, fastening his lips on her rouged ones, his hand cupping a half-bared breast. Resisting her own response to his ferocious appetite she pushed the young officer away.

‘You said there was something you had to explain,’ her voice was cool, ‘I would hear it first Alexander.’

He sighed and traced a finger across a bare shoulder as he considered how to tell her. ‘It is about the Ball, Natalya,’ he fixed her with his own steady look. ‘I have been prevailed upon to accompany someone else. It is tedious but unavoidable.’ He felt her stiffen and push away his exploring hand, pulling her robe about her.

‘A man like you is not free to take whom he wishes?’ she replied scornfully. ‘You cannot expect me to believe that!’

Alexander ran his fingers through his main of hair agitated by her reproof. ‘It is not to my liking, believe me,’ he retorted, ‘but my Chief has asked for this one favour. He has some dowdy goddaughter whom I must divert from her misery; her sister has recently married and left Moscow or some such. And her father Dr Putulo was good to me when I first came to Muscovy. She sounds a bore and I would have none of it, only–’

‘Go on,’ the Countess’s voice was steely.

‘Only, James MacQueen insisted he would like to accompany you himself if I would perform this deed. In fact he claimed to be an old friend of yours; is that true?’

Alexander tried to gauge his mistress's reaction as she sat motionless on the couch. It was too much that this evening should also be spoilt by the unwelcome Putulo girl.

'Yes,' she said quietly, 'many years ago we knew each other.'

'Then it will not be such an onerous task, Natalya?' he asked with relief.

'Not in the least,' she answered in the same controlled voice which unnerved him. Her face was hidden in shadow as the candles spluttered lower.

'Of course I will dispose of the Doctor's daughter as soon as possible and return here with you,' he added, wanting a more forceful response than this cold acquiescence.

'Naturally,' Natalya yawned and leaned across to him, her gown falling open, her heavy scent mixing with the waxy smell of the candles. 'Tell me about this girl. I do not like the thought of a younger rival.'

Alexander laughed, relieved by her familiar predatory response. He did not want his life complicated by young women either, except perhaps... Briefly he thought of the voluptuous uninhibited peasant girl, Katya, with a mixture of regret and angry frustration. Natalya began a skilful massage of his shoulders and neck.

'No prudish maiden would begin to compare with your charms,' Alexander declared as he shifted to embrace her. Natalya let out a gurgle of laughter as he kissed her throat and began to undo the pearl buttons of her *sarafan*.

***

Katya and Rosa had spent the last few days in a haze of excitement over the Ball, choosing materials for their dresses and begging accessories such as gloves and fans from those most newly arrived from Europe. The talk in the Foreign Quarter was of nothing else all week; each guest intent on out-doing the next in style and grandeur of costume.

Rosa eventually settled on the scarlet taffeta with layers of white lace bedecking the front and profusions of lace on the sleeves and cuffs. With some of the Panini jewels sparkling at her throat and in her hair, she would be a dazzling sight.

'Captain Paterson won't be able to keep his eyes off you,' Katherine grinned, looking up from her sewing as she put the final touches to her dress.

'I won't know what to say tonight,' Rosa gasped, suddenly overcome with the impending event.

'You mean he won't be able to get a word in edgeways,' Katherine laughed and held up her handiwork for inspection.

She had chosen silks of deep russet and flame orange that fell away from the gown in a striking train. Cream lace was gathered in ruffles on her bodice and at the elbows, though the front was much plainer than the usual formal style.

'I shall wear it with mother's amber necklace and pearl ear-rings,' Katherine announced with a tremor in her voice, her eyes pricking painfully at the thought that her mother would not be there to give her gasps of appreciation and encouragement as at her first ball.

'Just perfect,' Rosa squeezed her hand. 'Major Ballantyne will never look at that old widow of his again.'

'Rosa!' Katherine was shocked by her friend's unsubtle comment. 'I have no wish to separate him from anyone; I'm not the least bit interested in him anyway.' She pursed her lips primly, 'I only long for the dancing.'

'Of course,' Rosa could not hide her amusement, 'it doesn't matter to you who you dance with; you'd be just as happy with Hector Maitland.' She ducked as a pin cushion came flying across the room, to where she viewed herself in the mirror. 'I look forward to seeing you at the palace,' the Italian girl blew a kiss and pranced out of the room.

***

The Putulo's old housekeeper, Fiona, came to help Katherine get dressed. Having bathed in scented herbs, the young woman allowed her fussing Scot's maid to pull the new gown about her tall frame and fasten her in. She trailed some long dark tresses in ringlets about her bare shoulders, piling the rest on top of her head under the tall lace headdress. Pale orange ribbons fell from the crown onto her creamy skin. Silk stockings and satin shoes finished the stunning effect.

Fiona stood back and clucked approvingly at the young sophisticated woman before her. She had never seen her look as grown up, the almond-shaped eyes lively, the full lips and cheekbones heightened with colour.

'Even the Tsar himself will notice my Katherine,' her eyes shone with pride. 'How I wish your mother could see how lovely a picture you are.' Katherine was surprised to see tears in the older woman's eyes; she was not one to show her emotions easily. She hugged Fiona and wiped her cheeks with her lace handkerchief.

'This is a happy occasion Fiona,' she said gently, 'and I'm only going to a ball, not disappearing for ever like Elspeth.'

The servant sniffed and handed back the handkerchief. 'Don't worry about me; I'm just going soft with old age.'

Katherine smiled back. 'Look after Papa won't you? I think he misses Elspeth more than he cares to admit.'

'You just away and enjoy yourself, young miss, with your dashing soldier. Don't you be thinking of us, do you hear?' She began to bustle around her young charge, gathering up her velvet cloak and feather fan.

Katherine's heart lurched at the thought of how soon she would see Major Ballantyne again, sick with dread that he might recognise her instantly. Glancing one last time in the mirror, she saw a stranger with lively eyes staring back from under the high headdress. With luck he would never compare her to the simple peasant girl he had seen but a week ago.

'Chief James's carriage has come for you,' Ewen Putulo called up the stair. He crowed with pleasure as he saw Katherine appear in her finery and helped her into the waiting vehicle. James MacQueen made room for her in the warm leather-encased interior. With the crack of a whip the troika lunged forward into the darkness, speeding towards Moscow.

'We shall meet Lieutenant-General Ballantyne at the Kremlin palace,' the Chief explained, 'you will have heard he was honoured by Tsar Peter for his bravery?'

Katherine nodded, hardly hearing what he said, such was her state of nervousness. 'And who are you accompanying, Uncle?' she managed to enquire.

'An old friend, as a matter of fact,' he smiled back in the dimness of the carriage lantern, 'Countess Natalya Matrapov.'

Katherine was thankful of the dark, for she felt the fire in her cheeks at once. So she was to meet not only Ballantyne but his infamous mistress! Hating the idea as she did, she could not deny a strong curiosity at meeting the woman.

Presently her thoughts were jolted by the cries of guards at the city gates. Through the small window Katherine made out the high sweep of the Kremlin walls and then they were through into the Tsar's citadel.

CHAPTER 3

The sight before Katherine was breath-taking. Dozens of carriages and troikas were dropping off their occupants at the massive wooden doors of the palace. Inside, a marble staircase ablaze with lanterns swept into the upper gloom of archways and wood panelled ceilings. A myriad of colourful costumes mingled ahead, some of traditional Russian garb, others courtly European dress.

James MacQueen steered Katherine towards the stairs, while servants in smart blue livery hurried to the guests' bidding.

'I believe I caught a glimpse of Ballantyne at the top,' the Chief pressed his hand on her arm. 'I shall introduce you and then wait for the arrival of the Countess downstairs.'

Katherine gulped and mounted the stairs with as much reluctance as going to the gallows. She fought a desire to turn and flee from all the sumptuous grandeur which overwhelmed and made her dizzy. A group of young officers, laughing with the French diplomat, De Maton, parted as the Chief and his companion reached them.

'Alexander,' MacQueen cried and the broad shouldered man in the scarlet coat turned.

For a moment Katherine just stood and stared at the man before them. She did not recognise this tall elegant officer in his satin waistcoat, broad-sleeved overcoat and sword belt, the riding boots replaced by stockings and leather shoes. He wore a dark imposing wig that made him appear severely formal. Over the red uniform lay the blue-ribboned Order of St Andrew, the highest award for bravery the Tsar could bestow. Alexander came forward and greeted his kinsman.

'This is my goddaughter, Miss Katherine Putulo,' James MacQueen proudly made way for the young woman. 'Katherine, I have the honour of introducing you to Lieutenant-General Alexander Ballantyne.'

Katherine dropped in a curtsey, glad of the gesture to hide her nervousness. Several appreciative eyebrows were raised, but Ballantyne appeared not to notice her startling effect on the others. She could not resist a sly glance from under her long lashes as his square jaw descended on the hand she held out. He brushed it lightly with his lips and Katherine felt a delicious frisson up her arm. It was mere seconds, but Alexander hesitated, holding onto her hand and looked at her properly for the first time.

Their eyes met, yet she could not fathom the thoughts behind the piercing enigmatic blue of his. Her heart thumped under the constriction of russet-coloured silk, fear of sudden recognition tightening her throat.

'Enchanted,' he murmured, the bold gaze sweeping over her as it had done the other night.

'Sir,' Katherine nodded, her mouth dry, 'it is an honour to meet you.' She licked her lips as he stood back and hid her flushed face behind a large fan of feathers. James MacQueen left her with the group of officers and disappeared to find the Countess. Peering over the fan, Katherine was aware of the Lieutenant-General still eyeing her.

'Tell me Miss Putulo, how could I have overlooked such beauty in the Foreign Quarter? Does your father, the good doctor, keep you always at home?' This provoked amusement among the others. Katherine flapped her fan vigorously.

'I am surprised you do not remember, sir, my father is a cultured man who encourages my education in the arts and society,' she replied. 'But then you have not been to see him for such a long time and are, I believe, seldom in the Quarter. It is our loss that you are so often away on campaign, Lieutenant-General.'

De Maton guffawed, 'touché, Mademoiselle!'

Alexander gave her a sharp look and then laughed graciously too. 'I must make amends for past absences,' he acceded, taking her arm in his and leading her into the first reception room. 'How is your father?'

Katherine's hand shook as it closed around the stiff braiding on his coat sleeve, but she walked calmly forward. 'Very well thank you. He asks to be remembered to you and begs you come and visit before your duties take you from Moscow again.'

Alexander smiled and patted the hand on his arm. 'That I will most certainly do, Miss Putulo.'

Before them, a huge table was spread with tempting dishes of food; pastries, eggs, cheeses, meats, cakes and caviar stretched the length of the room. Alexander pressed her with a plate of salted fish, but she could not swallow a thing, her insides fluttered so violently in his presence. He took a mouthful and washed it down with a glass of vodka.

'Come and tell me about your sister's wedding,' Alexander led her to a corner couch, sensing her unease with him. It had only just occurred to him that she might be here under sufferance too, tired of the match-making of her father and godfather. He looked at the dark green eyes and rosy lips, the tendrils of hair curling about her neck, the cut of her shimmering dress across her creamy skin, and wondered. Of course it could not be, and yet this doctor's daughter stirred in him the same interest he had experienced in the peasant Katya's dark looks. How strange that they should resemble each other.

'I remember Elspeth as a small dark-haired girl who demanded I go on my knees and give her horseback rides,' he joked.

Katherine laughed. 'And I was quite relieved because being the taller sister, although the younger, that was usually my role in her games.'

'Yes,' Alexander watched her, 'I remember now. You seemed to find the way I spoke of great amusement; my youthful pride was quite hurt,' he laughed. 'The only time you weren't giggling was when you played the spinet quite beautifully. Do you still play, Miss Putulo?'

Katherine nodded bashfully, not wanting to be reminded of her childishness. Alexander saw her embarrassment and changed the subject. 'So the wedding was a grand occasion for your elder sister?'

'Yes,' Katherine faltered, trying to control her voice. 'There was feasting and speeches and dancing…'

'You like to dance then?' he asked quickly, turning to look at her fully.

'Yes,' she gulped, 'I enjoy a minuet, sir.'

Katherine could not bring herself to look into his face now, knowing how he scrutinised her. She felt overpowered by his closeness and the energy he exuded even in his relaxed pose. She smelt the muskiness of his cleanly shaven chin and swallowed.

'My sister Elspeth is a great dancer, you will no doubt recall, much better than I ever was,' she chattered. 'Elspeth is daintier, of course, and so nimble on her feet. She was always more accomplished at the social graces than me.'

Alexander leant over and covered her hands with his as they writhed in her lap. He could see her heart beating fast beneath the delicate silk and lace, her face glowing as warm as her dress in the lamplight.

'It is you I am interested in dancing with, Miss Putulo,' he spoke low, raising her gloved hand to his lips, 'not your sister, however perfect.'

Katherine's heavy lids fluttered and she stole a look at his face, the scar on his left cheek catching in the light like a branding. She felt again the mesmeric pull of his blue eyes, set in the strong-featured face and could not drag her gaze away. Her breath caught in her throat as he squeezed her hand and leant close so that his chin almost touched her cheek.

'Have we not met more recently than ten years ago, Miss Putulo?' he murmured. 'I feel sure that we have.'

She thought he must hear the hammering of her heart as it pounded like an iron bell. 'I don't believe so, sir,' she whispered, 'indeed I am sure we have not. Perhaps I remind you of someone else?' For a moment their eyes locked, and then he sat back.

'Perhaps,' he mused.

'It would be nice to join the dancing now, Lieutenant-General,' Katherine let out a long breath, feeling the moment of confrontation was past. He laughed and stood up, holding out his arm for her.

'It would be my pleasure, Miss Putulo.'

As they moved from under the archway, Katherine caught sight of her godfather and his partner. With a pang of envy she took in the latter's strikingly attractive Slavic face, delicate high-boned features like precious porcelain, highlighted by black face patches. She was small and still retained the curved figure of a much younger woman, set off by a sparkling gown of white lace and silver brocade, studded with diamonds and pearls. The only concession to her status as a widow, Katherine noticed, was a black gauze veil that covered her white blonde hair and black ribbons sewn into the bodice and sleeves of the dress which only enhanced its appearance. Her poise was almost regal.

'Let us join Penstroun,' Alexander said jovially, then noticed how Katherine hesitated. Following the line of her gaze, he saw that the Countess Matrapov appeared to be the subject of her concern. His first reaction was amusement; she too must have heard the gossip about himself and his mistress. Then, as Katherine's hand fell from his arm, he felt regret that their moment alone was over.

'Alexander,' Natalya Matrapov gave him a dazzling smile, 'you must introduce me to your charge.' She swung her gaze to the younger woman and fixed her with ice-blue eyes.

'Miss Putulo,' Alexander kept his voice light, 'this is Countess Matrapov. Countess; Miss Putulo is the daughter of the eminent Dr Putulo from Edinburgh.'

'And my dear goddaughter,' MacQueen added, beaming with pride. 'Is she not beautiful, Countess?'

Briefly the two women held each other's appraising look and then the Countess laughed. 'The child is certainly a pretty thing,' she said with a smile that belied her cold stare. 'I am delighted to meet you, Miss Putulo.'

‘And I you, Countess,’ Katherine replied, struggling to hide her fury at being called a child in front of the Lieutenant-General. She felt at once at a disadvantage with this sophisticated woman of the Russian court.

MacQueen took Alexander aside for a moment, leaving the two women together.

‘Your godfather has been telling me what a dutiful daughter you are, staying with your dear father,’ Natalya smiled. ‘But would you not rather marry and set up your own household like your sister? I hear you Scottish girls are so forthright.’

Katherine flushed. This woman was deliberately patronising her.

‘I am quite content, Countess,’ she managed to reply, wishing she could think of something witty instead.

‘How very noble, my dear,’ Natalya’s blue eyes glinted with bored indifference. Turning to the men she interrupted them. ‘I wish to hear all about the presentation of the Order of St Andrew, so well deserved I know.’ She smiled coyly over her lace fan.

Alexander sensed the frosty atmosphere between the women and said quickly, ‘Time enough for that, Countess.’

‘Quite so,’ MacQueen agreed hastily, recognising the awkwardness of the situation. ‘Now will you do me the honour of dancing with me, Countess?’

Natalya snapped her fan shut with a laugh and took the Chief’s arm. ‘With pleasure,’ she smiled, sweeping by Alexander with a swish of lace and a parting desirous look.

‘Shall we follow?’ he turned to his partner noticing the heightened colour in her cheeks and brow, where soft wisps of hair crept from below her headdress. She did not seem pleased and Alexander cursed himself for allowing Natalya to make barbed comments. No doubt she had delighted in making the younger woman feel uncomfortable. There was nothing for it but to endeavour to keep them apart for the remainder of the evening.

Katherine nodded stiffly without a word. She felt wretched. Just as she was beginning to enjoy this energetic officer’s company, the occasion had been spoilt by the appearance of his beautiful mistress; she reminded her of a hard but brilliant diamond. Even her godfather seemed quite entranced by the Matrapov woman, his gruff manner softened like a moonstruck youth. What chance was there that the handsome Ballantyne would prefer her company to that of the Countess?

He probably cursed the Chief's meddling in his affair and found being charming to her an onerous task.

'Come Miss Putulo,' Alexander's low voice broke into her morose thoughts, 'you do not seem happy at the prospect of dancing with a newly created Lieutenant-General?'

She winced at the gentle reproof, raising her eyes guiltily to his. He looked strikingly good-looking, his strong mouth curved wryly at one corner, the broad sweep of forehead and straight nose proud and aristocratic. The blue Order ribbon ran like a slash across the red breast of his uniform; at its end hung a miniature portrait of the Tsar beset in jewels.

Her heart squeezed at the thought that of all the men present in the great ballroom, she did not wish to dance with any other. For a brief heady moment, she, Katherine Putulo, was to dance with Tsar Peter's most celebrated foreign officer, and whether by duress or design he would partner only her. Smiling up at him, her jaw took on a delicate pink hue as she looked into the dramatic blue eyes.

'Please forgive me, sir,' her voice was husky with emotion, 'to dance with you would make me very happy.'

She noticed a muscle twitch momentarily in his cheek and he squeezed her gloved hand under his own. With a quickening pulse she allowed him to lead her forward.

***

The evening swept by in a wonderful haze of dancing and music, a glorious swirl of colour, light and gaiety as Moscow society celebrated into the early hours. To Katherine's delight, Alexander Ballantyne seemed to go out of his way to avoid the Countess Matrapov, content to entertain her with his tales of travel and adventure across Europe. He told her of the forays into the wild rocky terrain of the Crimea to battle with the Tartar hordes that ravaged into Russia each summer.

When she pressed him, he told her briefly of his escape from Scotland after the defeat of Claverhouse's Highland army by the government troops. Her father was a Presbyterian, approving of the regime in Scotland and she had never questioned that some Scots might not have been dealt with justly. In turn he listened with amusement to her anecdotes of romps around the Foreign Quarter with sister Elspeth as boisterous girls and the happiness of her childhood there.

‘So you have never returned to Scotland, sir?’ Katherine enquired. They had strolled for air along one of the draughty outer rooms and were standing on a balcony whose small window over-looked a quiet palace courtyard, above which blazed thousands of stars in a clear ink-black sky.

‘Never,’ Alexander answered. Catching her puzzled look he added, ‘I have sometimes thought of doing so, in my blacker moments. All exiles feel homesickness for the Highlands, I believe, like an itch that never quite goes away.’

Katherine gave him a quick side-long glance, surprised by the bitterness in his tone. ‘What about your family?’ she asked quietly. ‘You say your father is dead – but the others?’

He did not answer at once, a muscle in his cheek working while he struggled with some memory. Alexander rubbed the scar on his jaw.

‘My mother was – is – a Catholic, although the rest of the family were Episcopalian like my father and adhered to the Church of Scotland before it became Presbyterian. She went into exile in France and has remained there; your godfather says she has entered a convent.’ He sighed. ‘My Chief also tells me that my younger brother Hugh has returned to Scotland and is living with him at Penstroun. He wishes me to go back with him and do the same.’

‘And will you?’ Katherine probed.

‘I cannot,’ Alexander said defensively, ‘I have sworn never to return while King William sits on the thrones of Scotland and England.’

‘But if you do not return, what chance will you have of ever regaining your lands at Culduggan?’ Katherine asked. Alexander looked at her keenly.

‘So you are acquainted with my family’s history, Miss Putulo?’ he asked in surprise.

‘My godfather has talked of you these past few days,’ Katherine blushed. She had in fact asked many questions of the Tsar’s officer since the invitation to the Ball and had listened to conversations between her father and MacQueen when they thought her busy with her embroidery. ‘I know that Hector Maitland’s father runs Culduggan with a heavy hand and cares little for its tenants,’ she said with disapproval. ‘Uncle James says there have been the most terrible years of famine until recently and Sir Archibald Maitland has only sought to profit from the people’s distress.’

Katherine added, 'My godfather feels he still has some good influence on Hector and that is why he has brought him to Moscow. But I think he fears the older Maitland might have designs on Penstroun too.' Katherine said, giving him a sidelong look. 'And he has no immediate heir to help him curb the Maitlands' influence.'

Alexander was impressed by her observations, she understood the situation well. And yet he was irked by her reproving tone, as if it was somehow his fault. 'You think I should return and help him rid our lands of the troublesome Maitlands, don't you?' His voice grew terse.

'It is not for me to say,' Katherine flashed him a look, 'but you are a proud man and I cannot believe you are untouched by the suffering of your father's people. And you have a brother to consider, Lieutenant-General; one whose secure home was wrenched from him when he was very young.'

She watched his expression tighten, the scarred chin jutting stubbornly and eyes narrowing. She had said too much and Katherine cursed herself for having spoilt their moment of intimacy. Just as she expected him to turn away from her, his taut body relaxed and he rubbed his jaw.

'You may be right, Miss Putulo,' he agreed candidly, 'I am torn between answering my Chief's plea and remaining a loyal subject of Tsar Peter's.' He smiled ruefully. 'They are both exacting men.'

Katherine breathed again with relief and determined not to press him further on a subject which clearly cut him deeply.

'I have never visited my native land and have no real idea of what it must be like,' Katherine mused, 'and yet I have often yearned to see Scotland. Don't you think it strange to want something that can hardly be imagined? I know more about Muscovy than my homeland.'

She laughed softly and turned to face her companion. His chiselled features were illuminated by guttering candles in their embrasures.

'I don't think it strange to yearn for the unknown,' Alexander said, eyeing her keenly. 'I imagine you know a great deal about Mother Russia; perhaps more than a well-brought up young Scot's gentlewoman should know.' He sounded amused.

Katherine's heart began to drum furiously; had he guessed all along?

'I don't know what you mean, sir,' she gulped and moved away to grip the wooden sill.

'No?' he stepped behind her and stood so close she could feel his warm breath on the back of her neck. She shivered, not daring to turn.

‘It is cold and I think we should return to the Ball.’

‘Is not the doctor’s daughter who was capable of dressing up as a boy and climbing into kitchen gardens, capable of other such disguises?’ Alexander stroked the curls at the back of her neck as he spoke, sending delightful shocks down her spine.

Katherine’s chest constricted with panic. She must escape before an outright denial forced her to lie to him. Edging round the balcony away from his touch, she was suddenly acutely aware of their isolation.

‘Please, let us join the others,’ she avoided his eyes, feeling for the curtain hanging that half hid them from the other guests passing through the room. The lamplight caught his sardonic grin.

‘Of course there would be one way of finding out if we really have met before,’ he said, moving swiftly to block her retreat.

She gasped in shock at his quicksilver movement despite his size; his hands on her naked shoulders seemed to burn her skin. Any moment now he would stop her protest with one of his lusty kisses. She trembled at the thought, hating herself for not wanting to resist.

‘Ah, there you are, Miss Putulo,’ a loud voice intruded. The stout Hector Maitland pulled the hanging roughly aside. ‘My Uncle, Penstroun, is asking where you are,’ his plump face glistened above a heavily laced cravat, ‘I must say I’m surprised to see you out here.’

Alexander looked with annoyance at the plump interfering young man in peacock blue velvet. So this pompous sneaking youth was the heir to Culduggan; it was preposterous!

‘Miss Putulo does not need you to fuss over her like an old maid, Maitland,’ he said in contempt, ‘be gone with you.’

Hector Maitland flushed at the taller man’s dismissive gesture, his bulbous brown eyes narrowing with dislike.

‘That’s as maybe, Ballantyne,’ he answered peevishly, ‘but it appears your mistress cannot do without her toy soldier; the Matrapov woman demands that you return to the dancing too.’

‘You insolent pup!’ Alexander shoved him back.

Katherine intervened, piqued at the sudden reminder of the Countess and her claim on Alexander.

‘Stop it!’ she cried, pushing herself between the men and turning angrily on Alexander. He had no right to dictate what was best for her; he had merely been teasing her as a diversion to help the evening pass more quickly before returning to his lover. ‘If the Countess wishes to see you I shall not keep you a moment longer,' she said, tossing back her loose curls and turning from him to Hector. 'Please show me where my godfather is, Mr Maitland, we were on the point of returning as it was.'

Hector Maitland looked with triumph at the furious officer and then gloatingly at Katherine's silk-swathed frame. He had interrupted them just in time as he had judged. How he hated the handsome Ballantyne who appeared to gain everything he wanted so effortlessly. Still, he had what his rival wanted above all else and that was Culduggan, and now he had succeeded in stealing the delicious Katherine Putulo from under his disdainful nose! He gave the young woman, who was practically his height, his arm.

'Are you coming with us, Ballantyne?' he asked gleefully.

Alexander looked at Katherine but she glanced away; she seemed to have dismissed him. Well, let her go with Maitland; she did not appear to dislike his slavering over her like a dog. 'I have others I must speak with first,' he said, waving them away. 'I recommend you dance a minuet – Miss Putulo so enjoys the dancing.'

Katherine shot him an indignant look and caught Alexander's infuriatingly amused smile before Hector steered her away.

***

Alexander stayed and lit a cheroot to calm his frayed nerves, amazed at the force of his dislike for the young Maitland as much as his warm feelings for Katherine Putulo. He had nearly lost his head over the darkly bewitching woman he had so briefly held in his grasp. If the overbearing Hector Maitland had not intruded he would have had no hesitation in forcing his kisses on her without a thought for his Chief who had entrusted him with his goddaughter for one evening, or even for his mistress of five years' standing.

The green eyes and fleshy red lips were those of Katya the serving girl who had defied and eluded him before. The more he saw of Katherine the more he was convinced she was the same woman, though he was astounded by the recklessness and audacity of her actions if it were so.

Blowing smoke out into the room he remembered Katya had not been alone that evening; a small silent olive-skinned friend had accompanied her. She was the clue to resolving the mystery once and for all.

Extinguishing the burning cheroot between his forefinger and thumb, Alexander went to seek her.

***

Katherine finished yet another dance with the tedious Hector Maitland, beginning to regret she had left Lieutenant-General Ballantyne so hastily. The young man's conversation revolved around how to make money out of the Russians, how ill-mannered he found them and how he could out-drink any number of these foreigners. When she tried to get him to talk of Culduggan and Penstroun, he merely laughed and said the people were even more dull and wretched than the Russians and how, as soon as he could afford it, he would go to London and join the Court.

Katherine listened with mounting irritation, glancing around to see if Alexander still talked with the Countess Matrapov. Turning in the dance she saw them in animated conversation with her godfather and wished she was too. As the minuet finished she at last disengaged herself from Hector. Natalya Matrapov gave a brittle little smile as she approached.

'You have enjoyed the Ball, Miss Putulo?' she asked. 'It was enchanting to see you and the young Mr Maitland dancing so well together.'

Alexander watched the flush sweep up from Katherine's chest into her face. 'I have indeed enjoyed this evening, thank you,' she answered with dignity, aware of his appraising glance. She wondered if he too thought of their moment together in the alcove of the outer room.

'I have just been persuading your godfather to join my hunting party once the snows have melted,' Natalya continued brightly, 'we have not hunted together for such a long time.' She leaned towards MacQueen, putting a hand on his arm, a waft of heavy scent and low cut lace adding to her sensuality.

Katherine looked with quick interest at her godfather and saw his bearded face redden with pleasure. 'Well we cannot leave for Scotland until the ports are open,' he explained with gruff bashfulness, 'and that could be another couple of months.'

'Perhaps Miss Putulo would enjoy a few days of riding in the country too?' Alexander suggested. Katherine's mouth fell open in surprise, though she could not read his expression.

‘A splendid idea,’ MacQueen agreed, ‘Katherine is a fine horsewoman, I’m sure her father would allow it. What do you say my dear?’

‘I – I would be delighted to be included,’ she stammered, wary of being rebuffed by the Countess. But the fixed smile on the pale made-up face did not falter.

‘Of course you are welcome, child,’ Natalya answered lightly. ‘The Chief’s nephew, young Mr Maitland will be there, so you will have someone of your own age to entertain you.’

Katherine’s flush darkened, vexed that the older woman could make her feel so awkward and tongue-tied.

‘I think we should take our leave,’ James McQueen said at last, ‘it is late and my friend Putulo will be fretting about his youngest.’

‘Allow me to escort Miss Putulo home,’ Alexander stepped across quickly. ‘I am staying with De Maton in the Quarter tonight and it is on my way.’

Katherine saw Natalya’s face tense slightly but she said nothing. Her godfather seemed pleased at Alexander’s offer and bid them farewell with a smile. Descending in silence to the palace entrance, Katherine wondered if there had been an argument between the two lovers over the Countess’s obvious flirting with Penstroun. Alexander wrapped her velvet cloak about her shoulders and ushered her to a waiting troika. Inside the snug enclosed world, with its leather walls and furs to wrap around the occupants, Katherine was overcome with shyness. She could not think of a single thing to say and desperately wanted to break the intimate quiet as their carriage slipped over the frozen streets. Alexander reached for a bottle within his coat and pressed it to her lips.

‘It’s brandy,’ he said, ‘it’ll keep you warm.’

Katherine took a sip and spluttered at the fiery liquid on her tongue and throat. Within seconds she felt tingling warmth spread through her limbs.

‘Not so bad?’ he laughed, eyeing her in the gloom and took a large swig himself. They travelled for several minutes and then he spoke again. ‘Are you nervous of me, Miss Putulo?’

She slid him a wary look. ‘A little, I suppose,’ she admitted.

He grunted. A moment later he took her gloved hand lying on the fur covers.

‘You are a strange creature,’ he mused. ‘Sometimes you seem as if nothing ever daunts you – you speak freely and act with spirit – and at other times you withdraw into some secret world away from everyone else. You're like that now,' he regarded her closely. 'Am I so terrible that you wish for escape? Do you doubt that I would deliver you home safely?'

Katherine's heart began to thud. How was it that he could guess so much about her on their brief acquaintance? It was unnerving. She found him both frightening and exciting – unpredictable in his moods – yet she chose not to draw her hand away from his firm hold.

'As my godfather's kinsman, I trust you to behave like a gentleman, sir,' she answered huskily. 'And I do not find you terrible. I – I enjoy your company, Lieutenant-General Ballantyne.'

He leaned closer still and gently brushed aside a heavy ringlet from her neck, twisting it in his hand. 'That pleases me greatly,' he murmured, aware of a strong pulse beating in her throat. 'It is a long time since a gentlewoman has spoken so kindly of me, I assure you.' Tracing a finger across her neck, he was amazed by its softness, aroused by the flowery scent of her hair and skin. 'I wish I did not find you so irresistible, Katherine,' he spoke her name for the first time, 'or have such a desire to kiss you.'

She shrank back into the furs. 'You must not be so unscrupulous, sir,' she whispered, her eyes defiant. To her annoyance he leaned back and chuckled deeply.

'So you are a prudish doctor's daughter after all,' he mocked, 'I mistook you for something less tame, I must admit.'

'You are insolent!' Katherine flashed at him. 'I wish Uncle James were here instead of you; he is a true gentleman.'

'Do you really?' Alexander's breath was warm on her cheek. 'I don't believe it. I think you feel the same attraction I do Katherine. What was it you called me – a "coarse foreign soldier", wasn't it? Well that's what I am and you seemed pleased enough to kiss me then, didn't you, *Katya*?'

He slipped his hand behind her head and pulled her lips up to his, kissing her brazenly as he had done at the peasants' dance. For a moment she was quite taken by surprise, feeling the same headiness as before, enjoying the taste of his mouth on hers. Then she felt the indignity of having been taken advantage of so shamelessly. Pushing him away, she lifted her hand and smacked him hard across his scarred cheek, her large eyes blazing.

'I'm not your mistress to do with as you will,' she hissed. 'So save your unwanted kisses for your ageing Countess and don't dare to insult me further!'

Alexander grabbed her hand and pinned it back, seizing her chin in a painful vice. He would make her want his attentions and regret the blow she had just delivered. No one spoke to him like that! On the point of descending on her mutinous lips with another bruising embrace, he held back. Something in the dark eyes challenged him, spoke of their silent contempt for his behaviour. What had come over him?

'Damn you,' he cursed under his breath and released his hold on her.

They sat in silence, Katherine breathing fast. She loathed him now for his arrogance; he was no more than a common soldier, for all his grand title and award. He and the scheming widow Matrapov were well matched; both totally selfish in the pursuit of what they desired with no regard for the feelings of others.

She had been stupid to think that she could influence this man for her godfather's benefit, with appeals to his better nature to acknowledge his obligations and return to Scotland. He had obviously lost such feelings of loyalty and decency long ago and Penstroun was misguided to think of Alexander as his friend.

And now he knew it was she who had danced with him as Katya the peasant the other night. Katherine did not doubt that he would get a savage pleasure in embarrassing her with such intelligence, especially after she had insulted him and his mistress. Her best ploy might still be to feign ignorance.

'Why did you call me Katya?' she slid him a wary glance. Alexander considered her silently and she dropped her gaze.

'Don't be so coy,' he said. 'I spoke with your friend Rosa Panini tonight. I knew I had met you before, Miss Putulo.'

She squirmed with embarrassment; it was just as much her fault as his that things had gone too far. If only she had not been so impulsive in the *Khorovod.*

'Sir, you will not tell my father or godfather, will you?' Katherine asked nervously, not reassured by his mocking blue-eyed look.

'Tell them what?' his mouth twisted with amusement. 'That you flaunted their authority and roamed the dangerous streets of Moscow dressed in unseemly garb?' He paused. 'Or that you flung yourself at an uncouth officer and kissed him without even discovering his name?'

Katherine flushed and looked away. She wished she had not asked him now; he was enjoying her wretchedness. With a jolt the troika pulled up at her father's house. Alexander got out and held the door open for her. He stopped Katherine with a firm hand on her arm.

'We have misunderstood each other, Miss Putulo,' he said stiffly. 'I lack the polished manners you are used to, but I thought you had a certain liking for me, none the less. Perhaps I am mistaken,' his keen eyes searched hers. 'If you will forget the incident in the carriage, your secret over Katya is safe with me.'

Katherine began to shake uncontrollably as she nodded in reply.

'Good,' Alexander let go his hold, his manner now brusque. 'There is no reason for us to be further embarrassed by each other's company. You will not find me frequenting the Quarter. For the short time I remain in Moscow, I shall stay where I am wanted.'

Katherine's heart lurched at his obvious reference to the Countess and turned quickly from his cool expression.

Inside the house, she listened to his troika pull away and wondered why she was suddenly overwhelmed with the heavy weight of anti-climax. She bit her lip with disappointment, aware that she had lost Alexander's waxing interest in her. Katherine was annoyed at such feelings. What did it matter? They did not particularly like each other and had only made an attempt to be civil to please Penstroun. Well they had done their duty and that was an end to it. Exhausted, Katherine made her way upstairs.

CHAPTER 4

To Katherine's surprise she found herself continually thinking back to her stormy encounters with Lieutenant-General Ballantyne. To hear absolutely nothing of his movements since the Grand Ball was tantalising and she wondered whether he ever gave their brief meeting another thought. The weeks passed and the whole countryside began to wake from under its winter blankets and shake off the shackles of snow and ice. The rivers flowed again and the women returned to their banks to wash clothes. Meadows beyond the Foreign Quarter sprouted green once more and the larks could be heard hovering high above the gardens and parks of the Settlement.

Katherine's original anxiety at the outcome of the Grand Ball and whether Alexander Ballantyne would keep to his promise, gave way to the thrill of seeing the earth come alive again. The talk was all of planning excursions and picnics and parties as the days grew longer. Natalya Matrapov's hunting party was arranged for the end of the week and James MacQueen appeared to be spending less and less time visiting the Putulo household while increasingly being in the company of the Countess. Katherine wondered wryly what the insufferable Lieutenant-General made of that.

As she made her way home from visiting Rosa, Katherine was content to breathe in the sweet spring air and feel the tepid sunshine against her back as she walked. Her friend's talk had been only of Captain Paterson and she seemed to have forgotten her fear at her father's wrath should he discover their peasant escapade. Katherine on the other hand kept her thoughts of Alexander to herself and was evasive when quizzed about what had happened the night of the Tsar's Ball. Ballantyne at least appeared to have forgotten both events. Even Rosa did not seem to know if he remained in Moscow; with the advent of spring, Tsar Peter's army would be preparing to follow up their gains over the Swedes.

'Katherine,' a voice called to her from out of a passing carriage, 'allow me to give you a ride home.'

Her heart sank at the appearance of Hector Maitland at the window; she had managed to avoid his proposed trip with a variety of illnesses and family duties and had been assured by Rosa that he had found other young women to divert him. His face was flushed and jovial under a tight cravat, his large heavy wig hanging forward as he leaned out.

'I am enjoying the air, thank you, Mr Maitland, and am nearly home,' Katherine smiled politely and carried on walking.

'No, I insist,' Hector clambered out of the carriage. She heard laughter inside and saw that he had companions.

'Then that is kind of you,' Katherine let him take her hand. He was after all her godfather's nephew and she could be civil to him for a short while. He still knew embarrassing information about her.

'Let me introduce you to my new friends Rupert Crocker and his sister Sarah, from London,' Hector said expansively. 'And this is the Katherine Putulo I have talked about, Dr Putulo's youngest and prettiest daughter – and most elusive I may say.'

The young woman tittered and her brother stared at Katherine with pale eyes.

'Have you seen anything of the noble Ballantyne recently?' Hector lurched towards her. 'It must be quite frustrating for such an active man to have his place usurped by my ageing Uncle James.'

'What do you mean by that?' Katherine bridled.

'I mean his place in the Countess Matrapov's bed, of course,' Hector laughed and his friend, Crocker, sniggered.

'You are quite impertinent Mr Maitland,' Katherine coloured and looked at him with distaste, 'my godfather is an old friend of the Countess's from years ago and you should not speak of your own uncle so. As for the Lieutenant-General, his welfare is none of my concern.'

'I'm so glad,' Hector grinned and patted her hand which she quickly withdrew, 'and I did not mean to insult your sensibilities, Miss Putulo.'

It was only then that she realised they were speeding down the wrong avenue to take her home. The carriage was heading out into open countryside and away from the Quarter altogether.

'Your coachman has missed the turning, Mr Maitland,' she said, 'please tell him to turn about.'

'Oh come, Katherine,' Hector answered, 'we thought you would like to come for a jolly picnic with us on such a beautiful day.'

'My father is expecting me for the midday meal,' Katherine looked pleadingly at the others, but they just nodded and smiled.

'That has been taken care of,' Hector looked pleased with himself, 'we called at your house on our way. Your old maid said the good doctor would be out until evening, so we took the liberty of telling her you would be lunching with us.'

Katherine looked at him in dismay. He seemed very pleased with his 'kidnap' and continued to show-off in front of the others. She could see that to make too much fuss might just make matters worse and decided to remain mutely disapproving of his tactics.

Sitting back, she attempted to enjoy the ride and the sights and smells of the countryside, ignoring Hector's inane banter and the tittering laughter of the other two.

At last they stopped at the edge of a forest clearing with the distant sound of chopping wood ringing beyond and the rush of the swollen Moscow River. Birds sang and the meadow before them was damp and springy underfoot, smelling sweet and fresh.

Hector climbed out after her, hauling with him a casket of food and a large flagon of wine. 'Come on Katherine, we'll chose the best spot for lunch,' he ordered.

Glad to be out of the carriage she followed. Hector made towards the river where a circle of trees were in bud. Katherine shivered in a sudden gust of wind wishing she had put on her cloak that morning. As it was she only wore a light dress of pink satin and a lace cap and mittens.

'This looks a good nest,' Hector threw down his baggage, 'I'll get some furs for us to sit on.'

Katherine watched him go, wondering with irritation why the others were taking so long to join them.

'Come on Crocker,' she heard him call as he approached the carriage. From the door a large fur cloak was thrown onto the ground, then the door slammed and the coachman cracked his whip. With a jolt the horses set off at a trot leaving Hector shouting after them. He ran a short way behind the receding vehicle but was soon out of breath. Katherine caught a glimpse of Crocker's thin face laughing at the window and then he was gone. Annoyance swept over her as Hector panted back to the river.

'How are we supposed to get home now?' she snapped at his puffing figure.

'Sorry,' he wheezed, 'that Rupert's a bit of a joker.' He gave her a sly smile. 'But don't worry; I know they'll come back for us. In the meantime we might as well have something to eat, eh?'

Katherine put her hands on her hips. 'I think you knew fine well what they planned to do. I wouldn't be surprised if you arranged it to happen like this, Mr Maitland.'

Hector laughed indulgently, 'Don't let's spoil the fun. I've been trying to get you alone for weeks, you little minx.'

She wanted to place a well-aimed shoe in his fat ribs for the way he had tricked her, but stifled her anger with monumental self-control. It was no good crossing swords with him now, while he had her alone; she had no idea how far away the nearest people might be. In the vast silence of the forest, the woodcutter's noise could be miles off.

'Look, I'm sorry Katherine,' he gave her a puppy-dog look, 'I should have asked you first. But we might as well tuck-in now we're here. They'll be back for us soon.'

She sighed and sat down on the fur cloak he had spread for them, while Hector busied himself unpacking a huge selection of meats and cheeses, pies and chicken legs, cakes and fruit. Pouring red wine into two leather travelling goblets he handed one to her.

'Go on, it's spring and time to enjoy ourselves in this outlandish country,' he urged. Reluctantly she put the wine to her lips, tasting its mellow sweetness like summer orchards and Katherine discovered she was thirsty after her walk and carriage ride. Settling down, she found herself enjoying the food in the open air and listening to the sounds of old Mother Russia welcoming the springtide.

'Tell me about your family,' Katherine asked, 'what is the Chief's sister like?'

'Mama?' Hector sounded surprised that she should ask. 'Why, she is a kindly soul and runs Culduggan as best she can, which is not easy – it is such an uncomfortably bleak place. She enjoys the summer when she can visit my father's relations in the Lowlands and escape the tediousness and lack of society in the North. How anyone chooses to live there I cannot imagine; I spend as much time away as possible,' Hector said with disdain, chucking away a chicken bone.

'So why does your father choose to do so?' Katherine asked.

Hector shifted uncomfortably at mention of Sir Archibald. 'My father has pious notions of educating the Highlanders in the ways of God, though I think it a thankless task from what I know of them. They do not have our civilised manners and are keener on fighting and stealing from each other than making an honest profit.'

'You do not include your own uncle in this condemnation, surely?' she defended her godfather.

'Perhaps not,' Hector shrugged, 'though even he seems to devote too much energy in upholding outmoded practices on his estates and allows the labourers to get the better of him. My father is not so soft or easily taken in by their laziness,' he scoffed.

'Maybe Uncle James thinks it more important to save the lives of his people than to worry about profit,' Katherine chided.

'More fool him,' he laughed and picked up a chop, 'if the people were more industrious they would not starve.'

Katherine looked at him with horror, wondering if these were his own opinions or his father's words repeated so tritely. 'And is your sister so hard-hearted?'

'Sybilla does not concern herself with such things,' Hector munched as he replied, 'she cares only for new clothes and young men, neither of which are in plenteous supply at Culduggan.' He caught his companion's stony look and added hastily. 'You must not think me hard of heart, Katherine; I do not dislike your godfather's people, but it's not in my power to ease their situation. Let's talk of something more cheerful.'

Katherine leaned back on her elbow in the shelter of the ring of trees, too tired to argue with his callous indifference. She only half-listened to his gossiping about the Quarter as the warm sunshine fell on her face. Yawning, she thought she had eaten and drunk too much of the vast picnic and would struggle to keep awake during Hector's endless talk about himself. She would just close her eyes for a moment ...

***

Katherine woke to find herself alone. Glancing around drowsily there was no sign of the young Maitland. The heavy flagon of wine lay empty on its side and a small squirrel nibbled at a half-eaten cheese within an arm's reach. It was so peaceful that somehow she did not worry at her complete abandonment. It was like being a creature from the forest, enjoying the freedom of the countryside after months of hibernation.

A thump of feet behind made her turn to see Hector standing above. He had discarded his heavy green coat and his silk shirt flapped open at the cuffs and neck.

'Call of nature,' he grinned down, 'too much wine.'

Katherine was uneasy at the way he continued to stare down at her with his glazed prominent eyes.

‘Perhaps we should start back for the road,’ she roused herself, ‘someone is bound to pass sooner or later.’

He plonked himself down beside her. ‘No hurry,’ he slurred slightly. The reek of stale wine and garlic from his breath quite turned her stomach and she shifted away. ‘You’re not the first girl I’ve brought here,’ he leaned across, ‘but you’re by far the prettiest, d’you know?’

She rose to her knees, ‘I’d like to go now, Mr Maitland,’ she said as calmly as she could.

‘Ha!’ he laughed drunkenly. ‘Is this the coy game you played with Ballantyne? You’re even more desirable when indignant, my dear, I bet you drove him to distraction.’ Lunging towards her, Katherine dodged and Hector fell over into the damp grass.

‘Stay away from me or I’ll scream,’ she warned, scrambling to her feet as he regained his balance.

‘Katherine,’ he coaxed laughingly, ‘don’t play with me. You were ready for sport the night of your sister’s wedding and the night of the Grand Ball. I know you enjoy the company of men, for all your prim protestations. I just want a bit of harmless fun.’

He lurched forward. Katherine struggled with him, then raised her right arm and swung a fist at his left ear. Reeling from the blow, he grabbed at her dress to prevent himself falling. There was a rip of material as he went toppling awkwardly onto the leather food casket and twisted his leg.

‘Ah!’ he writhed in agony, cursing her loudly.

‘Stay down there or I’ll break your skull with this,’ Katherine warned, holding aloft the clay jorum of wine. Hector swore again, gripping his leg, but did not attempt to challenge her. ‘You can wait for your friends,’ she told him hotly, ‘but I shall make my own way back. Don’t you dare to call at my father’s house again, Mr Maitland. My godfather shall hear of your contemptible behaviour.’ She tossed the wine jar at him and walked briskly away.

Ducking, Hector shouted, ‘Then he shall hear of your peasant escapade too, Miss Putulo!’ The threat made no impression on Katherine and she continued without a backward glance. ‘Hey, you can’t leave me here!’ Hector called after her in panic. ‘I can’t walk on this leg, do you hear me. Katherine, come back at once!’

Katherine ran for the trees. If she remembered correctly it was only a short distance through the copse to the road. She had no idea what time it was, but there should be a few hours of daylight left, although the trees made everything seem darker.

Soon her shoes were squelching, stuck fast in the mud. Kicking them off, she went on in bare feet. Katherine felt her head and realised her cap had fallen off as she slept and the bodice and shoulder of her dress had been torn by the heavy-handed Maitland. Tramping on, she became anxious. Surely she should have reached the road by now? Perhaps she had taken the wrong track out of the river glade in her hurry. The sky between the trees was darkening and an eerie evening quiet had descended on the primeval forest. Only drips from the overhanging branches and the hoot from an owl disturbed the profound silence.

All at once she heard the distant drumming of horses hooves. If she were lucky it could be a woodman returning to his village with a cart of logs, from whom she could beg a lift. But what if it was some rough outlawed band of men, ready to take advantage of her defenceless state? People could go missing in these forest tracts, never to be found again.

With mounting alarm, Katherine crouched behind a thick tree trunk, pressing herself into the wet briars and foliage. As the riders grew closer, she thought her heart would explode with its hammering. From the sound there were at least two of them, maybe more. The horses slowed to a brief trot and then stopped yards away from her dank hideout. She peered through the grasses to try and view them. Her heart froze at the sight of a rough bearded thick-set man astride a black stallion. It was as she feared; the coarse skins he wore and the ugly looking sabre at his side confirmed him as a brigand.

***

Katherine tried to catch the words the ruffian called to his companion. They were obviously tracking someone and it was just her bad luck that they had happened upon her path. If they scoured the bushes to either side as they passed she was bound to be spotted. Her bright pink dress hardly blended in with the dark greens of the woods. She must move further into the undergrowth. Easing herself backwards, Katherine crawled through the grass. A moment later she heard the horses begin to walk on, the riders talking low.

Reaching for a branch to swing herself under, Katherine realised too late that it was rotten and half hanging from its tree. With an almighty crash it came down, pinning her beneath its weight. The forest echoed its protest at this disturbance with a flapping of birds above. She stifled a pained gasp in the hope the horsemen would think an animal had caused the noise.

'Over here!' a gruff voice called in Russian. 'I can see something.'

Footsteps thrashed through the bushes, the swish of swords cutting their way towards her. Katherine froze terrified and unable to move as a voice above sounded triumphant.

'Look what we have here,' the grizzled bandit with the thick moustaches leered close to her, 'a rabbit in a trap.' His laughter sounded harsh as his companion joined him. Katherine twisted her head, trying to make out her other captor.

'One of these days your high spirits will get you into serious trouble,' Alexander Ballantyne said with exasperation. 'Help me lift this branch Baturin.'

She gasped with relief at the familiar voice and the sight of Alexander's broad-shouldered frame bending over her.

'I thought you were–' she gulped, tears springing to her eyes as the shock passed. 'I was so frightened.'

Alexander looked at Katherine's muddy and bedraggled form. Her satin dress was sodden and torn, her hair undone and writhing about her face and shoulders. Grass stains and thorn scratches covered her face and arms. She crouched like some wide-eyed wild forest creature, trusting and relieved to see him, so unlike the haughty contemptuous woman he had parted from several weeks ago.

Up until now he had vowed never to bother with her again, after his initial fury at her stinging rebukes when vengeance seemed temptingly sweet. It would have been a double pleasure to have embarrassed James MacQueen with the scandal of his goddaughter's reckless behaviour and lessened him in the eyes of Natalya Matrapov. But his anger had abated and the best course of action had been to try and forget the Putulo girl altogether.

Watching her now, he was overwhelmed by a desire to protect her, to gather her up in his arms and crush her close to his body, gently kissing away the cuts to her soft flesh. Instead he answered her sharply.

'It was foolish of you to go off alone with that insufferable youth, Maitland. And it was even more stupid to run off into the forest, Miss Putulo; it's a miracle we found you.'

Katherine flinched at his words and the cold impatient look in his blue eyes. 'How did you know to look for me?' she whispered.

‘We came across your lover whining for help,’ Alexander answered grimly as he helped her to her feet. ‘We soon deduced that his quarry had run off in fright. I was surprised to find it was the good Dr Putulo’s daughter, I must confess. Maitland’s been making a laughing-stock of himself in failed seductions since he came here.’

Katherine closed her eyes at the reproof, the humiliation of the afternoon and her tattered state flooding over her. Fighting back hot tears she replied, ‘I was tricked into going. However little you think of me, sir, I thank you for coming to my rescue and regret the trouble I have caused. If you could deliver me home to my father I would be doubly grateful.’

Alexander turned away biting his lip. He had expected tantrums, tears or a furious denial, but not this dignified apology. ‘Come then, we shall surely do that,’ he said, hiding his confusion.

Baturin took her elbow and led her back to the horses, encouraging her with short grunts and chortles like a protective bear.

‘You will ride pillion with me,’ Alexander ordered. He helped her up behind him with Baturin’s aid.

As he gripped her round the waist Katherine was acutely aware of his eyes on her torn gown, her petticoats showing beneath and she clung to the damp shreds of satin self-consciously. He studied her for a moment, but she had no idea what private thoughts occupied him, no flicker on his scarred face indicating emotion. He was hard and pragmatic, his own dark auburn hair carelessly tied behind his head. No doubt he made a brilliant and ruthless leader of men, who at this moment viewed her as a minor irritation in his day’s hunting.

She sat side-saddle on the horse’s warm flanks, regretting she was now beholden to this man and reluctant to admit her initial pleasure at seeing him again.

‘What happened to Hector Maitland?’ she dared to ask as they moved off in front of Baturin.

Alexander snorted. ‘His friends arrived to collect him while we questioned the oaf.’ He glanced over his shoulder. ‘It was thanks to them we discovered who his victim had been. They seemed to find his embarrassment humorous and your flight of more amusement than we did.’

Katherine’s spirits plunged. What stories would circulate about her now? She was sure Hector Maitland would embellish them so as not to be held up to ridicule. And what would her father and the Chief have to say about it all?

'Am I to gather from your distress that you still care what happens to the pup Maitland?' Alexander mocked.

'No sir,' she was stung into a denial. 'In spite of him being nephew to my dear godfather, I dislike Hector Maitland and told him never to visit me again!'

Her rescuer laughed suddenly. 'I bet you did. I would have given up a day's hunting to witness Maitland being put in his place.'

'He deserved it – and the wine flagon I threw at his head too.'

This made Alexander roar with delight and he patted her knee. Katherine felt her leg tingle from the touch, her pulse quickening at the feel of his body so close to hers. She relaxed as they trotted on through the forest, the surroundings no longer sinister in the gathering gloom. She slipped her arms tentatively round the officer's riding coat and when he did not object she leant against him more heavily, overcome with tiredness.

Katherine came out of her doze to the sound of their horse's hooves clattering on stone and realised they were home. She disengaged herself quickly from her snug hold.

'Let me come in and explain the incident to your father,' Alexander offered good-humouredly.

'Thank you Lieutenant-General,' she replied gratefully.

As he dismounted, Katherine realised how chilled she was, her teeth chattering uncontrollably. Gently, Alexander lifted her down, her arms clasped around his neck. For a moment he did not let go, holding her firmly, amusement twitching at the corner of his mouth.

'Please put me down, sir,' she whispered, forced to look into his face too close to her own. His blue eyes glinted as he quizzed her.

'Am I still an unscrupulous and insolent common soldier, Miss Putulo?' His voice was too low for anyone but Katherine to hear.

'Perhaps I have misjudged you,' she murmured, unable to suppress the bashful smile that pulled at her lips.

Alexander chuckled and let her free as a shocked gasp came from the direction of the house.

'What in heaven's name–?' Fiona exclaimed. Much fussing and kindly disapproval followed as the old housekeeper bustled them all inside, including a reluctant Baturin who would rather have stayed with the horses. Fiona whisked Katherine away to change while Alexander was invited into the drawing-room by the Doctor. He poured them both some ale and listened to the officer's explanation.

'I am most indebted to you, Ballantyne, for rescuing my daughter,' Ewen Putulo said with relief. 'She can be too impetuous at times without thinking of the consequences.'

Alexander hid a smile. 'I think on this occasion,' he defended her gallantly, 'she was deliberately misled and taken advantage of, sir. Young Maitland is gaining a reputation for his indiscretions and my Chief would do well to take him in hand.'

Ewen Putulo studied him. He detected the relationship between MacQueen and this young kinsman was strained by rivalry over the Countess and Alexander no doubt felt it was time his Chief returned to Scotland taking Maitland with him.

'That I'm sure he will do,' the Doctor replied, then hesitated, wondering whether to take Alexander into his confidence. 'James MacQueen and I have also been discussing Katherine's future,' he continued, observing the young officer. 'It seems she will not take a husband and settle as her sister has done. Katherine spends too much of her time in idle pursuits and I have allowed her to have too much of her own way, I confess. This incident has brought home to me that life in the Quarter is too liberal and I no longer have the energy to contain Katherine's zest for sport.'

Alexander shifted uneasily, wondering why he was being told such things. He would not be dragged into some match-making game and have his life complicated by marriage even to the attractive Katherine. It would suit MacQueen, he thought bitterly, to have him wedded so he could continue his liaison with Natalya unrivalled. Yet he had to admit that his attraction towards the Countess was waning as his desire for Katherine flared.

'MacQueen has suggested that Katherine return to Scotland with him and remain a while at Penstroun. I myself will be retiring to Edinburgh in a year or so – I cannot face these harsh Russian winters much longer – and she can decide then where she wishes to live. Perhaps a suitable match can be found for my contrary daughter in Scotland; your brother, Hugh, for instance.'

Alexander looked at the Doctor in astonishment. The deep set eyes regarded him levelly as if wanting to provoke some reply.

‘Has Kath – Miss Putulo been consulted on any of these plans?’ he asked wryly. ‘She will no doubt have an opinion on the matter.’

Ewen Putulo laughed. ‘Not as yet,’ he admitted, ‘MacQueen intends to talk to her on this hunting expedition of the Countess’s. I also know that your Chief is keen for you to return and contest Maitland’s claim to Culduggan and help him at Penstroun; is that not so?’

Alexander scratched at his chin. ‘We have not talked much of late,’ he said brusquely, ‘but that was in his mind. He does not accept that I could be content to live out my life in Russia.’

***

Katherine’s arrival interrupted the men’s conversation and nothing more was mentioned on the subject. Instead, over supper, the two men argued and discussed across the table about Russia and the recent campaigns. Dr Putulo found himself enjoying the younger man’s company, eager to hear his opinions on politics and religion.

‘You are still a Jacobite at heart, then?’ Ewen Putulo questioned.

‘King James VII is dead and the Cause rests in the hands of his fourteen year old son; as you say, the chance of a Stuart restoration is slim,’ Alexander shrugged. ‘I have been too long away from Scotland to know what the people want, but I do know that our country has suffered much under the rule of William the Dutchman. Penstroun must have told you as much?’

Katherine watched his animated face, the brow furrowed between the thick eyebrows, jaw defiant; his words persuasive. She was secretly pleased that he was content to linger over supper with them and not hurry back to the Countess’s mansion. Suddenly Alexander looked across, catching her staring at him in the candlelight.

She had the sleek contented look of a cat, he thought, her eyes heavy-lidded and her long hair a luxurious informal tumble of curls. Delicate flounces of cream lace covered her bosom, their softness catching the warm light.

‘Well I have enjoyed our talk Ballantyne, but I have work to finish,’ Ewen Putulo got up, ‘if you will excuse me. Katherine, you will give our guest a nightcap before he leaves?’

Katherine nodded. Once he had left, they sat for a while in awkward silence. Alexander rose.

'You would like me to leave now?' he asked in a low voice.

Katherine stood up to stop him, realising how much she wanted him to stay. 'No please, you must do as my father wishes.'

'And what do you wish?' he stepped around the table and came closer. 'I will not stay where I am not wanted.'

The guttering candles threw light on his tall figure: the broad chest in the hunting waistcoat; the strong chin above the silk cravat. Desire twisted her stomach and quickened her breathing. 'I don't want you to go, sir; truly I do not,' she whispered, unable to meet his eyes.

She stared at his riding boots. In a swift move Alexander came to her and took her by the shoulders.

'Look at me Katherine.'

She gazed into his sky-blue eyes.

'Oh Katherine,' he murmured, 'all through supper I have been impatient to be left alone with you like this. Tell me you feel the same.'

'I do.' Her pulse began to race.

He bent his head and kissed her. Katherine's astonishment gave way to the quick flash of arousal as his lips consumed hers, hungry and demanding. Her head reeled and heart drummed. Unashamedly she thirsted for more kisses, searching for the taste of his lips until they broke away.

'You are the Katya I have desired since the night of the dance,' Alexander breathed hard. 'I couldn't get you out of my head. I had you followed you know? And then you were delivered to me the night of the Grand Ball,' Alexander laughed, 'it was fortune indeed.'

'And I was so afraid you would recognise me,' Katherine laughed, 'making myself sick with worry. I didn't want to go.'

'But you didn't regret our meeting again, did you Katherine, in spite of the way we parted?' Alexander held her face between his hands.

'No,' Katherine admitted, 'I wanted to see you, though I denied it to myself. I had no right to talk to you so harshly.'

'I was driven mad with thinking about you,' Alexander murmured in her ear, sending delightful shivers down her body. 'Why were you so scornful of my advances?'

'I thought you were merely having sport with me, angry that my godfather and the Countess seemed to be getting on so well together. I would not be teased in such a way.'

'You were mistaken; I was only reluctant to accompany you to the Ball when I did not know you were my Katya,' Alexander insisted, filling his hands with her luxuriant hair. 'I answered the call of the *Khorovod*, didn't I? It must have been obvious at the Ball that I would have kissed you again had the interfering Maitland not spoilt the opportunity.'

'And I wanted you to Alexander,' Katherine lifted her lips to his again.

They embraced with renewed force, her mouth crushed in his eagerness to taste it. He pulled her close, feeling the drumming of her heart beneath the thin silk. She smelt of sweet herbs and his desire for her creamy plumpness increased.

Footsteps sounded beyond the door. As it opened Katherine pushed Alexander away.

'What are you doing in the dark, Miss Katherine?' Fiona cried. 'You fair gave me a fright. Oh, sir, I did not realise you were here too.' Katherine's heart raced so fast she could not speak.

'Miss Putulo was about to show me out,' Alexander replied calmly, 'I'm sorry if we startled you, kind lady.' He knew neither of them could maintain the pretence of polite conversation at that moment.

'Oh sir, that's quite alright,' Fiona beamed at him. 'Your man Baturin was telling me how you boxed the ears of that wicked Maitland boy. He well deserved it.'

Katherine looked at Alexander in amazement.

'I confess it gave me great relief to do so,' he admitted.

'You look flushed, dearie,' Fiona fussed at Katherine, 'you must get some rest now. I will show Lieutenant-General Ballantyne downstairs.'

He turned and bowed briefly. 'I shall look forward to seeing you and your father at the hunting party, Miss Putulo,' he smiled, his blue eyes speaking much more. Katherine controlled her breathing long enough to reply.

'And I too, sir. I thank you again for rescuing me,' her full lips trembled in a smile.

With a nod, he was gone and Fiona with him. Left alone Katherine felt equally the thrill of their amorous encounter and an unease that she had succumbed so quickly to his advances. She was heady with his passionate words and the way her body responded to his touch, yet to what avail? They would next meet under the roof of Natalya Matrapov and for all she knew, Alexander was still her lover. Any furthering of their relationship would therefore be fruitless.

Could it be in his mind to merely make Natalya jealous over him by encouraging Katherine? He certainly seemed displeased with her godfather's presence at the moment. Thinking more calmly as she made ready for bed, she decided she would have to proceed cautiously at the hunting party and not allow Ballantyne to manipulate her in some empty affair.

***

Alexander rode towards the Matrapov mansion lost in thought, impervious to Baturin's chattering about the plump homely Fiona and her excellent broth. He dragged his mind back from the cosy dining-room and the intoxicating charms of Katherine Putulo. It had almost gone too far and he had spoken too much, drunk with desire for her. Such feelings were dangerous for a man who chose soldiering as his profession and he had sworn on leaving Scotland not to allow his emotions to rule his life ever again.

Spurring his horse on he knew he should try to harden his feelings towards Katherine and forget her dark beauty. Instead he should be putting up more of a fight to retain his comfortable arrangement with Natalya Matrapov before it was too late. As he galloped for the safety of her estates, Alexander had no idea of the shocking news that awaited him.

CHAPTER 5

By the time Katherine and her father were ploughing through the spring mud towards the Matrapov estate, she had decided to treat Alexander with politeness but caution. She had soon felt foolish about her show of ardour for him; the lusty Scots officer had been quick to take advantage of her overwrought state. While she would do nothing to encourage him in front of the Countess, Katherine could not deny her increasing nervousness at seeing him again.

As they swung into a tree-lined track, her mind was temporarily distracted by the magnificent mansion. Built in the traditional wooden style, its intricately carved windows, myriad of blue domes, spires and curved roof-tops spoke of past opulence. The main steps were covered in a wooden awning and servants stood waiting to receive them. To Katherine's delight, James MacQueen came out to greet them.

'Godfather,' she cried, 'we've longed to see you. You've neglected us of late,' she teased.

'I have had business to attend to,' he kissed her fondly, 'but now I can enjoy your company to the full. Ewen; welcome!' He turned to greet the Doctor, who raised an eyebrow but did not comment on his friend's lordly manner.

They were ushered into the huge rambling house with its air of faded elegance; the tapestries had lost their richness of colour and the painted woodwork was dulled and flaking. Katherine was surprised by the bareness of the vast rooms and the simplicity of the furnishings, yet there appeared an army of servants rushing to the beck and call of the guests.

Fiona helped her to dress in her favourite coral-pink silk gown while they chattered excitedly about their new surroundings.

'I have not seen the dashing Lieutenant-General Ballantyne,' Fiona said, yanking at the young woman's stays. 'It's not right that he continues to live here in an ungodly relationship with the Countess. He should have married her long ago.'

'Ouch!' Katherine protested at her sides being pinched so hard. 'It is not for us to comment on their behaviour, Fiona,' she remonstrated, 'we are the Countess's guests.' She felt herself blushing painfully at the mention of Alexander and determined to talk of him no more.

Thirty guests assembled for a gargantuan banquet of succulent meats and vegetables, huge salmon and caviar. Katherine was seated between her father and Alexander's amusing friend, the French officer De Maton, thankful that a subdued Hector Maitland kept out of her way and sat at another table.

Yet she experienced bitter disappointment that Alexander had spoken to her only briefly before dinner, exchanging small courtesies. It was as if the moment of intimacy between them had never been; he was polite but aloof, preoccupied by something else. Perhaps she had behaved too coolly towards him herself, or was he now regretting the endearments he had said to her? She certainly had not expected this casual indifference. Katherine watched him surreptitiously as he dined next to Natalya Matrapov. He was drinking heavily and appeared to be saying little, while Natalya conversed animatedly with her guests, her handsome face radiant in the candlelight.

Alexander sensed he was being watched and looked down the table at Katherine. She looked beautiful in the low-cut gown, her hair piled up revealing her slender neck and bare shoulders. The large dark eyes looked at him perplexed, the broad lips turned down in sadness. Her lids fluttered and she glanced away quickly. He felt very drunk. Dimly he wished he could talk to her, take her in his arms and kiss away her doubts about him. But he could not because he had decided to ignore his attraction for the Putulo daughter and all its consequences.

It was Natalya that he wanted, Natalya whom he must have to keep his ordered world intact and stop himself falling dangerously in love. James MacQueen was spoiling everything; acting like his rival and not his chief. Look at him now, his craggy bearded face close to Natalya's, as if he already possessed her, Alexander thought angrily.

They sat for five hours as course after course was served, the company growing more boisterous as vodka and ale flowed. Eventually, amid the raucous voices, James MacQueen stood to his feet and bellowed for quiet.

'Friends,' he growled, 'let us drink a toast to the Countess Natalya who gives her hospitality so lavishly.'

The assembled diners stood unsteadily and raised their goblets, crying, 'To the Countess!'

Katherine saw Alexander throw back his vodka in one and pour himself another. His mood was belligerent and she was sure he argued now with Natalya over something. To Katherine's amazement, he shook off his mistress's hold and pushed back his chair, knocking it to the ground.

‘I have another toast,’ he shouted as the hubbub grew again. ‘To my worthy chief, Penstroun – and my former mistress, Natalya Matrapov; may they be happy together,’ he slurred.

Silence fell like a snowfall, freezing the conversation as Alexander knocked back his drink. MacQueen’s face was full of wrath, but Natalya stayed him with a hand.

‘Alexander you have drunk enough,’ she cautioned quietly, ‘please sit down.’

‘What,’ he laughed savagely, ‘before we have toasted your betrothal to MacQueen? Don’t be so coy my dear.’ He seized a jug of vodka and poured it into her glass, letting the liquid slop over the top. ‘Come Natalya, drink to your future husband with me!’ Throwing back his drink he did not see James MacQueen step quickly round Natalya or anticipate the blow to his jaw that sent him crashing to the floor.

Katherine watched appalled, resisting the urge to run to intercept. Her godfather seemed like a man possessed, pulling Alexander to his feet.

‘I’ll not squabble with you in public Ballantyne,’ he said, his face stormy, ‘but I’ll not stand by and see you insult Natalya in front of her guests either.’

‘Then you will fight me fairly in a dual!’ Alexander pushed him away and stood glaring at the older man.

‘Very well,’ MacQueen snarled, ‘if it will teach you some manners!’

Natalya stepped between them her white powdered face strained with fright.

‘You will do no such thing. Do you both want to be sent to Siberia for your foolishness? I will not be the cause of your quarrel. Please gentlemen, come and sit down, you make a spectacle of yourselves.’

Alexander threw them both a thunderous look, his jaw and mouth tight with fury. Shamefaced, MacQueen took the Countess’s arm.

‘I apologise my dear,’ he said gruffly and turning to his kinsman he added, ‘you must accept Natalya’s wishes, Alexander. Can we not sit down and drink together as friends like before?’ He held out a conciliatory hand.

Katherine held her breath to see how Alexander would react to her godfather’s peace-making. She noticed a taut muscle pulling in his cheek, the blue eyes narrowed dangerously.

‘You are no longer my friend, Penstroun,’ he replied proudly, raising his chin, ‘you have betrayed my trust and taken what is not yours. I will not stay to be further insulted. Forgive me, Natalya, for spoiling your feast but I no longer have any appetite.' With that he wheeled round and stormed from the room.

The awkward silence was broken by Dr Putulo who got to his feet and raised his glass. 'Congratulations MacQueen,' he smiled across at his friend, 'let us all drink to the health of the Countess and Penstroun.'

The guests rose thankful at the easing of tension and the merriment continued. Yet Katherine's stomach churned at the awful fight over their hostess that they had just witnessed. It was a shock to learn in such a way of her godfather's intended marriage and she did not know how well she liked the idea of Natalya becoming his wife. But what distressed her more was Alexander's desperate behaviour, his misery over losing the Countess so transparent to all.

It explained only too well why the officer had made a play for her the other night, it was an attempt to rid his mind of his mistress, or worse, make Natalya jealous. He had spoken empty words to her and she had been stupid enough to believe them. Alexander had shown tonight how in love he was with his mistress in such a display of naked jealousy.

Her wretchedness was compounded by Hector Maitland's obvious enjoyment of the situation. He caught her as she made to retire.

'Is it not good news indeed to hear of your godfather's happiness?' Hector crowed, waving a lace cuff in their direction. 'They look so well together, don't you think? She will be a fitting mistress of Penstroun.'

'Yes,' Katherine replied frostily, 'and I suppose it pleases you even more to see the Lieutenant-General humiliated?'

'So he has a sympathetic ally?' Hector was sarcastic. 'A pity for you Katherine that his interests so plainly lie elsewhere. Perhaps now you will not dismiss my attentions so readily; I would never ignore you so, my dear.'

She itched to slap his fat jeering face so smug above the ruffles of perfumed lace but resisted, gripping her skirts tightly. 'Goodnight, Mr Maitland,' she brushed past him.

'Stay and celebrate with the happy couple, Katherine,' he called after her. She fled to her room with the mocking words ringing in her ears.

***

During the next few days Katherine shrugged off her gloom over the proposed marriage and her hurt over Alexander, riding hard in the warm spring air. She had to admit, watching her godfather with the Countess that he did appear to be in love with her and she returned his fondness. It was churlish of her to resent Natalya just because they had not liked each other on first impression and she was glad James MacQueen had found companionship after all these years. As for the Countess, she maintained a polite indifference towards Katherine which was preferable to the cutting remarks of their first encounter.

It was now nearly a week since the terrible scene at the opening banquet and Katherine had heard nothing of the Scots officer since; except that he now resided at the Scottish hostelry in Moscow. The Tsar's army was preparing to leave for Archangel and with a heavy heart she thought that it might be many months before they met again – if indeed he survived the summer campaign. Any special feelings that had flared between them would be long extinguished.

'You ride well, Miss Putulo,' the Count De Maton cantered up beside her. Katherine slowed and they fell into a walk behind the hunting party.

'Thank you sir,' she smiled, breathing in the scent of the meadows, 'I have not seen you these past two days.'

'I had duties to attend to in Moscow,' he smiled back, 'I am returning soon to France.'

'Oh, I am sorry to hear it,' Katherine said, genuinely disappointed, for she enjoyed his company.

They conversed as they rode and she listened with interest to his descriptions of Paris and the ways of the French compared to the Russians. It was only later that she realised the others were out of sight ahead of them, she had been so engrossed in their conversation.

'Shall we wait for them to return?' the Count asked. 'We are near the river here and can let the horses drink.'

Before Katherine could object he had led his horse off in the direction of the woods. They found a shady place, downstream from which a group of women washed clothes on the rocks by a ford. It was pleasant to hear them sing as they worked and Katherine dismounted and let her horse wander to the river's edge.

Moments later there was the sound of hooves pounding through the trees on the far side of the ford. Two figures appeared on horseback and splashed across the river, the women scattering in fright at their sudden appearance. With a start Katherine recognised Alexander with his rough

Cossack companion, Baturin, hailing Count De Maton as if they had been waiting for him. She rushed to her horse, but the Frenchman had it by the reins and trotted away to the edge of the clearing with the animal. Alexander dismounted and came towards her.

'Katherine,' he smiled, 'it is good to see you.'

She flashed him a disdainful look. 'What is the meaning of this?' she demanded. 'How dare you greet me as if we were friends?'

He stopped, flushing slightly. 'Forgive me, Miss Putulo, we have been tracking you. My friend De Maton agreed to bring you here so we could talk.'

'I have no wish to speak to you, Lieutenant-General Ballantyne,' she retorted. 'You have cruelly taken advantage of my feelings for you and behaved like a boor to my godfather and the Countess. Now you expect me to talk politely with you as if nothing had happened? Well I will not. Tell your friend I wish to go.'

Alexander went towards her and then hesitated. 'I'm sorry for the way I have acted – especially to you – and I don't blame you for despising me,' he answered. 'But I do need to talk to you, Miss Putulo. Will you grant me just a few minutes?'

His lively blue eyes looked down at her waiting for a reply, the chiselled features of his face impassive. He wore his officer's uniform and his chin was newly shaven. Gone was the drunken moody lover of several nights ago. Katherine nodded reluctantly and let him guide her out of earshot of the other two men. They walked in silence by the river for some minutes.

'I do not remember everything I did or said the night of the banquet,' Alexander said sheepishly, 'but I have been reminded by De Maton since. Will you forgive me?'

Katherine saw the tinge of colour on his jaw heightening his scar. 'It is not for me to forgive,' she answered stiffly, 'I was not the one you insulted.'

Alexander stopped and took her arm. 'Oh, but you were,' he insisted, 'after what had passed between us at your father's house, my treatment of you was damnable. I do not know what came over me.'

'It was obvious,' Katherine tried to steel herself against his touch, 'you behaved like the jealous lover that you are.' He dropped his hold.

'Perhaps I was jealous,' he said without bitterness, 'jealous that the woman I have lived with transfers her affections to another so quickly. But then MacQueen has a title and lands to offer her and not just a soldier's pay. It angers me that Natalya is only after my Chief's possessions – she has spent all of the Matrapov money – yet Penstroun cannot see it.'

Katherine looked at him coldly. 'Has it occurred to you that they might be in love with each other?'

'Love?' Alexander snorted. 'Natalya loves only herself. She fears being left alone in her old age or confined to a nunnery by her relations.'

'I don't really care why she wants to marry my godfather,' Katherine retorted, 'as long as he is happy with her. But then I don't expect a common mercenary like you to understand that; you have no idea what it is to love.'

She felt unwanted tears welling up in her throat and turned from him. 'If you have brought me here to try and persuade my godfather to break off his engagement then you are more callous than I imagined. I don't wish to remain here any longer.'

'Stop!' he caught her by the arm and swung her round. 'I didn't mean us to quarrel like this. Damn it, I don't care what Natalya does now. These past days I have thought only of you Katherine and I could not bear to think that I have hurt you by my actions. Can you believe me and forgive me?'

She felt herself weakening under his hold, wanting to trust his words. 'I don't know,' she agonised, 'I want to believe you.'

He pushed her chin up gently with his hand so that she had to look into his vivid eyes. 'I have been tortured with the doubt of not seeing you again before I leave to join the summer campaign.' He caressed her cheek with his fingers, pushing back the tendrils of hair.

Katherine felt herself tremble at the soft seduction of his words and touch. Her pulse began a slow thudding.

'I wanted to see you too,' she replied, 'but I thought I meant nothing to you.'

'My sweet Katya, you mean everything to me. I can no longer deny my feelings for you. I have never said that to any woman before.'

Katherine's eyes prickled with emotion. 'Oh Alexander; and I for you.'

Alexander bent and kissed her gently on the lips, his arms encircling her tightly. When she did not protest, his kisses grew more urgent, covering her mouth, her face, her neck. Katherine slipped her arms about him, rocked by the passion he awoke in her. They clung to each other while he whispered endearments and tasted the freshness of her skin. Katherine thrilled at the powerfulness of Alexander's embraces, not wanting them to stop.

Eventually he broke away, smiling into her dark eyes which mirrored his own desire. Alexander breathed unevenly. 'Katherine, will you do something for me?' he urged.

'What Alexander?'

'I want you to persuade your godfather to meet me at the Hostelry in Moscow.' Katherine pulled away. 'It is nothing to do with Natalya,' Alexander added hastily, 'I want to make amends but I know I am not welcome at the Countess's home.'

'What do you intend to say to him?' Katherine asked, curious.

'I have been thinking long and hard about his proposal for me to return to Scotland,' he replied, taking her hand in his, 'and I have decided to accept his offer of living at Penstroun – if I have not spoilt my chance by my outburst the other night.'

'But what of your pledge not to return while King William reigns?' Katherine reminded him, dismayed that he should be thinking of leaving Muscovy so soon, in spite of their feelings for each other.

Alexander smiled triumphantly. 'News reached Moscow yesterday that William of Orange is dead. He fell on a riding accident and did not recover.'

Katherine bit her lip in disappointment. 'Then you are free to end your exile with honour,' she disengaged her hand and turned back towards the others.

From her subdued look Alexander guessed MacQueen had not yet approached her about quitting Muscovy and going to live with him in Scotland. He hesitated about whether to tell her and then thought better of it; the words should come from her godfather.

'Come Miss Putulo,' Count De Maton called over to her, 'I can see the others returning this way.'

'May I call on you soon Katherine?' Alexander stopped her for a moment.

She nodded. 'I will speak with Uncle James today before we leave for the Quarter; I know he is already making preparations to secure a voyage home.'

'Thank you,' he kissed her forehead briefly and helped her up onto her horse. 'It is important that I talk with him soon. Tell him I will wait at the Scottish Hostelry for the next three nights. If he does not come I will leave with the advance party for Archangel and think no more of Scotland.' He held her hand a moment more.

'And Katherine,' he looked up at her intently, 'it is very important that no one else should hear of this meeting; it could endanger your godfather's life. Promise me?'

She nodded, startled by his insistence. He kissed her hand quickly and departed without further explanation, leaving her feeling uneasy.

As they rode out of the trees, Katherine glanced back to see Alexander's black horse disappearing in the direction of Moscow followed by Baturin. She was perplexed by their meeting and the obvious attraction they felt for each other. He had declared his love and yet was so eager to leave Muscovy now and end his exile. How, she wondered, could the Chief possibly be in any danger from reconciliation with his kinsman? Alexander was being melodramatic. Again she could not shake off the idea that he was manipulating her for his own ends, this time to secure his position with her godfather before his marriage to Natalya and return to Scotland. Or was his sudden disinterest in Natalya just a pretence? Perhaps his eagerness to return to Scotland was to follow his former mistress there. Katherine was left plagued by sickening doubt.

***

The hunting party returned to the Matrapov mansion in high spirits. Taking Katherine aside, James MacQueen became earnest.

'My dear, there is something your father and I would like to discuss with you.' Katherine shot him a wary look. Surely they had not learnt of her meeting with Alexander? The Chief smiled, 'Do not look so alarmed, our proposal may suit you very well.'

'Proposal?' Katherine was intrigued and followed him upstairs to his rooms. A moment later Dr Putulo joined them.

'Katherine,' MacQueen began, 'your father and I have been discussing your future during my visit here.' He considered her as she sat on the high-backed wooden chair, the green eyes in the oval face attentive. 'It seems you will not choose a husband from the cosmopolitan ranks of the Quarter and my friend Putulo has been tolerant and always put your wishes first.'

Katherine flushed pink and slid her father a look, but he remained silent. 'We have decided,' James continued, 'that a change would be good for you and that it is time you learnt something of your native land.'

'Father, are you thinking of returning to Edinburgh?' Katherine cried in astonishment.

Ewen Putulo nodded, 'It is in my mind to retire from Muscovy before long, but that is not our concern. Your godfather wishes you to go back to Penstroun with him and live there until my retirement. You could eventually decide whether to remain with him or come to me in Edinburgh.'

'By then I hope the question will be academic,' MacQueen grunted, 'and you will be settled in marriage with some Scots nobleman.'

Katherine gaped at them, her dark eyes wide. 'Father, do you wish this too?' she asked dumbfounded.

'I think your godfather does us a great honour by his offer and I'd be happy to think of you in Scotland while these wars with the Swedes threaten our security here,' he answered quietly. 'However, it must be your decision, my dear.'

'I – I don't know what to say,' Katherine stuttered, suddenly excited about the idea, especially if Alexander were to return with them.

She stood up and went to her father taking his hands in hers. 'I have always wanted to see Scotland I must admit, but I would be miserable at leaving you, Papa.' They smiled at each other, Ewen Putulo momentarily lost for words. The Chief looked on wistfully at the affection they so obviously shared.

'Then you must go,' the Doctor told her gently. 'I shall miss your company greatly but will not be long in following you home, Katherine.'

She reached up and kissed his cheek then turned to her godfather.

'I am pleased to accept your kind invitation, sir,' she smiled at him and his bearded face broke into a grin.

'Then that is settled,' he replied happily, glancing gratefully at his old friend. 'We shall travel back by way of Poland and Prussia, procuring a passage at Konigsberg.'

'Then we will see Elspeth on our journey!' Katherine cried with delight.

'Most assuredly,' the Chief promised. 'The Countess and I intend to marry immediately and it will be best to travel before the summer becomes too hot, we should not delay more than a month.'

Katherine glanced at her godfather awkwardly. 'What does the Countess Matrapov think to my living with you both at Penstroun?'

'Natalya will be delighted to have the company of her own sex,' MacQueen answered quickly, 'apart from my sister Christina and her daughter Sybilla, there are few of the gentility for many miles.' He walked briskly across the room and took Katherine by the arm. 'Now let us join the others, my dear.'

Katherine was not very convinced by his assurance of Natalya's willingness but did not say so. She hesitated, for now was the time to put Alexander's request to the Chief while he was in a jovial mood. It had occurred to her to stay silent about the matter, worried about the words of warning.

What if the young Ballantyne was intending to involve her godfather in some dangerous undertaking? However, if she did not bring about their reconciliation she might never see the tall officer again.

'There is one thing I would ask of you, Uncle James,' Katherine steeled herself to the task. He looked down at her quizzically. 'I have received an urgent message from your kinsman, Lieutenant-General Ballantyne.' She felt him stiffen and went on quickly, 'He wishes to apologise and make amends before it is too late. He asks that you visit him in Moscow before he leaves with his regiment, he says it is most important that he speaks with you at once.'

'And how did you come by such a message?' James MacQueen demanded sternly.

'I met him while out hunting today,' Katherine spoke quietly, but looked him straight in the eye.

'You saucy young maid,' her godfather exclaimed and then laughed. 'And you think I should talk with him after he has insulted his chief so badly?'

'I believe he is sincere in begging your pardon,' Katherine flushed under his grey-eyed scrutiny, 'and I do not like to think of you at odds with each other and parting with bitter words.'

'Perhaps you are right,' MacQueen patted her on the shoulder and gave Ewen Putulo a knowing look. 'And would it please you Katherine to think that the young Ballantyne might return to Penstroun with us?'

She felt herself grow hot with embarrassment, aware of both men's questioning gaze on her. 'If it would better the fortunes of Penstroun and Culduggan then certainly I would welcome his return,' she answered trying to hide a smile.

'Well spoken!' MacQueen cried. 'For your sake and Penstroun's I will endeavour to speak with my stubborn kinsman and hear him out.'

Katherine looked around quickly sensing another presence, but it was just a draught rustling one of the hangings. She dropped her voice.

'It was also his express wish that you tell no one of such a meeting, Uncle James.'

He looked at her sharply. 'Is that all that he said?'

'Yes,' Katherine felt a twinge of apprehension at his tone. James MacQueen nodded slowly, his face clouding in thought.

'Then this conversation remains between the three of us,' he agreed.

They left the chamber together and returned downstairs.

***

Later that night, once the guests had departed back for the Foreign Settlement, MacQueen set out for Moscow, telling Natalya that he had an assignation with a Polish merchant whom he must see in connection with their forthcoming journey.

She appeared put out that he left her in his nephew Hector's dull company and commanded him to hurry home where she would await him impatiently. He smiled at the thought of her lingering kiss and urged his horse into a canter. The Chief was secretly pleased that his young kinsman had decided to come to heel and co-operate with his plans, for he was sure this was the reason for the meeting. It was imperative that they kept their deliberations secret for the moment. They could decide on the journey home, which would be the safest way for Alexander to slip back into Scotland, for there were still those who might try to have him detained in spite of the King's indemnity.

***

The next day Katherine had just returned from visiting Rosa with the exciting news of her proposed adventure, when she saw Alexander ride into the courtyard followed by Baturin.

'Good day, Miss Putulo,' he called cheerfully as he dismounted and threw his reins to his servant. She smiled back regarding him from under thick lashes.

'You seem in a better temper, sir,' she replied archly, 'do you bring good news?'

Alexander came forward and took her arm. 'Indeed Katherine,' he lowered his voice and fixed her with his intense blue look, 'your godfather met with me last night and we understand each other well.'

'I am truly glad,' Katherine blushed with pleasure, returning his gaze. 'Does this mean you will be coming with us on our journey home?'

He squeezed her arm and gave his disarming smile. 'How could I refuse once I learnt you had agreed to live at Penstroun too?'

'And it will not trouble you that the Countess will live there as Lady Penstroun?' Katherine asked, her heart beginning to beat at his proximity.

He stopped and swung her around to face him, gripping both her arms, the scar on his jaw pronounced. 'Not in the least,' he was adamant. 'And you, Katherine, you are not still jealous of Natalya?'

'I have never been jealous of her,' she huffed in reply, squirming in his hold.

'Not even a little bit?' Alexander teased her, not allowing her to escape.

'Please let me go, sir,' she avoided the question, going red with confusion.

'There is something I wish to ask you first,' he held her firmly; finding her flushed annoyed face and pouting lips irresistibly tempting.

'Oh?' Katherine hesitated, her heart pounding at the nearness of his handsome face.

'Ballantyne,' the Doctor's voice interrupted them from the doorway, 'I had not thought to see you again quite so soon,' he said dryly.

Alexander dropped his hands and hid his vexation at Ewen Putulo's arrival. 'Penstroun and I have buried our differences,' he smiled.

'That gladdens my heart,' the Doctor held out his hand, 'please come inside and have some refreshment with us.'

Katherine felt frustration that her conversation with Alexander had been interrupted; it was tantalising that he had not been able to make known his intentions.

Sitting in the sunlit drawing-room watching him talking to her father with such charm, she found it difficult to reconcile this polished gentleman with the coarse and worldly soldier who had kissed her in the *Khorovod* and tried to take advantage of her on the troika ride after the Grand Ball. She felt even now that the hardened mercenary – headstrong and ruthless – lay close under the skin of the civilised Ballantyne. Katherine wondered with a mixture of unease and excitement whether she was part of Alexander's new plans?

'And will you not find life dull at Penstroun after the dangers and rewards of soldiering for the Russians?' Ewen Putulo asked his guest.

'I will not be idle,' Alexander answered with an evasive wave of the hand, 'and the skills of the soldier are still useful in the Highlands of Scotland.'

'Let's hope you will not have to use them,' the Doctor stood up to refill their glasses.

Before he could pour a drop, the door burst open and Fiona rushed in, breathless. 'Sir,' she panted, a hand to her chest, 'it's the Countess Matrapov and Mr Maitland – oh sir, she's in a terrible state–'

'Whatever's the matter?' Ewen Putulo demanded.

'I can hardly understand her–'

Fiona's announcements were unnecessary, for a moment later Natalya Matrapov swept into the room her pale face haggard from crying. Katherine tensed at the sight of Hector Maitland moving nervously behind her dressed in a lavishly embroidered pink coat and lace cravat. He was breathing hard and his eyes darted nervously around the room. Something had frightened him.

'My dear Countess, what is it?' the Doctor steered her to a chair, but she would not sit.

'The Chief,' she sobbed, 'my James–,' she broke off, putting a hand to her mouth. Katherine had never seen her in such a state and rose to go to her. Alexander had the same idea and leapt out of his chair.

'Keep away from me!' she almost screamed at him and shrank back.

'What in heaven's name has happened Natalya?' her former lover sounded impatient.

'So you profess not to know?' Hector demanded querulously as he gave the Countess his arm in a show of bravery.

'Know what, damn it?' Alexander rounded on him with irritation.

'My uncle has been found murdered,' Hector announced excitedly his brown eyes bulging, 'in an alley near the Scottish Hostelry. It appears he was dragged there having been shot in the back.'

Katherine's knees gave way as if someone had knocked her from behind and she sank to the floor in shock. 'Not Uncle James?' she gasped in horror. Fiona and Dr Putulo rushed to help her where she knelt and lifted her into a chair. 'Oh father, it can't be true?' she buried her face in his shoulder and clung onto him.

The Doctor looked over at the Countess and saw the truth of it in her harrowed face. 'Who could have done such a terrible thing?' he cried.

'Perhaps our heroic Lieutenant-General Ballantyne can tell us what my uncle was doing at the Hostelry?' Hector said viciously. 'He obviously hadn't gone to see a Polish merchant as he told us.'

Katherine looked up and saw Alexander's taut expression, the scar like a branding that slashed his jaw. Would he deny that he had met with her godfather last night?

'Do you dare to accuse me of murdering my own chief?' Alexander answered with ill-suppressed rage.

'So you admit that you saw him?' Hector needled.

'I did meet with Penstroun,' he answered coldly, 'but far from arguing, we were reconciled and I intended to return to Scotland with my chief to serve as his loyal clansman.'

'You lured him there,' Natalya spoke with hatred, 'you could not bear to see me happy with the man I loved. You killed him out of jealousy didn't you?' Her voice spiralled hysterically and she stepped forward, slapping Alexander in the face. He grabbed her hand and held it fast.

'You delude yourself Natalya,' he controlled his anger, 'I would not kill my father's greatest friend and the man who saved my life just for you.'

'We all heard you challenge him to a dual over the Countess,' Hector said quickly.

'I was drunk,' Alexander's voice was contemptuous, 'and this is preposterous. What would I gain by killing the Chief of MacQueen?'

'Penstroun,' Natalya spat at him, 'it should have been mine!'

'So that is what all this weeping is really about,' Alexander said bitterly, 'you cry for your lost title and not the lost man, that is more like you Countess.'

'No,' Natalya threw off his grasp, 'I loved him, but I would never expect you to understand that, you are incapable of such emotion.'

Hector pressed the advantage. 'But you are capable of killing for gain,' he sneered. 'You knew Penstroun could be yours with the Chief out of the way. You pretend that you settled your quarrel with my uncle, but you have no proof.'

'And you, Maitland,' Alexander looked as if he would take him by the neck, 'do you not have an equal claim, you and that thieving father of yours?'

'Maybe,' Hector looked triumphant, 'but I was with Natalya all evening and had no more idea than her where my uncle had gone.'

Katherine watched them all, stunned by the hatred and accusations. Alexander caught sight of her stricken doubting face and felt his heart twist.

'Tell me you do not believe I am capable of murdering your godfather, Katherine?' he pleaded.

Her mouth felt so dry, she could not utter a word but just looked at him appalled. She did not know what to think. Katherine had believed him when he said that all was well between himself and the Chief; yet no one else could have known of the meeting.

Unless it was some chance random murder, the finger of suspicion did point to the tall Scots officer. She could not imagine Hector had the appetite for cold-blooded murder even if he had known her godfather's movements, whereas Alexander was hardened to killing. If she herself had been a party to her godfather's death by arranging the tryst she would never forgive herself. Surely Alexander could not have so callously used her?

'My man Baturin can vouch that James MacQueen left my rooms alive last night,' Alexander's sharp blue eyes bore into hers, 'I would rather have lain down my own life than seen the brave Penstroun cut down in so cowardly a fashion.' Katherine's eyes stung to hear the proud hurt in his voice.

'A pretty speech,' Hector jibed, 'but we all know that your Cossack peasant would say anything you told him to. Your greed got the better of you, Ballantyne; like all common soldiers you will plunder where you can, even from your own kin.'

In one swift movement Alexander was across the room seizing his tormentor by his ornate coat. Hector tried to dodge him and move behind Natalya but was not quick enough. The taller man drew back his arm and jabbed a fist hard under his chin, sending the stout Maitland toppling backwards onto a delicate table which smashed under his weight.

'Stop this now!' Ewen Putulo cried, barging between them. 'You will not fight like dogs in my house.' Katherine watched her father's furious face; never had she seen him so upset. 'You make fools of yourselves bickering over something that you cannot have. How my friend MacQueen would have laughed at you all!'

'What do you mean father?' Katherine asked in distress.

'I mean that none of them stand to inherit Penstroun!'

'Then who?'

He opened his arms in a helpless gesture. 'You Katherine; *you.*'

All faces turned to him in astonishment. He looked at Katherine, her mouth open and eyes large with disbelief. He had not wanted her to find out in such a way; it should have been broken to her gradually at Penstroun when MacQueen had earned her confidence and love. The secret he hoped might never have to be told, now had to be laid bare. In cutting open the old wound he knew it would inflict new pain upon one he loved so dearly.

'You see my dear, James MacQueen was not only your godfather, as you know,' Dr Putulo sighed sadly, 'he was your natural father too.'

CHAPTER 6

For a long moment Katherine just stared at the Doctor with incredulity. It was impossible that the gruff bear-like James MacQueen was her father; she was the daughter of this quiet cultured man who stood before her in his sombre grey coat. She looked into his tired dark-ringed eyes for reassurance that she had misunderstood, but they were filled with a deep regret. Glancing at the others she saw the Countess drop into a chair, her face white with shock. Hector, still sprawled on the floor, gaped at her. Alexander's stern face regarded her with a strange tense look, but he said nothing. Rising slowly she went to Ewen Putulo and put her hands in his.

'How can this be?' she whispered.

'You were born here a few days after the bloody Streltsy Rising, nigh on twenty years ago,' Dr Putulo told her quietly.

'I know that,' Katherine said, 'mother used to tell Elspeth and I–'

'Not your mother,' he interrupted gently. 'You were born to Princess Katya Naryshkin; both of you were left in my care while your father avoided arrest and tried to secure a passage home for his family.'

'But you said the Princess and the baby died,' Katherine looked pleadingly.

'It was our own daughter who died just hours before you came into this world.'

'And Princess Katya – my mother?' Katherine pressed.

She saw his chin tremble and he cleared his throat with difficulty. 'She was still distraught after seeing so many of her relations murdered before her very eyes at the Kremlin. Her mind never really recovered, poor woman. The Princess believed she had been abandoned by your father and that he would never come back. She could not bear the thought of returning to her own people in such disgrace, after all, there had been fierce opposition to the marriage in the first place.'

'She was right wasn't she?' Katherine's eyes pricked with angry tears. 'Why didn't my father come back for us?'

Ewen Putulo lifted her chin and looked directly at her. 'Your father never abandoned you. He waited at Archangel for word that you both followed, but when none came he risked all by returning to find you. I had to tell him that his wife was missing – she had escaped the house – leaving you wrapped in her own embroidered silk shawl, the only possession of value she had managed to save when they fled the uprising. Fiona found you alone.'

Katherine looked quickly at their housekeeper. The ageing woman's cheeks were damp with tears and she nodded her be-capped head in agreement.

'And did you ever find her?' Katherine croaked.

'Her body was eventually washed up on the banks of the River Yauza,' the Doctor spoke with difficulty.

Katherine flung her arms about his neck and shut her eyes tight to hold back the painful tears she felt for the mother she never knew. Ewen Putulo stroked her hair comfortingly.

'Your father was heart-broken and he made a great sacrifice in leaving you, his only child, to be brought up as ours. MacQueen wanted to give you a happy home, whereas life with him at that time was uncertain and dangerous. You were a great comfort to Sybil and myself and a precious sister for Elspeth.'

Katherine shook as she cried in his arms. 'Why did he never tell me who he really was?'

'Because he saw how happy you were here,' the Doctor answered simply. 'If he had married again and had heirs there would have been no reason for you to ever know; it was a burden he was prepared to carry as long as you were content. But my friend never did re-marry,' Dr Putulo glanced sadly at the distraught Countess, 'and he seemed eager to settle his affairs on this visit. The Chief was so pleased you had accepted to live at Penstroun and he fully intended to tell you in the course of time.'

Katherine raised her tear-stained face to look at him. 'I wish I had known,' she whispered.

'I'm so sorry my dear,' Ewen Putulo looked pityingly at the young woman, 'perhaps we were wrong not to have told you sooner.' He pushed her gently to arm's length and turned to the others. 'There is something else you all should know about my friend's last will which he intrusted to me, though in the present atmosphere of suspicion it could prove awkward.'

Hector Maitland got to his feet and looked in anticipation. 'He has left something for me I am sure?'

The Doctor regarded him coldly, 'He did not Mr Maitland.'

Katherine glanced at Alexander. He was looking at Hector with contempt but seemed too shocked to speak.

Hector's eyes narrowed at him as he caught the look. 'You will not be so insufferably calm soon Ballantyne; even the Tsar's favourite officer cannot get away with murder.'

'Be quiet,' Natalya spoke at last, her pale blue eyes still fixed on Katherine's face, 'Dr Putulo is trying to tell us something.'

'Indeed,' the Scots doctor continued, 'it was as if MacQueen knew that his life was in danger. He wished to appoint a guardian over Katherine until she reached the age of twenty-one. This person would be her advisor at Penstroun and negotiate any marriage plans. At the time I thought it strange for he was in rude health, but then he may still have had worries over revenge from his wife's family I suppose.'

'And who is this guardian?' Natalya asked in a tremulous voice.

'Lieutenant-General Ballantyne,' Ewen Putulo turned to the man he named.

Katherine spun round too, eyes wide in amazement. He appeared equally aghast at the news.

'It cannot be; Penstroun mentioned none of this to me,' Alexander retorted.

'No,' the older man nodded, 'in this way he insured you returned to Scotland even if he was dead.'

'I wish to God that he had lived,' Alexander said with feeling.

The men exchanged looks, each sizing up the other.

Katherine was torn by conflicting emotions. Did Alexander mean that he did not want to be her guardian? Her bruised heart leapt at the thought of them being brought together until she came of age; but he seemed suddenly reluctant. Had his feelings for her been superficial and his talk of feelings merely empty flattery? Scanning his hard features the horrifying thought came to her that he might have murdered her real father in the hopes of gaining Scottish lands. If so, she now stood in the way of such ambition. Then she felt ashamed of her suspicions. Alexander might not feel for her as strongly as she felt for him but she did not doubt his passion as a Highlander and loyal clansman. He had gone into exile for his chief and his clan; it was unthinkable that he would have murdered Chief James in such a cowardly way.

'It's too late now to wish him alive,' Hector said waspishly. 'But you shall not be troubled with such onerous duties, shall he Countess?' He turned to her gleefully. She looked on the point of speaking when they were all distracted by loud hammering and the crash of splintered wood below.

Katherine was rooted to the spot at the sound of raised voices and scuffling, followed moments later by steps clattering up the staircase and the door bursting open. Russian soldiers rushed in. An unshaven officer brandishing a pistol barked, 'Which one of you is Alexander Ballantyne?'

'What is the meaning of this?' Dr Putulo stepped forward, outraged. The Russian pushed him out of the way and Katherine clung onto his arm.

'I am he,' Alexander raised his head proudly. He suspected this was one of the Tsar's new secret police officers, but did not flinch. 'What do you want with me?'

'You are under arrest. Take him,' the officer ordered and two others seized him by the arms. Alexander struggled to throw them off.

'In the name of St Andrew, what for?' he demanded scornfully.

'The murder of some foreigner,' his captor spat at his feet.

'This is a matter for our own community,' Dr Putulo protested.

The surly Muscovite snarled at him to stand back or be arrested too. 'We don't want you foreigners here,' he shouted, 'it is time we made an example of one of the infidel.'

Katherine was galvanised out of her shock by his disdain for them all. 'But you would take the word of the infidel who accuses Lieutenant-General Ballantyne, one of the Tsar's trusted officers?' She gave Maitland a withering look.

'No,' the policeman snapped, 'we would not come so quickly on a foreigner's bidding. But for the Countess Matrapov, we come swiftly.'

Katherine stared appalled at Natalya and her pale expressionless face. So this was her revenge for Alexander's insults; surely she could not believe he was her betrothed's killer?

The guards dragged Alexander forward and pushed him towards the stairs. Katherine rushed after them. 'You're mistaken, let him go!' she screamed, tumbling after them.

'Stay where you are!' Alexander barked, before a boot jabbed him in the back. Her last sight of the tall officer was his resolute face, the eyes shining fiercely as he looked back at her.

The Doctor reached her and pulled her to him.

Katherine wailed, 'Stop them please, Papa.'

'We can do nothing,' he cried in agitation.

Natalya confronted them at the top of the stairs.

'Weep for your dear father and not for the worthless Ballantyne,' Natalya said bitterly, 'he deserves his punishment.' For a moment she looked at the young woman regretfully. 'You are so like the Princess Katya, why did I not see it before?' Katherine regarded her with angry silence. 'You won't believe this,' the Countess met her hostility with dignity, 'but I would not have begrudged your place at Penstroun as my step-daughter. I never had children of my own.'

She passed with a brief nod at the Doctor and Hector hurried after her without a word to either. For what seemed like an age, Katherine stood with her step-father staring after them, numb with shock, unable to take in the enormity of what had just happened.

Hardly aware of Fiona's gentle coaxing, her old servant and the Doctor steered her back into the drawing-room and sat her down.

'We must do something for Alexander,' she fretted, 'I cannot believe the worst of him. Oh, my poor dear father!' Katherine buried her face in her hands.

'Do not worry, we will do what we can for your guardian,' Dr Putulo promised, though his look was full of doubt. 'We will petition the Tsar if necessary. As a foreigner Alexander comes under his protection and should be judged by a special tribunal and not by Russian law.'

Katherine looked up at him with the rekindling of hope. 'Perhaps Tsar Peter will listen to me as the daughter of a Russian princess? I will plead his case,' she declared. 'You do not think my father's kinsman is his murderer do you?'

Ewen Putulo hesitated. The evidence did appear to incriminate the tempestuous officer and it was true he had been violently jealous over the Countess for good reason. But instinct told him that Ballantyne's code of honour would never entertain the cold-blooded murder of his own Chief; certainly the youth who had escaped execution in Scotland would not have done so.

'I do not really doubt Alexander's loyalty to your father,' he squeezed her hands, 'there must be another explanation. But first,' his voice trembled with emotion, 'we must burry my good friend MacQueen.'

***

The next days passed in a blur as word spread of the murder and Katherine's new found fortune as heiress to the Penstroun estates. Members of the foreign colony and fellow Scots came to pay their respects to the tall, sad-eyed young woman in mourning who received them with a brave dignity. Rosa attempted to raise her friend's desolate spirits but Katherine could not hide her increasing worry over Alexander's well-being as they failed to get near the Kremlin fortress where he languished.

It had taken all the Doctor's persuasive powers and diplomacy to discover where he was held, but his enquiries came up against an implacable Russian stone wall. He rode out to the palace at Preobrazhenskoe, headquarters of the Secret Police, but the chief officer refused to see him and left Ewen Putulo feeling that he too was under surveillance for asking so many questions.

The Chief's funeral was a quiet affair by Highland standards. Katherine was aware that had he died in his own beloved Penstroun, people would have travelled for days to attend the funeral and paid tribute to him in the music of the pipes and in much drinking and story-telling over his embalmed body. As it was, the small Presbyterian Church in the Quarter was packed to overflowing with mourners and afterwards, Dr Putulo held open house for the funeral feast.

Katherine could not avoid Hector Maitland's unwelcome presence near her, dressed in a coat of black velvet, black stockings and buckled shoes. She wondered briefly how he could afford to dress as he did and whether his strict father would condone his son's extravagance on clothes.

'Dear cousin Katherine,' he leaned close to her as she gazed from the upper window towards Moscow, 'as we are now related I want you to forget the unfortunate incident which passed between us at the picnic. I would never have behaved in such a way to a daughter of Penstroun.'

'But you would to a daughter of Putulo?' Katherine looked at him coldly.

Hector blushed in confusion. 'I merely ask your forgiveness. As we shall be travelling back to Scotland together, I wish us to at least be on speaking terms.'

'I cannot leave without my guardian,' Katherine replied dismissively, 'perhaps you can secure his release as effectively as you did his arrest?'

'It was not I but the Countess Natalya who accused him,' Hector sniffed, taking Katherine by the arm. 'You cannot delay return indefinitely, Cousin Katherine, else we shall not be able to complete the journey before the autumn gales set in. As Mistress MacQueen of Penstroun you have duties to consider above your concern for Ballantyne. I find it strange that you should take such an interest in your father's killer.'

'Let me alone,' Katherine shook him off, 'I wish for as little of your company as civility allows and no more.'

'Mr Maitland will you give me a moment with Miss MacQueen?' Natalya interrupted their argument. Hector flushed beetroot red and stalked off.

'And have you come to taunt me about Alexander too?' Katherine reproached.

'No,' Natalya met the challenge in Katherine's green eyes, 'I think I may be able to arrange for you to visit him in prison.'

Katherine gasped, 'When?'

'It may take a few more days to arrange,' Natalya answered cautiously, 'but the prison governor is not above bribery and I still have influential friends in the Kremlin.'

Katherine was still suspicious. 'I am glad you wish to help me, Countess, but why do you care what happens to Lieutenant-General Ballantyne?'

'I don't,' she snapped, and then her tense face relaxed. 'You are the daughter of the man I loved,' she said awkwardly, 'and I do not like to see you suffer as you do. If it gives you comfort to see Ballantyne then I shall try to arrange it. I do not believe in his innocence as readily as you Katherine, but that is not for us to decide.'

Katherine looked more closely at the woman before her, so pale and drawn against the black of her mourning robes, her hair completely hidden by a soft gauze veil. She looked much older without her painted face and elaborate hairstyle; Katherine saw the tight lines of sorrow around her blue eyes and thin mouth. Instinctively she put out a hand to comfort.

'Thank you, Natalya,' she replied as her step-father approached.

'Countess,' he smiled at the Russian widow briefly, turning his attention quickly to Katherine. 'My dear, Count De Maton brings encouraging news. The Tsar has agreed to hear our plea before he leaves for Archangel.'

'Oh father,' her face lit up, 'then there is hope?'

'That may depend on you,' he answered, touched by her unconscious use of the endearment. 'The Count thinks the Tribunal will decide his fate swiftly; the Tsar wants it settled before he departs. I think Alexander's best chance for clemency is for you to face Tsar Peter alone.'

'Then it shall be done,' Katherine agreed without hesitation.

***

A court official appeared through the large double wooden doors. Dr Putulo stopped his pacing and Katherine rose in anticipation. Sitting in the dark draughty antechamber of Granovitaya Palace within the Kremlin, they had waited all day for a glimpse of Tsar Peter, while scores of soldiers and officials bustled to and fro in the chaos of war preparation.

The official dressed in the German fashion of short coat and breeches and beardless by the Tsar's decree waved his papers at them.

'His Royal Majesty, Our Lord the Tsar, has no time to deal with requests from foreigners now,' he said breezily, 'he has too many matters of state to attend to before he leaves. You will have to go.'

'But we have waited all day!' Ewen Putulo protested, his patience at breaking point. The official was dismissive.

'You cannot expect our *Batushka*, the Father of Great Russia, to bother with the petty complaints of foreigners when there is a threat to the motherland from the Northern infidel. Be gone with you,' he sniffed at them with unveiled disdain, 'come back in the summer when His Majesty returns victorious and may look favourably upon your plea.'

Dr Putulo bit back his annoyance but Katherine could bear the insufferable jibes no longer. She drew herself up tall in the cream lacy dress ordered the previous summer from Paris and worn specially to please Tsar Peter's Western tastes.

'You speak to the daughter of Princess Katya Naryshkin, a Russian noblewoman and relative of the good Tsar,' she said, her pale cheeks enflamed and eyes flashing. 'You will tell Tsar Peter I am here to speak to him, or do you wish him to discover you have kept his relation waiting all day? Perhaps you would prefer to spend the rest of your working days in the wastelands of Siberia rather than preening at court like a peacock?'

The official gaped in surprise. He had never been spoken to so forthrightly by any woman. His face tightened.

'Madam, there is nothing I can do. The Tsar is at this very moment leaving the palace for Preobrazhenskoe to fetch the Tsarevich Alexis and liaise with his officers. There is little point in wasting any more time here.'

Before Katherine could release a second tirade, the doors opened and into the dim lamp-light stepped a familiar figure.

'Count De Maton,' she cried with relief, 'we have been refused permission to approach the Tsar by this servant here,' she pointed an accusing hand. 'Can you do something, please?'

De Maton flinched at the open expectant look in the sad eyes and cleared his throat.

'It is not good news, Miss MacQueen,' he said gently, 'a hastily called tribunal has found Ballantyne guilty of your father's murder, I'm sorry,' he laid a hand on her shoulder.

'No,' she shuddered, 'it can't be true? They have no evidence that it was Alexander!'

The Frenchman glanced at the official and lowered his voice further. 'The incident has given certain boyars the ammunition they need to attack the foreign contingent in Moscow and Alexander is the scapegoat they want, in spite of him being a friend of the Tsar's. They have found servants at the Hostelry who swear that they heard Ballantyne and your father in a dispute and a shot fired in his upstairs rooms. Tsar Peter looks very sternly on the whole affair and is furious with Alexander for getting mixed up in it when he is so needed by the army. In the light of the court decision the monarch appears to have changed his mind about your petition.'

Katherine felt tears of frustration sting her eyes. She would not give up without a fight. 'If only I could be allowed to see the Tsar,' she urged, 'he might relent. Please De Maton; can you speak up for me?'

He looked at her for a long moment, struck by her courage and felt a twinge of envy for his Scottish friend imprisoned deep in the Kremlin, who inspired such devotion.

'Wait a moment,' he came to a decision and bracing himself for the royal wrath, returned into the state apartments. Long agonising minutes of silence ensued, the affronted official leaving them in almost total darkness. At last the doors swung open once more and De Maton appeared in a glow of light.

'Come Miss MacQueen, you have ten minutes to persuade the Tsar not to execute your kinsman.'

She followed him nervously through two rooms still crowded with courtiers and officers and was left in a large chamber hung with rich tapestries. Katherine instinctively fell to the ground before the immensely tall dark man who stood at a distance and touched the floor with her head in the Russian mark of respect. Suddenly she was terrified of the task ahead and her bold insistence on seeking audience with the Tsar when his mind could only be on the threats to his country's security. It was sheer folly and Katherine was seized by doubt over Alexander's innocence.

'Please Miss MacQueen,' a warm hand touched the back of her head, 'there is no need for this.'

Shaking, Katherine found herself looking into the swarthy face and dark alert eyes of Tsar Peter. His wiry dark hair, roughly parted in the middle, fell in waves to his shoulders. A stern face, heavily furrowed, surveyed her and then he smiled beneath the thin moustache and his whole face brightened and lost its severity.

Katherine gave a nervous smile as he helped her to stand. Holding onto her arm for a moment, the Tsar gave her an appreciative look.

'Is this beautiful woman the same young girl, skittish as a kitten, whom I met at her sister's wedding?' he teased.

Katherine blushed in confusion; she had not expected flattery.

'Your Majesty,' she replied huskily, her throat dry, 'I did not know then that I was the daughter of both a Naryshkin princess and a Highland chief, else I might have acted with more nobility. I am indeed proud to be related to your royal person.'

Tsar Peter chuckled loudly and patted her hand, pleased with the compliment. 'And so you should be,' he agreed. 'Your father was a friend of mine during my childhood before he fled Russia, did you know?' Katherine murmured that she knew he had served as a loyal soldier of Muscovy. 'He used to instruct me in my war games,' the Tsar smiled, 'we would inspect and drill my playfellows and MacQueen would describe to me the battles of his ancestors and the Highlanders' fearful charge.'

He broke off and they regarded each other in silence. Tsar Peter abruptly dropped her hand. 'His murder was a terrible crime and one that shall not go unpunished,' he turned quickly and marched back to a long table strewn untidily with plans. 'I give you foreigners free reign in my capital and I am repaid with undisciplined behaviour. Well you shall not carry on your feuds in my streets!' he shouted.

Katherine watched him in dismay. 'Your Majesty,' she stepped after him, 'I loved my father greatly and his death was a grievous blow. We shall never be able to enjoy that special relationship between father and daughter which should have been ours–' her throat constricted with tears but she forced herself to continue.

'You are right to punish the perpetrator of this crime, but the man you hold is not he, of that I am certain. He was as loyal to his Chief as he is to his Tsar. They held each other in great respect and I know my father wished Alexander Ballantyne to return with him to Scotland. If he had not trusted him so completely he would not have made him my guardian.'

The monarch strode up and down, agitated by her remarks, his hands clasping and unclasping behind his back, his green coat flapping against his boots as he moved.

'And who else would have had cause to murder your father?' he turned to face her, his visage grim. 'Ballantyne will say nothing to save himself.'

'It could have been a random attack by robbers,' Katherine stood her ground, 'or revenge. There are Russians who hated the Chief for marrying one of their own kind and blamed him for my mother's death. They would be happy if this provoked a backlash against your foreign subjects.'

Katherine held her breath wondering if she had gone too far. She saw the left side of his face twitch violently and his lips purse. She knew this last comment had struck home, for he himself was criticised in private for cultivating friendships with the Europeans, a source of contamination to the traditionally conservative Muscovites.

Tsar Peter looked at the tall young woman standing with quiet poise in layers of soft cream, her luxuriant dark hair tied back under a simple black veil to denote her state of mourning. Her large green eyes held his, mutely pleading.

She was brave, he mused for a moment, ready to defy all for her kinsman. Ballantyne was a lucky man, he thought ruefully, to have such a beautiful woman plead his cause.

'Lieutenant-General Ballantyne was my friend and comrade,' he came forward and looked down at her from his great height. 'I cannot deny I shall miss him greatly on my next campaign. But he will not tell us what passed between himself and MacQueen that night, so all the evidence is against him, you must see that?'

Katherine felt her eyes blur as she stared up at the tall monarch; she was losing the argument and the helplessness of the situation overwhelmed her.

'Then I beg Your Majesty to pardon him,' she whispered hoarsely. 'His loyalty to his Tsar is without question ...' her voice cracked.

Tsar Peter gently lifted her chin and smiled sadly. 'And your loyalty to him is equally touching, my dear.'

To her mortification, tears streamed down her cheeks; she had not wanted to resort to an emotional scene to sway him.

'Come, come,' he cajoled and dabbed her face with his silk cuff, 'this is no way for a daughter of a Highland chief or a Naryshkin to behave.' Katherine smiled through her tears and sniffed vigorously into her own silk handkerchief.

Pausing, he strode back to the gilded table and picked up a drawing, studying it hard. 'You must understand that Ballantyne is in the pay of the Russian army and not free to leave its service unless I say so, even if he were not imprisoned for murder. But I have listened to your plea, Miss MacQueen, and am much moved by it. Your kinsman's life will be spared.'

Katherine nearly fainted with the relief that hit her with the force of east winds across the Russian plains. 'Thank you–' she whispered.

'However, he will have to serve a term of exile in Siberia for his crime,' the Tsar added sternly, 'it will be a lesson to others.'

Her heart sank at the harsh alternative, her hopes for Alexander's freedom dashed as soon as they were raised. She would have to return to Penstroun without him, with the desolate thought that she might never set eyes on him again. She curtsied to hide her bitter disappointment, but Tsar Peter seemed to have lost interest and was engrossed again in his plans. Just as she reached the doors to leave he called after her.

'You shall be allowed to visit the Lieutenant-General before he is moved.'

Katherine managed to stutter a thank you as, picking up her skirts, she fled from the room.

***

With the extinguishing of any hope of Alexander's release Katherine listlessly accepted the plans for her departure and journey. It was some small comfort that her step-father and Count De Maton would accompany her and Hector Maitland as far as Prussia, the latter on his return to France. Fiona would go as her companion to Scotland. Messages were sent ahead to Hugh Ballantyne and the MacQueen gentry that the heiress's return was imminent.

In spite of the Tsar's assurances, once he had left for the north, it proved exceedingly difficult to procure a visit inside Alexander's prison. Only with the Countess Matrapov's help did the governor finally relent to a brief interview a matter of days before their departure to Poland.

Resigning herself with the same fatalism that her mother had displayed all those years ago, Katherine determined to be stoical in Alexander's presence. She would upset neither of them by a display of emotion, for any relationship was now pointless. She could not however, deny herself this last chance of seeing him.

On first entering the fortress Katherine could see nothing after the blinding light of outside, aware only of the cold smell of stone and centuries of damp around her. Gradually her eyes became accustomed to the dimness and she could make out the low honeycomb of passages leading them deeper into the solid tower, with its walls the thickness of three grown men laid head to foot.

Dr Putulo gripped her hand in encouragement as they stumbled after the guards, trying not to knock his head on the arched ceiling. Katherine shuddered in the cold, trying to fight off the terrifying feeling of the dark walls closing in around her. No natural light filtered into the stronghold and thoughts of past prisoners incarcerated for years on end filled her with panic.

Their footsteps rang on the hard uneven floors and steep stone steps as they climbed past locked doors and dark passages that trailed away into the blackness. In her imagination she had expected to hear the cries of the captive, but this awful silence was more frightening, as if they were the first people to have disturbed the dank air for years.

All at once the passage opened up into a round guardroom with candles flickering in wall brackets and a rough wooden table and chairs the only furniture. A gaming-board with dice lay beside wooden cups. The younger guard nodded at the Doctor to sit while the older gaoler began to unlock a heavy wooden door and remove its iron bars with laboured wheezing.

'Your visitor,' he mumbled and stood back as the door swung open with a grinding clang. 'You may go in madam,' the grey-haired guard bowed at Katherine.

Taking a deep breath and heart hammering, she moved forward into the cell. The door remained open behind her.

To her surprise she felt a thin rug beneath her feet and the candles that flickered in the recess of the nearest cell wall half-illuminated a wall hanging of red and gold wool. Searching the dim room, she could at first see no one. There were a few rugs piled in the corner for a bed and a table and chair stood under a slit high up in the wall that allowed a crack of daylight to enter the tomb-like chamber. The spluttering candles smelt waxy but did not hide the sickening stench that permeated the very walls.

'Katherine?' a questioning voice rang out from the dark corner where the rugs lay.

'Alexander?' she gulped in reply, still unable to make him out.

A tall shadow detached itself from the general darkness and moved slowly across the room. She strained to make out his face. Taking a candle from the table he shone it at her, making weird shadows leap across his features; the heavy stubble, the livid scar and the dark eyebrows. His hair fell loosely about his neck, while the blue eyes seemed darker and hollowed.

'They did not tell me it was you,' he whispered just audible, taking in the sweep of her pale green and black satin dress and the black lace cap, trying unsuccessfully to hide the riot of dark curls. Her face seemed younger and nervous in the glow of the candle; the soft lips pressed tightly together, the large dark eyes cautious behind the almond-shaped lids.

'Who were you expecting?' Katherine stiffened and pulled out of the light.

'No one as welcome as you,' he said hastily, but held back.

'Natalya Matrapov arranged this visit,' Katherine broke the silence. 'She has been a good friend to me these past days.'

'Ha!' Alexander gave a mirthless laugh and banged the candle back on the table. 'That is truly touching; my accuser has a heart after all. But you can save me Natalya's blessings, Mistress MacQueen, I would rather trust to the Devil.'

Katherine was hurt by his bitterness, she had come to comfort him and all he could do was jeer at her in her misery. 'So even now you cannot accept the fact that she loved my father more than she cared for you,' she retaliated, 'perhaps she was right and you did kill my father out of jealousy for her and the Penstroun lands!'

Alexander leapt forward and gripped her. 'Is that what you believe?' he demanded. 'Tell me.'

She was suddenly afraid of him, unable to read the expression in his searching eyes. 'I don't know,' she whispered, 'I don't think I know you at all.'

He dropped his hold, running a hand through his tangled hair in exasperation. Alexander had been overjoyed to see her standing there in his cell like some vision conjured up out of his imagination. He had filled the long empty hours between brutal interrogations by the secret police with thoughts of Katherine and the revelation that she was his Chief's daughter.

His last sight of her pale distressed face watching him being forced out of Putulo's house had haunted him but made the pain bearable when Romodanovsky's men had whipped his back to ribbons. Strangely the torture and questioning had ceased two week ago when his sentence of death had been commuted to banishment and these crude furnishings had been brought to his cell.

'I can't blame you for hating me,' he said bleakly, 'this has been a terrible time for you. But I wish you could believe I had no part to play in your father's death; it would make my exile the easier to bear when you are gone.'

Katherine felt her heart twist painfully, unwanted tears oozing from below her downcast lids. 'Would I have risked the Tsar's displeasure by pleading for you if I hated you Alexander?' she said. 'At least I can leave Muscovy knowing I have spared your life if not your liberty.'

Trembling and exhausted by the strain she felt, Katherine reached out for the rough chair. Alexander caught hold of her quickly.

'You spoke on my behalf to Tsar Peter?' he asked incredulously.

'Yes,' Katherine blushed, 'surely they told you that? He promised me you would not be executed.'

Alexander cursed himself for having been so ungracious towards her; he had repaid her great courage with cruel words. 'Forgive me Katherine,' he brought her close to him, roughly brushing her hair with his lips, 'I did not know.'

With a deep sob she gave way to his hold, burying herself against his chest, unable to stop the shaking that wracked her body. He tightened his arms about her to share his warmth. 'I would almost welcome death rather than live out my life in Siberia knowing you are out of my reach,' his said with feeling. 'You are a brave daughter of Penstroun and I am a boorish soldier not worthy of your consideration.'

For a moment their gaze locked, and then Alexander cupped her face in his hands and found her lips with his own. His fingers reached into her hair, loosening the wayward curls from their cap and pressing her tightly to him, kissing with urgency. Katherine moaned, overwhelmed by a longing that left her dizzy. She kissed his chin and cheek and then his lips again, slipping her arms around his back. Alexander winced with pain at the pressure on his wounds and Katherine drew away.

'You're hurt?' she gasped.

'No,' he caught her hands, 'it's of no matter. You can only hurt me by denying your sweet kisses Katherine.' He cut off her protest with another desperate embrace. She tasted exquisite, her flowery perfume filling his nostrils like fresh air. 'You are so beautiful,' he kissed the hollow of her throat.

Katherine's heart beat rapidly. She thrilled to his dextrous touch and the searching lips on her skin. How could she bear to leave him here, knowing that once they were parted she would see him no more?

'Oh Alexander,' she cried, 'would that you could come with us.'

He cradled her head on his chest and covered her forehead with gentle kisses. 'Do you not know how much it pains me that I am powerless to protect you?' he answered desperately. 'What use am I now as your guardian?'

She raised her face to his. 'What was it you meant to say to me in the courtyard that day, after you had agreed with my father to return to Penstroun?'

Alexander did not answer immediately, a muscle working in his tight jaw. It was useless now to tell her he had thought of proposing marriage that very day. He had been euphoric with his decision to return to Scotland and the secret plans that his Chief had discussed and the thought of securing the hand of Dr Putulo's daughter had excited him to a reckless gesture, only interrupted by the Doctor himself. But the terrible news of his Chief's murder and the revelation of Katherine as his heiress had changed everything. A bid for her hand would have confirmed suspicions that he would go to any lengths to grasp Penstroun for himself, even Katherine might have doubted his sincerity and that he could not bear. Furthermore, he was now her legal guardian and could not abuse his position of trust by entertaining a union with his charge, even if he were free to do so. His future was now one of indefinite banishment – ten years minimum had been mentioned – and it was unfair on Katherine to burden her with his private hopes.

'I cannot recall,' he answered with a sad smile, pulling her closer.

The old gaoler appeared at the open door and jangled his keys impatiently. 'We change guard soon,' he grunted, 'I must take you back now, madam.'

Alexander and Katherine exchanged desperate looks though he still held her in his arms. 'When do you leave?' he asked hoarsely.

'At the end of the week.' Katherine saw him through a blur of tears. 'We make for Elspeth in Konigsberg and then sail for Scotland.' She broke down and wept.

'Do not cry for me,' he gently wiped her damp cheeks with his hand. 'One day I shall be free to follow,' he assured her, bending to kiss her one last time. Neither of them admitted how unlikely was that hoped for outcome.

'Come, Madam,' the guard moved across and took Katherine by the arm, prising her from Alexander's hold. She stumbled after him, her eyes not leaving the tall prisoner's face. Resisting the gaoler a moment longer, a thought came back to her.

'Alexander,' she croaked, 'you knew my father was in some kind of danger didn't you? That's why you asked to meet him in secret.' Her pleading look willed him to tell her. 'If you know his murderer why don't you reveal him and save yourself?'

Her urgent appeal cut him like a sabre slash. 'I cannot,' he rasped.

'Not even for me?' Katherine's voice choked with misery. His gaunt face was rigid as he answered her with silence.

She turned from him, numbed by his passive acceptance of his fate and engulfed in her own grief. She remembered nothing of their retreat through the warren-like fortress, as Ewen Putulo supported her faltering steps. All she could recall was the lasting image of Alexander Ballantyne's harrowed face and the fierce pride in his handsome eyes.

CHAPTER 7

Scotland

Katherine's first view of Penstroun was in the late summer, when the mountainsides were a hazy purple from the heather bloom and the steep-sided fields of barley were turning golden. The sky receded into a washed-out blue and a stiff breeze tugged at their cloaks and packs as the party made the descent out of the pass to the sea loch below.

For a moment she reigned in her horse and gazed down at the blue-grey loch, a wide sleeve reaching out into the distant sea, patches of green pasture and the mottled browns of thatched dwellings clinging to its edge. All was tranquil, save the cry of the gulls as Katherine breathed in the sharp salt air, exhilarated to be at last within sight of home after months of exhausting travel.

Penstroun Castle appeared to grow out of the promontory on which it stood, square and solid, staring defiantly out to sea. Lapped by the loch on three sides, a small plantation of beach and oak trees protected it from behind.

'Fiona,' Katherine turned excitedly to her companion, 'is it not a noble sight?'

The nurse's drawn face looked too tired to express any enthusiasm; she had suffered much from seasickness and the squalor of the country inns at which they had rested between Edinburgh and the Highlands.

'If it means parting from this nag and using the feet God gave me, then it is indeed a noble sight,' she rallied with some of her old spark.

'Come then,' Katherine kicked her horse into a trot and followed their guides who had been sent to meet them, though she understood none of their Gaelic speech. Hector Maitland had left them at the mouth of Culduggan glen earlier that day and handed them over to these men on squat sure-footed ponies.

The young heiress had had only a tantalising glimpse of the thickly forested glen where Alexander had grown up, but no sight of Culduggan House itself. What a relief it had been to say goodbye to the young Maitland and his incessant whining about the discomforts of the journey; the filth of the inn servants, the rankness of the food and the ignorance of everyone they had met, from Polish shopkeepers to English seamen.

Yet, riding so close to Culduggan had brought on bitter pangs of longing for the man she had left incarcerated in a Moscow prison, who by now must have reached the desolate isolation of Siberia and its cruel winters. It seemed in another lifetime that she had experienced the heady attraction for the Tsar's Scots officer and the flowering of love between them. Or did she delude herself that Alexander had felt anything more than a physical attraction to her?

For all his robust flattery he had never promised any lasting commitment and he had shown in his liaison with Countess Natalya that he held marriage in contempt. If he ever survived the rigours of a Siberian exile, it was almost inconceivable that he would remember his fondness for her and return to Scotland on her account.

As Katherine rode down the hillside towards Penstroun she shook off her sad recollections of leaving Moscow and Alexander and the tearful parting with her step-father and then Elspeth at Konigsberg. Now she was the mistress of Penstroun and was about to meet her kinspeople.

Approaching the Castle through the woods, Katherine was amazed to see the pathway thronged with people. They greeted her with Gaelic calls, standing barefoot in colourful woollen plaids of green, saffron yellow, purple and brown, the men in blue bonnets. Delightedly she waved back, her thanks drowned by the blast of a piper who stood by the castle gate. Katherine laughed at Fiona's mutterings about an unholy row and slipped gratefully from her saddle as a servant took the reins.

Before her, standing in wait, was a group of bewigged gentlemen. A broad-shouldered elderly man with a long hooked nose and grey-green eyes stepped forward. He wore checked hose and a green and scarlet plaid belted around his waist and draped over a plain doublet.

'Welcome Mistress MacQueen of Penstroun,' he smiled, 'I am Alastair MacQueen of Buala, a cousin of your late father.'

Katherine remembered her father talking fondly of him and curtsied in respect of his age which delighted the old man. He introduced the six other senior men of the clan, all holders of tacks of land on the Penstroun estate. As Katherine reached the end there was a clatter of footsteps down the outside stairs immediately beyond the gate, accompanied by laughter.

A tall fair-haired young man in plain brown trouse and waistcoat, followed by a petite young woman with hair the colour of white-gold sand, rushed up to the solemn group. The first latecomer, interrupting old MacQueen, seized Katherine's hand and kissed it.

‘I’m your kinsman Hugh Ballantyne,’ he grinned breathlessly, ‘we were watching your arrival from the top of the keep.’

Katherine smiled back at the handsome boyish face that greeted her, the broad sweep of forehead and straight nose so reminiscent of Alexander’s. But the friendly eyes were hazel and his eyebrows and wavy hair reddish-fair compared to his older brother’s dark auburn.

‘I have been looking forward to meeting you,’ Katherine answered warmly, ‘I know your brother well.’ She blushed as Hugh regarded her with the same keen-eyed interest as the older Ballantyne.

‘What news of Alexander?’ he questioned eagerly. ‘Surely he is free by now and is following?’

Katherine braced herself to tell him.

‘I’m sorry, I bring unhappy news. His sentence of death was indeed lifted, but he has been committed to at least ten years in Siberia.’

There were murmurs of disbelief among the gentry.

‘My brother would never have murdered his chief,’ Hugh shouted angrily, ‘none of us would. Your father was a great leader and our hope for the future–’

‘That’s enough,’ Alastair MacQueen broke in with a hand of caution on the young man’s arm. ‘You must forgive your young kinsman, Miss Katherine; this news comes as quite a shock.’

‘There is nothing to forgive,’ Katherine replied with kindness, ‘my sympathies lie with Lieutenant-General Ballantyne too and I, for one, do not believe him guilty of my father’s death.’

Fiona spoke up unafraid of the stern-looking Highlanders. ‘My mistress pleaded with Tsar Peter himself for Ballantyne’s release; if she had not he would be dead by now.’

Hugh shot Katherine an admiring look, his fair face flushed with remorse at his outburst.

‘Then I shall serve the Lady Penstroun in any way I can,’ he said fervently and bowed.

Katherine glanced over his head to the girl behind him, meeting the bashful inquisitive face. Alastair MacQueen took charge once more and beckoned the stranger forward.

‘This is my youngest daughter, Anne,’ he said with pride. She curtsied quickly at the tall dark foreigner who spoke English with a strange accent. Anne noticed with a touch of envy that her clothes were travel-stained but of rich fabrics, and her high-boned features and dark lashes quite beautiful.

Katherine smiled readily at the small woman with the darting blue eyes, pleased to think there would be a young companion for her after all. It had been so hard leaving behind her good friend Rosa and she sorely missed the Italian girl's intimate conversation and sense of fun.

'I would be very pleased if you would help me settle in here and show me the ways of a Highland gentlewoman, Miss MacQueen,' Katherine said.

'I would be honoured,' Anne MacQueen nodded, her face alighting with pleasure.

Katherine did not notice the smile on Anne's small mouth falter as Hugh offered Katherine his arm, leading her through the gate and up the narrow stone steps to the gun court. He chattered about Penstroun, making wicked comments about some of the household at which Katherine could not help laughing. They proceeded up a further stone spiral staircase through a large dark oak-panelled dining-room and a smaller drawing-room hung with tapestries, its wooden doors painted with landscape scenes.

'How beautiful,' Katherine cried as she saw them, 'I'm surprised my father had an eye for such decoration.'

'He did not,' Hugh answered rather tersely, 'it was commissioned by his sister, Christina Maitland.'

'I'm sure she had it done as a welcoming gesture,' Anne cut in quickly. 'Chief James told her he intended bringing you back here to live.'

'How kind of her,' Katherine said, eyebrows raised.

Hugh snorted, 'It was more likely done in expectation of removing here herself; the Maitlands have an eye on Penstroun as well you know, Anne.'

The girl coloured pink at his rebuff. 'Well, this was once her home,' she reminded him. 'I don't think it was done out of any selfish motive, but Hugh will think the worst of the Maitlands,' Anne apologised to Katherine.

Katherine decided not to pursue the subject.

'Will you show me to my apartments, Miss MacQueen?' she slipped an arm through the other girl's.

'Please call me Anne,' she blushed, pleased at the friendliness and glad that her fears of a haughty Russian princess were unfounded.

Hugh said he would meet them again later; they could play a game of bowls before supper. He watched Katherine go, quite enchanted by his new kinswoman. For a moment he had forgotten his other worries and the meeting with Sir Archibald that loomed ever closer. His need for money was acute even though, this past year, he had been able to take advantage of the lax overseeing of the estate by the elderly MacQueen of Buala.

It irked him to be beholden to Maitland in any way, a man for whom he had a deep loathing. Had he not treated the people of Culduggan mercilessly during the recent dreadful years of starvation? He had even imprisoned children who stole kale from his yard and held back stores of grain until they reached famine prices. The day of revenge would come, he vowed.

Staring after the plucky chief's daughter who had not blanched at confronting the Tsar of Russia or undertaking a dangerous journey across Europe, Hugh believed that day might come sooner than he had dared hope.

***

Those last blustery weeks of summer passed quickly into a red-gold autumn, as Katherine settled into Penstroun, guided by old Alastair MacQueen in the affairs of the Castle and by his daughter, Anne, and her kinsman, Hugh Ballantyne, in getting to know the countryside and its people. She had been shocked by the poverty of the barefoot tenants who lived in windowless smoked-filled houses with their animals. Yet she responded to their welcoming manner and delighted in watching the girls spin with their distaffs and spindles, listening to them sing and soon picked up their Gaelic conversation. Alastair was teaching her the language of her people.

Katherine's favourite ride was across the tract of open moorland above her home, to the headland with its dramatic drop below to the sea and the shingle beach. From this height she could look down on the seabirds which wheeled crazily beneath and watch the sea hurl itself onto the rocks. It was a new sensation which mesmerised and excited.

On a wild autumn day, when the wind was whipping in off the grey sea and storm clouds loomed like titanic shadows overhead, Katherine and Anne took the familiar path through the copper-coloured bracken.

Further up the coast they caught a glimpse of the white sands of Buala Bay, Anne's former home.

'I never tire of looking at the sea,' the mistress of Penstroun smiled at her companion, 'you must think that strange having lived with it all your life.'

'I certainly have no desire to sail on it,' Anne shrugged, 'the sea is just something that helps provide a living for our people.'

Katherine laughed at her ever practical friend who was baffled by her romantic notions about the place.

'And is this where you first espied Hugh as he returned from France?' she asked wickedly, knowing the girl's fondness for the younger Ballantyne.

'I had better things to do than stare out to sea,' Anne rose to the bait, 'I recall I was sewing shirts when the Chief called with his newly arrived guest.' She caught Katherine's amused looked and laughed too. Turning her horse back, Anne asked curiously, 'Is Hugh like his older brother? I wasn't born when they left Scotland; it's tragic that they were so cruelly separated.'

Katherine felt her insides twist at the sudden reminder of Alexander. She would always remember him as she first saw him in his uniform, half-bearded and confident in his actions, taking enthusiastically to the *Khorovod* in spite of his weariness.

'In some ways the brothers are quite similar,' Katherine mused, 'they both display a stubbornness of character and a quick temper when roused.' Anne nodded in agreement. 'Men of passion, I suppose,' Katherine blushed as she admitted it. 'But in looks Alexander is much darker and he bears a scar on the left side of his face which he received from a Tartar's sabre.'

'And you were fond of him?' Anne slipped her a look. Katherine nodded. 'And Hugh; are you fond of him?' Anne persisted. 'I know he likes you.'

Katherine glanced at her quickly but her friend now concentrated on the path ahead.

'I find Hugh handsome and good company,' she was candid, 'but he is not Alexander and I cannot feel the same way about him.' She noticed the younger woman's face relax a little. 'Tell me Anne,' Katherine remembered a recent puzzling incident, 'where does Hugh go on his evening rides? He refuses to take me with him and is so secretive I cannot bear it!'

Anne gave a nervous laugh. 'Oh, he just goes to see friends,' she answered vaguely, 'he used to visit us at Buala before your father brought us here to keep him company at Penstroun.'

'And is our own company so dull that he must seek out others so frequently?' Katherine asked rather piqued.

‘I’m sure he means no slight by it,’ Anne said quickly, ‘it is for your own safety that he does not let you ride abroad after dark.

Katherine let it pass and they left the cliff top, taking the more sheltered deer path that wound back along the lochside. Something made Katherine look back and, for the first time, she noticed a small vessel lying off the rocky isle opposite Buala.

‘Look Anne,’ she called, ‘I wonder what that ship is doing there?’

Her companion squinted and looked taken aback. ‘It could be a government boat patrolling these waters for French privateers. Father says they are a menace to our merchant ships since war was declared with France,’ she gabbled. Then her tone became resentful. ‘Of course, Hugh blames the English for forcing us into reluctant hostilities with our ally France; the southerners commandeer our sailors but care little for protecting our coastal trade.’

‘Then it is unlikely that this is a government frigate,’ Katherine grew inquisitive. ‘So why does it shelter there, I wonder? We would never have noticed it if we had not taken the deer track; the ship is quite hidden from above.’

‘Who knows,’ Anne shrugged, ‘let’s go home now, the weather is about to worsen.’ With a shiver she set off ahead.

They continued in silence, Katherine wondering if she had said something to offend her friend, for she seemed in no mood for speech. The rain came on swift and heavy; as they reached the edge of the village, Hugh rode into sight.

‘Katherine, come!’ he shouted with glee. ‘You must witness this spectacle.’

‘What is it?’ she smiled.

‘You’ll see,’ Hugh could hardly contain his mirth, ‘just come quickly!’ They trotted after him and reached the Castle gateway bewildered at seeing nothing out of the ordinary. ‘Up there,’ he pointed, ‘on the top road.’

The women followed his hand and saw what had caused Hugh’s merriment. A large cumbersome coach pulled by six straining and stumbling horses lurched precariously in the rain along the brow of the hill, following the drovers’ track. Two servants in gaudy blue and green livery stood behind the carriage and another two ran in front clearing boulders out of the way. As they watched its slow progress, the vehicle shuddered and wobbled unsteadily like a portly gout-ridden old gentleman and toppled sideways into a rut. The coachmen leapt off and tried to lever the coach out of its hole with their long poles, but it refused to budge.

'I've never seen a coach in these parts,' Katherine said, transfixed.

'That's because everyone else has the sense to go by horseback or on foot in the Highlands,' Hugh laughed. 'I've been stalking them for two hours and they've only moved a stone's throw since noon!'

'Who is it?' she asked in amusement.

'The Maitlands,' Anne answered with a giggle.

'Who else would show off their wealth in such a ridiculous way?' Hugh added scornfully.

Katherine's heart sank to think Hector might be in the lumbering carriage. Let it stick fast, she thought unsympathetically. Her interest quickened, however, when the occupants emerged defeated from their confinement and two women clambered out aided by their menfolk.

'Come, Anne,' she turned to her friend, noticing the liveliness in her brown eyes as she exchanged looks with Hugh, 'we must alert the kitchens that we have guests arriving. Hugh; send some of the men up to help them. Now, let's get out of the rain.'

***

She gave speedy instructions to the servants to open up rooms for the Maitlands, who could not possibly return home with a storm coming on. The kitchen staff were instructed in what to prepare for supper; it would be a feast to show them that she was a worthy successor to Chief James.

It seemed an age while Katherine waited in the upper drawing-room for the Maitlands to finally reach the welcoming walls of Penstroun. The women entered first, shoes and skirts bespattered with mud, the younger one's face twisted in annoyance.

'Aunt Christina,' Katherine came forward to greet the handsome older woman, guiding her into a high-backed seat. 'You will take some claret to revive you?'

'That is most kind,' she replied still flustered, her brow creased in worry, the dark grey eyes searching the room as if she had misplaced something. Her daughter threw herself down in a chair before being asked, her pretty plump face and brown eyes sizing up her hostess.

'I'm Sybilla,' she announced.

Before Katherine could respond, a voice commanded from behind, 'Miss MacQueen, we meet at long last.'

She turned to see a stocky elderly man in black coat and breeches enter in front of Hector and Hugh. He wore a tall black hat, from whose rim droplets of rain still spattered onto a full-bottomed wig. But it was his one unblinking eye which held her attention, his other masked behind a patch. He came forward and kissed her hand.

'It's a pleasure to meet my wife's niece; Hector has told me much about you, but even his admiring description does not do you justice.'

Katherine gave the Maitland heir a dismissive frosty look, but he said nothing, just grinned foolishly. She noticed he was dressed soberly for once in grey, with only a dash of lace lining his cravat and none at his cuffs. Obviously his father did not approve of foppery even though he rode ostentatiously in a coach.

'And I have heard much about you, Sir Archibald,' Katherine replied guardedly, gesturing for him to sit down, her interest in him aroused. She had not expected such courteous flattery from the man everyone described as an ogre.

'Please, you must call me Uncle,' he smiled and his whole face creased into deep channels like cracks in dried leather, his nose and cheeks patterned with tiny red veins. It was a face that had not been spared life's indulgences and belied the impression she had of him as a strict and pious parent. He accepted the pewter bowl of claret with alacrity and drank deeply.

'Aunt Christina, you will stay with us tonight and take supper,' Katherine insisted, ignoring Hugh's look. Her aunt did not answer, but turned to Sir Archibald and waited for him to accept.

'We would be honoured,' he dabbed his lips, 'Culduggan could not be reached again before nightfall.'

'Not in that coach,' Hugh added under his breath, provoking Maitland's sharp one-eyed look of displeasure. He ignored the jibe and turned back to his niece.

'You are settling in to life at Penstroun, I hope? It must be quite dull after Moscow society.'

'I love it already,' Katherine replied, giving Hugh a warning glance. 'Anne and Hugh are the best of companions.' She smiled encouragingly at the young MacQueen girl who had not uttered a word since the Maitland's arrival. 'Besides, there is much to do about the Castle and I am being tutored in Gaelic, so my days are well occupied.'

'So it would seem,' Sir Archibald eyed her, 'my family have been disappointed not to see you over at Culduggan before now. But you will visit us before winter sets in, I trust?'

Katherine felt it was more of an order than an invitation, so parried with a question of her own.

'Do you entertain much at Culduggan, Uncle?'

'We never have visitors,' Sybilla interrupted moodily, twirling her curls and trying to catch Hugh's attention.

'Be quiet, daughter,' Sir Archibald snapped and she threw him a reproachful look. 'Sybilla complains overmuch about most things at Culduggan. She would spend her days in dancing and other godless entertainment, I'm afraid it is her mother's overindulgence. There is only one way to correct such vanity and that is daily meditation and instruction in the ways of God,' he lectured.

To Katherine's surprise her aunt did not protest at this criticism; she felt a pang of sympathy for the Maitland women.

'Then I'm sorry you will be inconvenienced here, Uncle; the old chaplain died last year and has not been replaced.'

'That is regrettable,' he sucked in his lips and toyed with the empty vessel which he had already drained without passing on, 'but understandable as your father left his affairs in the hands of Buala. I fear he remains at odds with the new established Church of Scotland.'

Katherine was aware of both Hugh and Anne stiffen at the attack on Anne's father and quickly intercepted.

'This is a Presbyterian household and I was brought up believing in the same doctrines as yourself, Sir Archibald. The post remains vacant because of a lack of trained Presbyterian ministers in the district and nothing more sinister,' she smiled.

'Then, dear niece, you shall have the services of my own chaplain, Stevenson, while we are here, tomorrow being the Sabbath,' he insisted. 'He travelled with us and is taking prayers with the servants at this very moment.'

Briefly Katherine caught a pleading look from Anne and a nod towards the young Ballantyne, as if she did not trust him to hold his peace.

'Well, Aunt,' Katherine changed the subject swiftly, 'you'll want to change out of your wet clothes before supper. Please come with me.'

She experienced a wave of relief as they escaped and saw Christina Maitland's fretful face relax as they made their way up to the small chambers above. From the high narrow window Katherine could see geese being chased through the pelting rain for the evening meal and a drenched hound rounded up to turn the large spit.

‘I thought you would have worn more interesting clothes,’ Sybilla said tactlessly as she held up the dresses set out for them. ‘Hector said all the ladies in Muscovy wore the latest French fashions,’ she swept disappointed eyes over Katherine’s woollen gown of black and white checks.

‘I find simple dresses and plaids far more practical here than the constricting dresses I wore in Moscow,’ Katherine laughed unoffended.

‘Did you bring them with you?’ Sybilla asked eagerly.

‘A few,’ Katherine admitted.

‘Then let me have them if you won’t wear them.’

‘Sybilla,’ her mother murmured in a half-hearted attempt to admonish the girl.

‘I’ll look them out for you,’ Katherine closed the tiny casement window against the increasing blustery air, ‘though you are smaller than me and may need to take them up.’

‘Yes,’ she preened, ‘mother says I have petite good looks; it is not becoming for a woman to be too tall.’

Katherine flushed at her rudeness and bit back a retort. Anne slipped an arm through hers in solidarity.

‘But you would agree, Sybilla,’ Anne countered sweetly, ‘that in Katherine’s case, height and beauty are equally matched?’

The Maitland daughter threw them both a surprised look and muttered a grudging agreement. Katherine thought it best to steer the conversation away from herself, asking her aunt about Penstroun and what it had been like when she had lived here as a girl. Strangely, the older woman’s face took on a look of girlish pleasure, the grey eyes lighting with fond memories and she talked freely about former days when her own father had held court as chief with bards and harpists, pipers and a jester.

‘What a happy time it was,’ Christina spoke wistfully, ‘but things changed for my brother once King William came to the throne and he could not afford to keep up a large household.’

‘Are you not content at Culduggan then?’ Katherine probed.

Christina’s expression grew guarded.

‘It is not such a grand house as Penstroun certainly, but we are comfortable.’

‘What mother means is that Culduggan is cold and dismal and deadly dull,’ Sybilla piped up, as she regarded herself in the mirror. ‘The only company my father keeps is that of Captain Leighton, the Governor of

Fort William – and he is deadly shy in female company. He blushes red as a rose when we speak to him.'

'Sybilla, that is enough,' Christina chided.

'Well, it's true,' her daughter pouted, 'you are only happy when we remove to the Lowlands for the summer and father stays to do endless business.'

'That's not so,' the older grey-haired woman grew agitated, 'I do not like to leave your father here on his own.'

'Well I do,' the girl answered moodily, 'it is the only chance I have of enjoying the society of young men. And Hector couldn't wait to get away from Papa last summer and travel with Uncle James, he told me as much.'

Katherine and Anne exchanged wary looks; it seemed all was not harmony in the Maitland household. Christina turned and picked distractedly at the dress on the bed.

'We shall leave you to change,' Katherine said swiftly, 'if you prefer, Sybilla, I will look out an evening dress of mine for you to wear.'

'Oh yes,' the girl agreed in an instant, seemingly oblivious to the upset she had caused her mother. 'I would feel so much better in silk.'

***

By the time they were assembled again for supper, including some MacQueen gentry caught in the storm, the wind had grown ferocious outside and the rain lashed tirelessly at the deep-set windows in the solid Castle walls. Katherine revelled in the wildness that marooned them as they sat cosily in the panelled dining-hall with its blazing fire and candlelight flickering crazily in the gusts as servants brought in food.

She wore a gown of soft rust-red satin, cut away to show the lace of her petticoat that framed her bosom. The front strands of dark hair were pulled back from her face and caught with ribbon under a simple black cap to denote her mourning; the rest tumbled naturally about her bare shoulders.

She noticed with amusement, Sybilla's almost pained imperious look as she sat bound in swathes of cherry pink and lemon silk, her breasts squashed by the tight bodice. Her father had exploded when first he saw her dressed in such wanton finery, until Katherine had interceded and told him there was nothing else to fit her. His daughter had looked exultant at his blustering acquiescence and manoeuvred herself next to a sullen Hugh.

MacQueen of Buala and several of the other gentry had joined them at the large table and Katherine was pleased at the ill-concealed look of envy on Sir Archibald's face as the laden traunches of food appeared. They began with oysters and buttered crabs, followed by roasted hare, wild fowl, mutton collops and succulent goose cooked in its juices with thyme and sage picked by Katherine.

At the end of the meal, Maitland wiped his mouth with his napkin and drained off another mazer of claret.

'This is indeed a feast, Katherine,' he allowed his cup to be refilled, 'and excellent claret.'

'We find it more difficult to procure now that trade has been interrupted with France,' Katherine answered dryly, eyeing him, 'but our guests shall enjoy it while there are casks to be drunk.'

'We have good stocks of wine, my dear,' Maitland leaned across and gave her a lopsided smile, 'you must let me know if you ever run dry, we can give you a good price.'

Katherine felt offended that her uncle would think of charging her in return for her hospitality, but decided to ignore his miserly attitude.

'Let us drink a toast to our neighbours and guests,' she said brightly and then regretted her impulse as she felt her kinsmen stiffen around the table. Raising her glass she caught Hugh's look of displeasure, but they all followed her lead. Maitland responded enthusiastically with a toast to the Mistress of Penstroun.

'And now let us drink to the new Queen Anne and her government,' he remained on his feet. This was met with a stony silence. Katherine felt uneasy as she surveyed the grim set faces of the MacQueen gentry who had never before been asked to show such allegiance at her table. Nothing had ever been said, but she guessed their sympathies still lay with the exiled Stuarts, as Hugh's so patently did.

'We will all be under the table, Uncle, if we drink too many healths,' Katherine kept her voice light. 'Perhaps you would enjoy some entertainment now?'

'Once we have drunk to our sovereign as loyal subjects,' he shot her a challenging look with his one brown eye glinting in the candlelight. 'Surely you would not want the Governor of Fort William to hear that Penstroun was disloyal to the Crown or harboured Jacobite sympathisers, my dear? That would be most foolish.'

Hugh moved to stand up and Katherine quickly held him by the arm, to stem any impetuous outburst.

'Then you shall have your toast, Sir Archibald, but it will be the last time you ever give an order to my household at Penstroun,' Katherine answered his look coolly, showing her displeasure at his threat. Personally it was no hardship for her to make such a show of allegiance; she had no strong political ties. But she would not have her kinsmen slighted by this bullying man. She saw his flushed face deepen in colour and continued quickly.

'To our sovereign!' she chose the ambiguous words deliberately and raised her glass. The others followed. Katherine was just aware of Hugh passing his glass over the water in his finger bowl before he drank and wondered if the allusion to the Stuart King 'over the water' had gone unnoticed by Maitland.

Her uncle sat down abruptly with a fierce scowl at having been outmanoeuvred. The rest of the Maitlands sat tensely, as if awaiting some imminent explosion.

'Well Katherine,' Hugh beamed at her delightedly, 'will you play the spinet for us? It is a treat your dear cousins have been denied so far.'

'Yes, Katherine, do,' Anne urged, 'and then perhaps we could have some dancing?'

'Of course,' their hostess agreed, noticing Sybilla's round face light up with interest.

Archibald Maitland pushed back his chair noisily. 'Then you'll forgive me if I retire to bed, Miss MacQueen–'

'Please stay for a while, Uncle,' Katherine smiled at him sweetly and took his arm. She did not want to turn him against her over such a trifling incident, for she suspected he could be a vindictive enemy.

For a moment he looked quite taken aback by her coaxing, and then he shrugged off her hold and nodded his heavy wig. Christina Maitland gave out a small sigh and relaxed her tight expression. The guests rose from the table and followed Katherine into the drawing-room where she forgot the difficulties of the evening and threw herself into playing the spinet. Anne and Hugh accompanied her in song.

Finally the elder Maitland, full of good wine, made an unsteady retreat from the room. The proceedings grew livelier and they returned to the dining hall for dancing accompanied by the pipes. Even Christina allowed herself to be led in a reel by her cousin, Alastair MacQueen, and Sybilla brazenly claimed Hugh as her partner.

To Katherine's dismay, Hector appeared by her side.

‘I hope you have not been avoiding Culduggan on my account?’ he leaned his plump red face close to hers and ogled her. ‘I have missed your company, my dear. I know you misunderstood my intentions in Moscow but hope you sometimes think fondly of our time travelling together, as I do?’

‘Oh?’ Katherine answered offhandedly. ‘I was quite glad when that awful journey was over. Indeed, I have no wish to leave my home at Penstroun and am content with the company I keep here.’

Hector went puce at her snub and ran a finger under his tight cravat, jutting out his fleshy jowl.

‘I see you are quick to encourage the ardour of another Ballantyne,’ he said huffily, ‘it is foolish of you to make the same mistake twice.’ Katherine went hot with annoyance, but he caught her hand as she attempted to move away. She felt nauseous at the heavy smell of his powdered wig. ‘I am a better prospect than Hugh Ballantyne,’ he persisted under the noise of the bagpipes. ‘He is a worthless fortune-seeker, just like his older brother. I at least have estates and a title to offer you, Katherine.’

She looked at him with distaste, leaning her head away from his.

‘I see you still overestimate your charms, Hector,’ she answered disdainfully. ‘I would rather remain an old maid than marry you.’

‘We’ll see,’ his thick lips drew into a cruel line as he tightened his grip on her. ‘But let me warn you, you’d do well to disassociate yourself from young Ballantyne, he keeps some dubious company.’

‘I don’t need your advice,’ she flared back, ‘and anyway Hugh and I are merely friends.’

The music stopped and the noise of conversation could be heard again.

‘Katherine,’ Hugh strode towards her smiling, ‘you should be dancing too. Hector, stop boring Mistress MacQueen with your tedious conversation, I insist you release her.’

Hector looked at him sullenly but dropped his hand. Katherine gave Hugh a grateful smile and accepted his proffered arm.

As they moved away, Fiona entered with a serious face. She had aged since the journey, her legs stiffer in their movements and her hair now quite grey. Katherine wondered if she had come to complain about the noise of the pipes as it was nearly midnight and the Sabbath was about to break.

‘We shall be going to our beds soon, Fiona,’ her mistress pre-empted any criticism.

‘And so you should,’ Fiona gave her a stern look. ‘But that is not what I’ve come about. I was on my way upstairs when I thought I heard shouting down below. It may just be the noise of the storm, but some of your Highlanders heard it too. They’ve gone to investigate.’

‘Perhaps someone has got caught in the gales and needs shelter?’ Katherine queried, turning to Hugh. ‘Though it is late in the year for packmen.’

She noticed his youthful fair face pale at her words.

‘I’ll go and see,’ he said hastily, ‘there is no need to tell anyone else, Fiona.’ He glanced around nervously as he went. Katherine felt his unease and hesitated, undecided whether to follow. Hector’s words about Hugh’s dubious companions came back to her. Was he expecting someone? Around her the guests were drinking deeply and someone called for the dancing to begin again. She took Fiona by the arm and steered her from the room; whoever was at her door she ought to learn their identity.

By the light of Fiona’s candlestick they descended the steep steps to the cold draughty antechamber below. The heavy wooden outer door was only slightly ajar but already the stone floor was awash with rainwater and the torch flames of the servants had gone out.

‘Where is Mr Ballantyne?’ Katherine asked them as she peered in the dark.

‘He’s gone to the main gate, Miss Katherine,’ one of the retainers replied.

Before Fiona could stop her, Katherine was out of the door and groping across the gun court after him. Within seconds she was soaked through, her dark hair lashed across her face from the ferocity of the rain-laden gale. Reaching the shelter of the outer wall and the guardroom by the iron gateway, she found Hugh at the top of the steps while her retainers unbarred the door below. Her sudden appearance startled him.

‘You shouldn’t have come,’ he sounded almost frightened.

‘Who is it, Hugh?’ Katherine asked unnerved by his behaviour.

The outer door swung open with a clang and two figures wrapped in plaids staggered up the narrow stairway, pushed by the elements at their backs. Katherine went to Hugh instinctively and held onto his arm. The men behind the strangers heaved the thick door back again and the noise of the storm abated. In the sudden tense quiet of the guardroom, Hugh and Katherine watched the figures in their course bulky plaids, dripping with rain and salty sea spray.

'Who are you?' Hugh whispered, as it suddenly unsure of their identity.

The taller of the two unwrapped his plaid from about his head. All Katherine could make out was the outline of a gaunt bearded face framed by wet strands of long hair. He seemed too exhausted to speak. Hugh thrust the candle he held at the stranger's face, his own expression one of perplexity. He did not recognise him or the wild grizzled companion.

Katherine's heart lurched as the flame flared to show the hollow eyes that regarded her and the curved scar on the man's jaw. Feeling her legs give way, she clung to Hugh's arm for support. Her voice came from far off, a dry strangled cry deep in her throat.

'Alexander, can it be you?'

CHAPTER 8

Alexander stared exhaustedly at the woman before him, with her writhing black coils of hair stuck to her pale face and neck, the huge dark eyes regarding him with fear. She was dressed like a Highland gentlewoman, the plain satin dress folded loosely around her body, the simple lace trim of her low-cut petticoats stuck to the curves of her bosom from the rain. For a moment he had not recognised this noblewoman, dishevelled from the storm and clinging onto the tall fair-haired man beside her. Then she had spoken and he knew it was Katherine.

'Yes, Katherine, it is I,' he answered hoarsely, the weight of his sodden plaid adding to the weariness he already felt from days on foot. Yet his spirits lifted to see her at last. 'Baturin and I have been on the road for days, this Cossack has never seen so much rain,' Alexander gave a faint smile.

But to his disappointment, she did not move forward to greet him in the way he had yearned for during the long months of escape and evasion. She just gaped at him as if he were a ghost and sheltered behind the tall frame of her young companion.

He noticed this man for the first time – his sweep of long fair hair, firm chin and lively eyes – who turned to Katherine for confirmation as if Alexander was not there.

'Tell me who this is Katherine,' he demanded, catching her around the waist as he felt her lean against him heavily. She looked up anxiously as if afraid to speak the name again.

'This is your brother, Hugh,' she whispered and dragged her gaze back to Alexander's.

He looked so thin and exhausted, his handsome face gaunt in the feeble flame. She could not believe he stood before her; she was too frightened to reach out and touch him in case he was not real. She longed to rush to him and throw her arms about his neck, but her feet were rooted to the spot and he did not move towards her either.

Alexander and Hugh stared at each other as the full implication of what Katherine had just told them struck home. The older brother saw at once the similarity between this fresh-faced, handsome gentleman and the energetic, sandy-haired youth he had last seen scampering among the rocks in Culduggan River.

'Alexander!' Hugh cried and rushed forward to embrace his broad-shouldered older brother.

Alexander clung to him in silence, the sudden constriction in his throat cutting off the greeting he wished to give. He had not expected to feel such emotion for his sibling after all this time; it was as if the intervening years had been mere months. They stood clasping arms, taking in the look of the other.

'How do you come to be here?' Hugh asked incredulously. 'Katherine said you had been banished to Siberia.'

Alexander glanced at the mute woman behind his brother.

'So I had,' he said grimly not taking his eyes from her. 'But my good man Baturin affected an escape during my transfer out of Moscow. In the confusion of Tsar Peter and his army leaving for the north we managed to slip my escort. I was nearly recaptured outside the city, but bribery was the only weapon needed.'

Baturin gave a racking cough and sneezed violently over the others. Alexander smiled as Hugh stepped back in distaste. 'He does not understand our speech, brother,' Alexander defended him, 'we are very tired and would tell you our adventure at greater length after some wine and a warm bed.'

Katherine stirred herself at this modest request after the harrowing journey they must have experienced.

'I will arrange quarters for you at once,' she said nervously, 'and there is plenty of food left from the banquet, I shall have it brought up to you. Hugh, you can give Alexander some dry clothes and I'll arrange for Baturin to sleep with the servants.'

'Of course,' Hugh agreed at once, 'come with me, Alexander.'

'We have interrupted some entertainment?' Alexander questioned, his mouth twisting in a wry smile. 'I'm glad to hear the traditions of Penstroun are being upheld.'

Katherine and Hugh glanced at one another; this was not the time to tell their kinsman to whom it was they gave hospitality. Without replying, Katherine led them back across the gun court and into the shelter of the main fortress. As the travellers were ushered up the back stairway, Alexander heard the muffled sound of raised voices and the welcome tune of the pipes.

'Who is it making merry in the great hall?' Alexander asked with curiosity.

Katherine felt her throat go dry, but managed to say, 'neighbours and MacQueen kin. You will meet them in the morning, but now you must get some rest.'

Alexander watched her as she disappeared towards the kitchen, the lumbering bulk of Baturin following at her heels. He had an odd feeling that she was keen to get away from him, as if she resented his presence at Penstroun. It had been half a year since they had seen one another, yet he had been desperate to reach her as soon as possible, surprised by his own strength of feeling.

Now it appeared she did not need him as he had assumed she would. Katherine obviously ran the Castle well and was quite at home entertaining the clan gentry. Half-listening to the rapid talk of his younger brother, Alexander realised with vexation that she already had someone on whom to depend. He remembered how she had kept to Hugh's side on first seeing him and how familiar was their talk to each other. Had she already found another lover to replace him, he thought wretchedly? But then she could not have been expected to wait for him for ten years or more; neither of them had imagined he would make such a dramatic escape.

'You can share my room tonight,' Hugh said opening the door to his chamber.

As Alexander turned to follow him, a stocky figure lurched up the stairs behind them, belching loudly. Something about the portly gait and perfumed smell was instantly familiar to the older Ballantyne. The figure swayed with his lamp and brushed heavily against him.

'Who're you?' he slurred, his bloated flushed face scowling at the man in his way.

Alexander recognised with revulsion the over-weight Hector Maitland. In spite of his fatigue, he felt a quick stab of anger that this man, who had accused him of James MacQueen's murder, was now staying under the dead chief's roof. Things had changed indeed in the past few months.

'Come Alexander,' Hugh beckoned to him quickly, not wanting a scene. His older brother gave young Maitland a hostile look, but kept a steely silence. Hugh shut the door behind them and listened for Hector's unsteady footsteps retreating into the opposite chamber. He turned to face Alexander's grim look.

'It is the first time Katherine has had the Maitlands to stay,' he began to explain. 'They just arrived unannounced and were caught by the storm.'

'Do you mean to tell me, Archibald Maitland sleeps sound at Penstroun too?' the other asked incredulously.

'She could not turn him away,' Hugh defended his kinswoman, 'he is a powerful neighbour and Katherine has no quarrel with him.'

Alexander regarded him with impatience. 'You are quick to come to her defence, brother,' he spoke with derision, 'do you all forget our family's enemy so easily?'

'We do not forget,' Hugh answered hotly, pricked by his brother's accusation, 'and he will not be at Culduggan for ever, on that I swear. But it is easy for you to criticise us, you have not had to live here and stand by powerless while he ruins the lives of our people. Even his own children despise their father. How I hate him!'

Alexander stayed him with a hand.

'Forgive me, Hugh,' he answered, 'it was just the shock of seeing Maitland's brat that made me react so. I do not blame you. As for Katherine; she has the right to give hospitality to whom she pleases, though as her guardian I wish that it were not the cursed Maitlands.'

At that moment there was a knock and Hugh opened the door to Penstroun's new mistress and a boy carrying a plate of meat and jug of claret. The servant stared at the scar-faced traveller but Katherine bade him serve the food and leave. She hovered in the doorway.

'I hope this will do,' she said, twisting a coil of damp hair. 'It must be an age since you last ate. Baturin is devouring a side of mutton himself.'

'This will do very well,' he replied, eyeing her. She smiled awkwardly, clasping her hands in front, waiting for him to eat. He bent hungrily to the food and began.

While Hugh chattered on about his life in France and his mother's decision to take holy orders, Katherine watched Alexander tear at the meat, the strong bearded jaw working hard, his hair tousled about his neck. She could hardly relate this half-starved man to the sophisticated officer of the Tsar's foreign regiment. Yet the sharp blue eyes and the sweep of forehead and nose were achingly familiar. He still sat in his wet all-embracing plaid; under it she could see the dirty white of his plain linen shirt. His bare legs stuck out, hard and knotted from days of walking.

Katherine could not steady the hammering in her chest at being so near him and yet she acted like a polite stranger attending to a guest's needs. She wished Hugh would leave them alone for a moment so she could say something encouraging to him, but her friend was in full flow telling all about the years the brothers had been apart. Alexander nodded as he ate but said little.

Finally, Alexander took a long swig at the claret, wiped his mouth on his sleeve, and looked up at her. Was it emotion or tiredness that made his eyes glint?

'You provide excellent fayre, Lady Penstroun; I should be grateful the Maitlands have left me so generous a portion.'

Katherine felt a deep flush rise from her chest. She looked at Hugh.

'Hector ran into Alexander on the stair just now,' he explained.

'I'm sorry, Alexander–'

He laughed hollowly. 'Why should you apologise to me? I was the last person you expected at Penstroun. I can see my presence here embarrasses you, Katherine, while you are making merry with my father's old enemy. I can assure you, if I was not under an obligation as your guardian, I would leave tomorrow.'

The words stabbed her. How could he be so unkind when all she wanted was to see him safely installed at Penstroun? Did he really think so little of her or was he just annoyed to see her in command at Penstroun and managing well without his guardianship? Well he would not make life more difficult for the MacQueens by persisting in his hatred of the Maitlands, however tiresome a family they were.

'You are indeed my guardian, as my father wished,' she raised her head proudly, 'and as such you are welcome at Penstroun. But you will take care not to offend my aunt and uncle while they are our guests. As a clan, we rely on them for good relations with the garrison at Fort William; Sir Archibald has much influence with the Governor there. Penstroun will be a peaceful place while I am its mistress,' she challenged him with a bold look.

Alexander was stung by her rebuke. He clamped his mouth shut, not trusting himself to reply. How haughty she had grown with her new position; her disdain for him was unbearable.

Hugh cleared his throat, baffled by their hostility. 'Katherine, I think we should leave Alexander to get some sleep.' He touched her arm and she turned from the roughly clothed Highlander who glared at her from the bed.

'Goodnight,' she said coolly without looking round and heard his gruff farewell.

The party below was breaking up and some of the MacQueen tacksmen were making themselves comfortable by the hall fire for the night. Katherine retired thankful to get out of her wet gown, followed by an excited Anne who was sharing her room while they had visitors.

'Hugh has told me about Alexander,' she said breathlessly once they were alone, 'you must be so pleased he is here.' Katherine shrugged off her dress and did not reply. 'Is there something wrong?' Anne asked with concern, wary of these moments when Katherine became withdrawn.

'No.'

'Please tell me,' Anne said gently and went to help her out of the damp petticoats.

Katherine turned and looked unhappily at her friend.

'He blames me for finding the Maitlands here,' she said in exasperation. 'I could see the look of accusation in his eyes, as if I had betrayed him. You see, Hector Maitland was instrumental in having him arrested for my father's murder – and you know how the Ballantynes hate Sir Archibald.'

Anne nodded.

Suddenly Katherine flung her arms around the Highland girl's neck and hugged her. 'Oh, Anne, I have often dreamed of Alexander returning in just such a way, but I never imagined we would be like strangers to one another.'

The slim fair-haired woman patted her comfortingly. 'He must have suffered much these past few months and no doubt it was a shock to find his enemies here. Don't judge him too harshly, Katherine. Give him time to adjust to being back at Penstroun.'

Katherine looked forlorn, her green eyes moist. 'I hope you are right.'

***

On his way down to breakfast, Alexander ran straight into a disgruntled Sir Archibald escaping the merriment in the great hall at the news of the rightful Culduggan's return. Neither man moved aside.

Alexander regarded the heavily jawed man blocking his way. He had last seen him thirteen years ago, when Maitland had ordered him to be imprisoned with the other survivors of Claverhouse's shattered army. The man's dark wig belied his age though the deep scored lines and veined drinker's nose spoke of the passing years.

'Well, Ballantyne,' the older man broke the silence, 'I confess I did not expect to see you again.'

'And I did not expect to find Penstroun crawling with Maitlands,' Alexander replied with a steely look.

Sir Archibald's left cheek twitched below the masked eye, but he kept his voice level. 'And how is it that a man convicted of his chief's murder finds himself free in Scotland?'

'Wrongly convicted, sir, as my kinsmen well know,' Alexander answered coldly. 'Besides, in Scotland I am beyond the jurisdiction of Muscovy.'

'You would appear to make a habit of escaping your captors,' Maitland sneered. The allusion was not lost on Alexander; Maitland had allowed him to escape all those years ago so that he could snatch Culduggan from James MacQueen as compensation.

'I have no intention of running from anyone again,' said the young soldier, 'least of all you, Sir Archibald.'

'You will find things changed in the Highlands now, Ballantyne,' the other snapped. 'We have a good understanding with the Queen's garrison at Fort William; we acknowledge their authority and in return are allowed to carry on running our lands as we see fit – as long as the people are peaceable.'

'No doubt you go to great lengths to enforce your so-called peace on my clansmen?' Alexander's voice was flinty.

Suddenly Maitland moved forward, his one good eye narrowing as he stared at his rival.

'Listen here,' he snarled, 'my niece very sensibly concerns herself only with the day to day running of Penstroun. That is how the Governor of Fort William likes it and that's how I like it. For her sake, Ballantyne, do not think of interfering.' He dropped his voice lower. 'I suspect there are already some here who hold questionable loyalties that could put your young kinswoman in danger were Captain Leighton and his troops to learn of them. They shall not, as long as you follow Miss MacQueen's prudent example and do not cause trouble.'

'Don't threaten me, Maitland,' Alexander said, his jaw clenching. 'As Miss MacQueen's guardian I shall do what is best for her and Penstroun, not what is most convenient for you and your government friends.' Without further argument, he barged past, angry that his cunning old enemy could still provoke him so easily. Trying to calm himself, he entered the dining-room where others still breakfasted.

Katherine's heart lurched as Alexander entered, dressed in trews and a shirt belonging to Hugh. He looked more like the man she remembered, his chin newly shaven and his dark auburn hair tied back behind his head. He stepped into the room confidently, his vivid blue eyes taking in the scene. With a short bow he acknowledged her and took the seat offered him.

'I trust you slept well, sir?' she asked him politely, thinking how little she had slept as a result of his arrival.

'Very well, thank you,' he answered briefly and looked away.

Katherine saw Sybilla slip Alexander a pouting smile as she regarded him across the table. She realised now why the young girl had lingered after her family's departure to their rooms.

'I am keen to hear your tale of escape, Lieutenant-General Ballantyne,' she told him, 'I think you are quite the bravest man I know.' She gave him a coquettish look.

To Katherine's annoyance, Alexander smiled back at her saucy plump face and replied, 'I am flattered to have such a pretty admirer. I have been away too long and am eager to get to know my relations again. May I ask your name, madam?'

'Forgive me for not introducing you,' Katherine cut in quickly. 'Alexander, this is Sybilla Maitland, Sir Archibald's daughter.'

She watched triumphantly as his face fell and his mouth pursed into a tight line. Sybilla shot her a resentful look then recovered.

'I hope you will not hold that against me, sir?' she replied, a hurtful expression on her face. 'I have no wish to be your enemy.'

Alexander relaxed at the girl's appealing look; his argument was not with her or her mother. With a quick flash at Katherine he answered gallantly, 'And I have no wish to quarrel with you, Miss Maitland. I can see you have the MacQueen charm of your mother and not the offensive manners of your menfolk.'

Sybilla gave him a bold stare and simpered, 'Then we can be friends, sir?'

'Indeed, I hope for better acquaintance,' Alexander returned her smile, hoping to provoke a reaction from the proud woman at the head of the table.

Katherine rose, nettled by the blatant flirtation going on under her nose. 'We shall all meet in the drawing-room in an hour's time for the morning service with Mr Stevenson,' she ordered primly, ignoring the mocking blue eyes that followed her as she left the table.

Let him play his little games if he wished, she thought angrily, he deserved a dose of Sybilla for his pettiness. He had condemned her quickly enough for sheltering the Maitlands and yet was charm itself for their spoilt daughter. It was too aggravating!

She hurried away, climbing the back stairway to the top of the old keep until she reached a favourite small chamber that looked out over the loch. This was where her father had done his correspondence and entertained his most intimate friends. The view from the narrow window was of relentless rain; Katherine surveyed the scene dismally. The Maitlands would be here for another day at least.

Sitting back in the cushions of a large dark oak chair, she felt overwhelmingly alone. She had made such an effort to settle in here and learn the ways and language of the people, burying her sadness at leaving behind her home and friends and the man she still loved as her father. Now the shock of seeing Alexander again had stirred up all her longing and homesickness for Muscovy, as well as her yearning for him. Yet she did not recognise this cold and callous man. Had prison damaged him beyond repair? Why had he bothered to return when he did not feel for her as he once had? Then it occurred to her that as a fugitive from his adopted country he had no choice. He probably blamed her for the upheaval in his life that had torn him away from a celebrated career in the Russian army and a cosy alliance with the widowed Countess Matrapov. She sat in the dim room cradling her arms about her, wishing she was still the light-hearted Katherine Putulo of a few months ago.

Katherine started at a knock on the door.

'Who's there?'

The heavy low door opened and Alexander stooped to enter. For a moment he hovered suddenly hesitant at interrupting her reverie.

'What do you want?' she demanded.

'To talk with my charge,' Alexander answered evenly. 'Am I to be permitted a few minutes of your time, Mistress MacQueen?'

Katherine ignored the mocking note in his voice and indicated for him to sit down.

'You must make it brief, sir; I do not wish to be late for the service.'

He sat across the tiny room, watching her pace to the window in the alcove. Her dark hair cascaded about her shoulders and the soft woollen dress the colour of rowan berries. He noticed her wan expression, the large eyes sad, and the corners of her full mouth drawn down pensively. At this moment the concerns of Penstroun seemed to weigh heavily on her young shoulders.

Or was it just his presence that upset her? There was no resemblance to the brave young woman who had penetrated the Kremlin prison to see him one last time, distraught at the thought of his exile. Could she have really changed so much in so short a time? Was it possible his gregarious young brother meant more to her than he, Alexander, had ever done? If he was to be any use to Katherine as a guardian, he must curb his feelings for her.

Alexander cleared his throat. 'We must go over the affairs of the estate at a convenient moment. I will be taking over from Alastair MacQueen as your advisor.'

Katherine threw him a disappointed look. He had come merely to talk business.

'Surely we can wait a few days,' she sighed, turning away, 'or are you so keen to take over the reins of authority?'

He bristled at her indifference to him. 'I did not ask for this position as your guardian,' he stood up in exasperation, 'it was forced upon me by your father, remember?'

'Oh, I remember,' Katherine spun round, 'you have made it quite clear what an onerous task it is for you. Well by next summer I shall come of age and you will be able to go where you please. I shall be the last person to stop you!'

She saw his sharp blue eyes narrow in anger, the firm mouth twist into a mirthless smile. 'Perhaps I should go now? It seems you have no need of me with my capable brother around and your friends the Maitlands. I see you have no shortage of suitors. Of course, while I am your guardian I must agree the husband of your choice.' He stepped closer to her. 'Which will it be Katherine; Hector or Hugh?'

Katherine gasped in fury, raised her hand and slapped his scarred cheek. 'You have no right to insult me so,' she blazed at him, 'you are not the man for whose life I pleaded to the Tsar of all Russia.' Her face went crimson as she spoke. 'I was a fool to think the noble Alexander Ballantyne ever existed, you will always be the vain common soldier I first took you for.'

In one swift pace, the broad-shouldered Highlander seized her by the shoulders and glared into her face.

'Then let me see if you are still the passionate peasant girl that I mistook you for – this disguise of a cold and haughty princess's daughter does not fool me.'

Bending his head, he forced his mouth onto hers, still parted in protest. Even as she struggled against him, he tasted her lips with sweet desperation, willing her to succumb to his embrace. He would make her remember the way she felt about him, he raged inwardly.

Katherine, taken completely by surprise by his brutal kiss, was for a moment overwhelmed, her arms pinned by his grip. She felt small pulses explode in her neck and temples at his touch and her heart pounded. She had longed for his kisses since his arrival home, but not like this, so full of contempt for her.

Twisting from his mouth Katherine leaned away from his consuming look.

'Leave me,' she whispered hoarsely, tears pricking her eyes beneath the downcast lids.

Alexander dropped his hold realising the futility of his impetuous behaviour. She did not care for him and could no longer bear to be intimate with him. What a bleak homecoming this had proved to be. Just as he turned from her he caught sight of slow tears rolling down her cheeks. It cut him like the thrust of a dirk to see how he hurt her.

'Katherine,' he spoke her name low, reaching forward to brush a tear with his finger, 'please forgive me.'

She raised her eyes warily and saw the look of concern replace the harshness of moments before. But how could she trust him?

'I cannot bear that you despise me so,' she held his look, 'but I will do whatever is best for Penstroun, and I will marry whom I please.'

He was stung by her dignified reproof and cursed himself for his cruelness to this woman whom he found himself loving no matter how much he denied it.

'How could I ever despise you, Katherine?' he held out his arms pleadingly. 'I have risked my life to return to the Highlands and be with you. I too wish what is best for Penstroun and for you. But what am I to do? You are indifferent to me as if our attraction for each other in Muscovy had never been.'

Katherine felt her insides dissolve at his sudden tenderness. She stepped towards him. Why did they have to argue so? She touched his cheek.

'Oh Alexander, I am far from indifferent. I have thought of you every day since we parted, fearing I would never see you again.'

His hands cupped her face, but this time his touch was gentle. He stroked her hair away from her damp cheeks.

'Forgive me, my sweetest Katya.'

'I thought I had lost you,' she whispered and brushed his mouth with a kiss. He responded with soft pressure on her lips, slipping his arms about her protectively.

'Never,' he said, holding her tight, 'it was the thought of you which kept me going during these past terrible months.'

'Why did you not show your pleasure in seeing me again?' Katherine chided. 'You were like a stranger.'

Alexander murmured, 'I was consumed with jealousy at seeing you so at ease with my brother.'

'Hugh has been a good friend to me since my arrival, as has Anne,' Katherine admitted.

Abruptly, he loosened his hold. 'Tell me there is nothing between you and Hugh, Katherine.'

'Oh course there is nothing,' she stiffened at his aggressive tone. 'It is Anne MacQueen who loves him; she would do anything for your young brother.'

'I'm sorry,' Alexander flushed, disengaging. Why was he so bedevilled with jealousy and for his own brother? And what was he doing, allowing his feelings for Katherine to run unchecked? Others would see it as taking advantage of his ward. His role was to advise and protect her; nothing more. 'I had no right to ask,' he said, forcing himself to step away. 'I am not surprised Hugh finds himself attracted towards you, what man would not?'

'It is not like that,' Katherine blushed, 'he has been a good companion; that is all.'

Alexander gave a dry smile, 'You may see it that way, my dear, but I'm sure Hugh hopes for more. I saw at once how much he admires you.'

'Don't!' she pleaded. She could not bear his teasing at this moment.

'Where is he anyway?' Alexander asked, trying to make light of their conversation. 'It is unlike him to be so long from your side.'

Katherine looked away, confused by his sudden taunting. It was his own fault if he would not be reassured by her word. 'I have no idea,' she answered impatiently, 'I have seen neither Hugh nor Anne all morning.'

'You better find them for Maitland's service,' Alexander said, 'we can't have any Papist accusations thrown at the name of Penstroun.'

'You are right,' Katherine replied crossly, 'perhaps you might have some idea where they might be, as you seem to know your brother's thoughts so well.'

He threw his arms wide in a careless gesture, 'I shall leave you to hunt them down, while I see that old Baturin is not fighting with your servants. My brother probably quite rightly hides from the Maitlands.'

'You are mistaken,' Katherine was piqued by his mocking, 'Anne says Hugh is quite friendly with Hector, despite being Sir Archibald's son. Apparently Hector resents his father as much as the Ballantynes do, even Sybilla hinted as much.'

Katherine saw brief surprise register on his face and then it twisted into a smile again.

'And you believe everything the young Miss Maitland says, I suppose?'

Katherine clamped her lips shut and regarded him with annoyance. She had not forgotten how he had flirted so easily with Sybilla and yet he had the gall to insinuate a liaison between her and Hugh. She brushed passed him but he did not try to prevent her going.

Reaching the door, she stopped abruptly at a strange sound beyond the wall. Katherine listened again and heard dull thuds like descending footsteps behind the chimney breast.

'What is it?' Alexander strode over. She put her finger to her lips. Again came the ring of distant steps on stone; they grew nearer and then tailed away again.

'That's odd,' Katherine's face wrinkled in thought, 'there is no room beyond this one. Those noises came from inside the old wall of the keep.' Alexander did not answer; he touched the wall and looked about him. 'Can you explain it, Alexander?'

He shrugged, 'Perhaps it was just an echo from below.'

'But it sounded so close–'

'Old MacQueen ghosts,' Alexander suggested wryly and opened the door for her. To his relief she let the matter drop, though he was no less intrigued than her. He intended to find out where the footsteps had come from in due course, for he did not believe in wandering chiefly spirits.

As they reached the floor below, Hugh and Anne appeared, followed by Alastair MacQueen, from out of his chamber.

'Where have you all been?' Katherine cried.

'At prayer,' Hugh replied jauntily, giving her a wicked grin, 'just like Sir Archibald.'

Anne shot him a worried look but Katherine let the teasing remark pass.

'Then you will be ready for Mr Stevenson's sermon?' she smiled and turned to lead the way to the drawing-room.

'I will join you later,' Alexander said offhandedly and continued down the stairs. Katherine felt her annoyance mount at his deliberate snubbing of Maitland's chaplain. She took a deep breath and entered the room, brightly decorated with Christina's painted panels. The Maitlands were already waiting.

***

The grey gloomy day which had never really lightened into daylight, darkened into twilight early. Alexander knew he had lost Katherine's confidence in him again by his accusations over Hugh and his avoidance of Maitland's pious exhortations. Well, he could not suffer the man's presence even for Katherine's sake. And it was best for Katherine if he kept his desire in check while he stood as her guardian; she needed someone she could trust to serve her best interests at Penstroun.

Taking himself off to the gun court and sheltering in the doorway of the guard chamber he lit a cheroot. The wind had dropped but the rain fell vertically and splashed on the stones at his feet. He blew smoke morosely into the darkness, wondering about the green-eyed mistress of Penstroun. She had been in charge only a matter of weeks, yet her dedication to the place was obvious. Katherine would put it before everything else; how proud old chief James would have been. Alexander forced himself to think dispassionately about Katherine's and Penstroun's future; what would the dead chief have wanted?

Should he, as guardian, encourage Katherine to accept a proposal from Hugh should he press his case, in order to provide the chiefly family with heirs? His younger brother was certainly a dashing prospect, though, like himself he had no lands or title to offer her. Still she had enough wealth of her own.

How should he deal with Hector Maitland, should the odious man offer his hand in marriage? Katherine despised him but Alexander did not underestimate Sir Archibald's ruthlessness in trying to forge a match that would give him Penstroun as well as Culduggan. Maitland was a threat to the MacQueens; he would manipulate both his son and Katherine to further his own ends. As guardian he would oppose such a match.

Grinding the spent cheroot beneath his shoe, Alexander pulled his plaid about him to face the rain. At the sound of voices emerging from the Castle, he hesitated and hung back.

'I have already extended the time, Ballantyne,' a man's voice spoke curtly, 'my patience is spent.'

Alexander gaped thinking for an instant that the man addressed him and then realised he could not possibly be seen in the dark doorway. The squat figure, huddled under a large cloak, was talking to Hugh, whose expression he could not see.

'Just give me a few more weeks, Sir Archibald,' Hugh pleaded, 'I intend to pay you back in full.'

'And how do you propose to do that?' the older man demanded.

'My kinswoman, Miss MacQueen, will help, I'm sure of it,' Hugh insisted.

'For your sake I hope she does,' Maitland said with contempt, 'then she need never find out how you arranged a wadset for half of her land. Be in no doubt, Ballantyne, if you do not repay me I will claim every inch of the estate you have given in guarantee of my generous loan.' He shook the water from his cloak. 'I'll give you one more month, though you don't deserve it. After that Penstroun's coastal lands will be mine – unless you conjure up the fortune you owe me,' he grunted and turned back inside the Castle.

Hugh gave out a low howl of frustration and anger as the stocky figure of Sir Archibald disappeared without further discussion. 'Damn him!' he cried to the damp night.

To Alexander's relief he did not come any nearer, but stormed back into Penstroun's keep. The older brother stood for shocked minutes, trying to digest the fact that Hugh had been meeting secretly with their sworn enemy Maitland. Worse still, Hugh was deeply in debt to him and to the detriment of Penstroun and Katherine if he could not deliver. What had his wild brother been up to in Chief James's absence, he wondered in horror?

He had to discover what was going on behind the tranquil facade of this Highland estate. The scheming Sir Archibald Maitland had a hold over his volatile sibling; that was obvious. Forced into such a corner, Alexander doubted if Hugh could be trusted to act with caution.

CHAPTER 9

The following morning the mist lifted from the loch and the rain ceased, leaving a washed-out grey light illuminating the sky and sea. Waterfalls coursed down the hillsides, frothy and brown. Katherine escaped for an early ride, her Highland pony kicking up spray from the sodden bracken and boggy moor, soaking the hem of her riding skirts.

She gulped in a lungful of the clear air, revelling in its salty freshness. At least the Maitlands would be able to depart today, she thought with relief. She longed for life to revert to its normal leisurely pace in the company of her new friends and kin, and it would give her a chance to prove to Alexander that there was nothing between her and Hugh. They had misunderstood one another and spoilt their reunion with silly jealousies, but that could change. She had tasted his passionate kisses again and knew he still felt the same desire that she did.

As Katherine gazed out to sea she caught the barest glimpse of the small frigate slipping out of sight around the islet where it had sheltered the other day. It had chosen a good haven from which to weather the storm and she supposed it was now on its way out to sea. It must have decided to drop anchor in Buala bay faced with the worsening weather and now continued its voyage, saved by the prudence of its captain.

On her return, Katherine saw the Culduggan servants attempting to pull the abandoned carriage out of the mire where it had stuck fast since Saturday afternoon. With the help of several local men they appeared to be making progress. By the time she reached the Castle, Sir Archibald was pacing restlessly by the guardhouse, dressed in his thick black coat and boots, his tall severe hat jammed onto his full square wig. He smiled at Katherine as she appeared.

'You have been most generous, dear niece; you do the name of Penstroun proud,' he nodded at her. 'But now I have business to attend to and we must be going. Come along Christina,' he called imperiously to his quiet wife, who hurried behind wearing her most worried expression. Hector strolled out, giving the appearance that he did not jump to his father's order.

'Thank you, dear Katherine,' Christina Maitland brushed her hostess's cheek with a kiss, 'I hope we will meet again soon. You are most welcome at Culduggan.' From the look in her soft grey eyes, Katherine felt she meant it.

'I would like to visit you there sometime,' Katherine smiled back.

Hector stepped up to her quickly.

'That would give me great pleasure too, my dear,' he grabbed her hand and planted a wet kiss. He stared at her, his face florid even in the cool morning air. 'My offer still stands,' he murmured closely, 'we could be the most powerful partnership this side of the Great Glen, Katherine,' he encouraged. 'Do not let your MacQueen pride dismiss me so completely.'

She froze at his unwanted touch and the distasteful suggestion he made.

'Goodbye, Mr Maitland,' she answered coolly and pulled her hand away.

She turned at the sound of Sybilla's shrill voice and with vexation saw her emerge from the Castle with Alexander.

'Now I have your promise that you will call on us at Culduggan, sir?' she fluttered coy lashes at the tall soldier, pressing up against him as she hung onto his arm.

He looked down at her soft upturned face and the rounded figure that she brushed against his side and thought how dull life must be for this pretty young girl, with her reserved mother and over strict father.

Smiling back he squeezed her hand, 'I intend to see Culduggan again soon, Miss Maitland. Your being there will make the visit far more enjoyable than I had anticipated.'

She gave him a dazzling smile and, turning to her cousin, was delighted to see the disapproval on her proud Russian face.

'Goodbye, Sybilla,' Katherine held out her hand stiffly. 'You are welcome to keep the dresses I gave you, they are of little use to me here and you might enjoy wearing them when you are away in the Lowlands. Your mother tells me you plan to be there this winter.'

'Thank you, cousin, but I may not go away this year. No doubt we will see you at Culduggan; I know my brother longs for your company.' With that she threw Alexander one more adoring look and flounced after her parents.

Katherine's face was stony as she walked after them and watched them disappear down the steep steps and out of the Castle's protective wall. Footsteps clattered behind her and she turned ready to give Alexander a cutting rebuke. But it was Hugh who joined her breathless.

'What a pleasant sight that is to see the Maitlands go,' he said with a harsh laugh. Katherine was surprised by the bitterness in his voice.

'And why were you not here to see our guests away, Hugh?' she chided him gently. 'I have seen nothing of you or Anne all morning, it was very remiss of you both.'

Hugh gave a mock bow of shame and seized her hand playfully. 'Please do not throw me in the dungeon, Lady Penstroun,' he gasped, 'I will do anything for you to make amends – accept run after the Maitlands and beg their forgiveness.'

Katherine laughed and shook him off. 'I must admit I'm relieved they are gone too.' Then catching Alexander's appraising look, she jutted her chin and added, 'Though there are some who seemed surprisingly reluctant to see our neighbours leave, is that not so, Alexander?'

The older Ballantyne hid his annoyance. He resented the accusation; even Hugh's look was suspicious. Well he would not be censored by them for being civil to Sybilla; he had a good mind to expose Hugh there and then for his underhand dealings with Sir Archibald. But he checked himself, not knowing how much of a threat Hugh might be to Katherine or how deeply he was involved with the enemy.

'I have no quarrel with your aunt or your fair cousin,' he answered, 'and you cannot accuse me of being discourteous to your guests. In fact, I was left to entertain Christina and Sybilla this morning while you went off for a ride, Katherine.'

He saw her flush pink above her green riding habit.

'Thank you, Alexander,' she replied, flashing him a spirited look, 'I'm glad you found it so enjoyable. Perhaps you would like to accompany me when I go to visit Culduggan?'

'I expect business will take me over there before you are ready to see the Maitlands again,' Alexander smiled sardonically.

'What kind of business?' Hugh demanded.

Alexander turned to him in surprise. 'There will be things to discuss between the two estates once I have acquainted myself with the affairs of Penstroun.'

Hugh recovered quickly and smiled, 'You should not be rushing into such tedious tasks, brother. You still have not rested completely since your arrival and should enjoy what respite we have from the winter gales. When we are all snowed in for the winter you will have time enough for book work.'

'I agree,' Katherine said briskly, 'I would rather spend the next few days in exercise and leave the accounts until later.'

'Good,' Hugh looked relieved, 'Anne will accompany you if you wish to ride again.' He took her arm and steered her back across the gun court to the keep. 'Perhaps Alexander would like to do so too?' Hugh glanced at his tall brother warily, unnerved by his scrutinising gaze.

Katherine looked at him hopefully, but said nothing.

‘I prefer to remain here for the moment,’ Alexander watched him cautiously, ‘I have no desire to climb into the saddle after these past weeks on horseback.’

Rebuffed, Katherine turned away in disappointment. ‘Then we shall ride alone,’ she said and swept past him.

It rankled with Alexander that it was Hugh and not Katherine who pressed him to ride, but he wished to keep a close eye on his brother and would sacrifice the more pleasurable prospect of cantering out across the hillside with Katherine.

Later he watched the two women set out across the wet moorland towards the sea and experienced a stab of frustration that he was not with them. He restrained himself from rushing for his horse and galloping after the dark-haired woman who rode out purposefully in front. If only she knew that he remained behind to safeguard her own interests, she would not take offence so easily at his refusing to ride with her.

***

Katherine set an exhausting pace; Anne had difficulty in keeping up with her companion. They rode along the cliff tops further than they had ever gone before, almost to the edge of the MacQueen lands. Finally Katherine drew her horse to a walk and began to lead it down a deer track that dropped precariously to the shore.

‘This is too dangerous,’ Anne called after her anxiously, ‘we must turn back and go the way we came, Katherine.’

Katherine dismounted and continued on foot, encouraging the reluctant beast. ‘We can ride back along the beach from here, Anne, we’ve never done that.’

‘No Katherine,’ her friend sounded severe, ‘you must come back at once.’

Katherine looked back in astonishment at the commanding tone of her younger kinswoman. ‘What are you frightened of?’ she asked, noticing the worried frown on the fair face.

‘There may be smugglers and such like, dangerous men,’ Anne fretted, ‘we should not be here on our own.’

‘Smugglers?’ Katherine queried in amusement. ‘Well, if there are such suspicious characters around the coastline of Penstroun, then I ought to know about them.’

‘No,’ Anne pleaded, ‘Hugh would never forgive me!’

'For what?' Katherine asked, baffled by the distress on her friend's face.

'For leading you into any kind of danger,' she answered unhappily.

'Oh come,' Katherine coaxed her, 'we shall ride without stopping if that makes you happier.' With that she led her horse forward down the steep cliff path. Glancing back she saw Anne standing rigid like a stack of rock on the headland.

'I cannot follow,' she called, 'these heights make me dizzy.'

'I'll beat you back home, then,' Katherine waved and smiled, hoping to reassure her timid companion. Neither Hugh nor Anne had ever allowed her to ride along at sea level, insisting the boulders made it impossible. But from what she had glimpsed, there were good stretches of sandy beach in between the shingle which she and her stout horse would delight in exploring. She was tired of being told what was best for her by her over-protective kinspeople.

The pearly-grey light was beginning to fade from the sky by the time she reached the bottom and the wind was chill again, so Katherine nudged her beast into a brisk trot, his nimble hooves muffled in the soft ripples of sand and grass. It was a magnificent sight with the tall black cliffs standing guard to her left and the sea crashing on the shore to her right, spitting white foam and clawing at the rocks. From far above a huge bird of prey wheeled and followed her in silent pursuit.

Round the next bluff, Katherine knew must be Buala bay and from there she could join the deer tracks that led her back to the boggy moor above the village. There was a series of slabs of rock dividing the two bays and she dismounted again to negotiate the slippery outcrop.

To her surprise she found herself in a narrow horseshoe-shaped cove, set into the cliff to the north of Buala bay. Delighted by its sheltered seclusion she splashed through the lapping waves on the edge of the beach to the far side. Turning to give it one last look, Katherine's breath stopped to see a wisp of smoke billow from a fissure in the cliff face. She peered harder but could not make out any entrance to the rock, but she was sure she had not imagined it. Leaving her horse by the shoreline, Katherine edged closer to the bald rock that rose all about, the silence only disturbed by the reedy call of some orange-beaked sea birds.

Suddenly a figure appeared out of the very wall of the cliff, a large boulder hiding the cave's entrance. Katherine froze back against the rock, Anne's words of smugglers making her fearful. She had been stupid to ignore her words of warning and now she was completely alone within sight of some secret hideaway. She prayed hard that she, or the dark squat pony waiting patiently at the bay's edge, would not be seen.

Thankfully the strangely dressed man, in a long coarse woollen robe, did not appear interested in the beach and without glancing in her direction, disappeared inside another dark crack in the cliff side. Again she saw a ribbon of smoke issue like a signal from the rock and then dissolve into the air. The stranger did not look like a smuggler, though he had been too far away to recognise his face for any of her clansmen.

With hammering heart, Katherine slipped and crawled frantically over the rocks and pulled her horse away from the tufts of long grass he had happily discovered. Once on the main shore of Buala bay she mounted and kicked the animal into a canter, nervous of being followed. She did not stop for breath until she had cleared the shore and climbed the hillside whose far slope reached to Penstroun.

All the way back she puzzled over the identity of the solitary bearded man and the seclusion of his cave dwelling. It was completely undetectable from above and well away from any township. It would only be possible to spot the cove from the sea and even that view must be screened by the craggy isle opposite. A hermit perhaps? But if so, she would have been told about him by Anne or her father, surely?

All of a sudden it struck Katherine that the ship recently anchored offshore would have been able to watch the comings and goings on the tiny beach. Had it had anything to do with the man in the cave? And why had Anne been so against her scouting along the coastline? Katherine grew uneasy. She remembered now how nervous her friend had been when Katherine had first drawn her attention to the ship. Perhaps she and Hugh knew of things happening on her own land that they did not wish her to discover. It would explain Hugh's frequent evening absences from Penstroun. Could he possibly be involved in some intrigue such as smuggling?

Katherine swung her horse round towards home and with a troubled heart, set off for the Castle, the evening gloom advancing.

***

Alexander shook his head, groggy from the sleep that had overtaken him so easily that afternoon. Judging from the darkness descending outside the narrow window of his room, now vacated by the Maitlands, he must have slept for hours. He cursed himself for allowing a few moments of rest when he should have been watching the movements of his brother like a hawk.

He descended to the great hall and the drawing-room but no one was about. The two women must still be out riding, Alexander thought with a prick of concern at the gathering dark. There was no sign of Hugh anywhere and the various MacQueen tacksmen who had stayed during the bad weather appeared to have departed too.

Yawning and stretching to jerk himself awake, Alexander went to seek out Baturin in the kitchen quarters for some company. He found him talking with Fiona who mended a cap by a roaring fire and was trying to tell him things about Scotland in her stilted Russian. His servant's craggy face broke into a grin of welcome at the sight of his friend.

'You have something for me to do?' Baturin got up quickly.

'No,' Alexander stayed him with a hand on his shoulder, 'I'm afraid I merely came looking for company,' he smiled wistfully.

Fiona put her sewing down and got stiffly to her feet. 'I will get you some wine or a morsel to eat, sir? You look in need of feeding up.'

'Please do not worry on my account,' Alexander began to protest, but the old nurse pressed him to sit while she bustled around in concern.

'I thought you would have been out riding with Miss Katherine?' Fiona handed him a cup of claret.

'She went alone with Miss MacQueen.' Alexander took a long gulp and nodded in appreciation. 'This is fine wine Fiona; I see your mistress keeps a good cellar.'

'Oh it is Mr Hugh who brings in the supplies of wine and brandy,' Fiona said with a sniff of disapproval. 'According to the servants' gossip that awful Maitland boy arranges for cases to be delivered without his father knowing. I believe it is a scarce commodity since the war with France, but that is no bad thing.'

Alexander shot her a look of amazement. 'My brother is buying wine from Hector Maitland?' he said with disgust.

'Oh, I don't think it is a matter of buying, sir, it comes as a gift. No doubt to try and sweeten Miss Katherine towards him,' she answered warmly, 'though no amount of French wine could do that, I'll warrant.'

'And Katherine – Mistress MacQueen accepts these gifts?' he demanded.

'I suppose so,' Fiona drew herself up defensively, 'after all she has a large household to maintain, with people appearing out of the mist daily.'

Alexander knew he was being put in his place and he drained the rest of the cup silently. A young servant entered with a tray of discarded bones and an empty vessel.

'Is somebody ill?' Alexander asked in Gaelic, not sure why his curiosity was aroused.

'No,' the boy replied, 'Alastair of Buala has been taking his meals in his room – this is left from this morning, sir.' He carried on into the main kitchen where preparations for the evening supper were already underway.

'Have you seen this boy carrying trays of food before, Baturin?' Alexander asked the Cossack quickly.

'Yes,' the older man grunted, 'usually it is just bread and ale, but this morning the guest was given meat. He must have been feeling better. I thought it might have been for you,' Baturin gave a crooked grin, 'wishing to avoid the company of the Maitlands.'

Alexander got swiftly to his feet. 'No, it was not for me,' he answered in Russian, 'and neither was it for Alastair of Buala as the boy claimed – he has taken his meals in the great hall, until he left for Buala early this morning. I want you to come with me, Baturin, and make sure I am not followed,' he ordered.

With a polite bow to Fiona he apologised for leaving her, but explained there was something he wished his servant to do for him.

They mounted the back stairs with stealth, Baturin not questioning his master's actions, just pleased to be active at last. The dining-room door was ajar. Alexander could hear Hugh and Anne in heated discussion; he slipped past unnoticed with Baturin following. At least, he thought with relief, the women were safely home before dark.

Trying the door to Buala's chamber he found it unlocked and empty. There were a couple of bits of clothing lying over the bed in the cramped room, but the old MacQueen gentleman must have left with his sword and dirk for there was no sign of them. Alexander began to feel his way around the walls of the chamber.

Baturin watched him mystified as he tapped at the panelling and lifted the tapestries on the wall.

'What are we looking for?' the servant growled.

'A door,' Alexander whispered, 'and a hidden staircase. I heard footsteps in the wall yesterday. I think they have something to do with those trays of food – and I think my brother's mixed up in something. I caught him and Buala and Anne coming out of this room just after I heard the footsteps.'

‘What’s that there?’ Baturin pointed.

One strip of dark wood seemed cracked all the way to the floor and Alexander levered at it gently. With more pressure the panel gave way and swung open revealing a heavy wooden door behind it.

‘Good man!’ But to Alexander’s frustration, it was locked. ‘Help me search for a key. Let’s hope Buala hasn’t taken it with him.’

They wasted several minutes of fruitless searching, then on the point of giving up, his fingers closed around a large iron key jammed into the recess of the fireplace, behind a stack of peat.

He tried it in the rusty lock and it clicked open. Alexander spun round in triumph. ‘Guard the door, Baturin,’ he ordered, ‘and make sure no one comes in.’

Lighting a candle from the mantelpiece, Alexander heaved open the old door and found it led to a narrow stone staircase carved into the thick wall of the Castle. He followed its curve, dirk in the other hand, not sure who or what he might find at the end. A strange pungent smell of herbs grew stronger as he ascended the steps and then a second door confronted him.

Cautiously, Alexander pushed it open and peered into the small tower room which he never knew existed. It was bare, but for a rough table covered in a linen cloth and a bed of rushes in the corner. No one was there now, but the embers of a modest fire showed it had not long been vacated. A half familiar smell lingered in the room like traces of the person who had lived here. He swept the tiny chamber with one more circle of his candle, disappointed not to find any more startling evidence. Who was it that Hugh and Alastair of Buala had been hiding? Whoever it was they had not wanted Katherine to find out about it, for she plainly knew nothing of the hidden stairway and room.

Something glinted gold in the flame and Alexander stepped closer to the corner with the piled reeds. A gold cross, elaborately carved with wild beasts lay nestled in the dry rushes next to a silver chalice, half wrapped in a piece of checked cloth. All at once it dawned on Alexander what he had discovered; he sat down stunned on the makeshift bed. This was a priest’s hole, a secret sanctuary where someone had recently prepared and celebrated mass. The aroma which lingered was that of incense; he had not smelt it for years.

So Hugh and Buala and his daughter Anne must all be practicing Catholics; Alexander was astounded by the thought. But then his brother had been brought up at the Catholic French court by their Catholic mother, it was hardly surprising.

His blood ran cold to think that they must have been harbouring some priest or travelling friar at the very time when the Maitlands were staying at Penstroun. The thought filled the elder Ballantyne brother with anger. Sir Archibald would have been merciless in his retribution against a household of Papists; not only had they risked their own lives, but they had put the safety of Katherine, their patron, in jeopardy.

'What could Hugh be thinking of?' Alexander cried aloud in his fury at his brother's foolish behaviour. Was he not in enough trouble with the wily Maitland without endangering them all and their future plans?

He began to wonder if Chief James had ever taken Hugh into his confidence over his schemes for the future of Penstroun and Culduggan as he had done with himself. The old MacQueen soldier had foreseen a time when the rightful Stuart monarch would be restored to the Scottish throne and he had finally persuaded Alexander to return home to help in the cause of the young King James VIII in exile at Saint-Germain. Events had overtaken them and he had come as Katherine's guardian, but he still harboured ambitions under a Stuart restoration.

Alexander cursed roundly at his wild younger brother for complicating matters. If Maitland knew Hugh was Catholic and had him under surveillance, what hope was there that they could spin a web of resistance among the clans ready to entrap the government supporters when the rising came? What was it Sir Archibald had said about Hugh holding questionable loyalties? Hugh was probably a supporter of King James but what use was that when Sir Archibald had a financial hold over him? From what Fiona had said, he was also involved with the self-opinionated Hector on some trade deals over wine. What he wondered did Hugh give in return for the French claret? He needed to know exactly how far his relationship with the hated Maitlands went. Alexander bundled the precious relics into the reeds again and made for the door.

***

Katherine had retreated to her small private withdrawing-room next to her bedchamber in a quandary as to what to do about her recent discovery. She had meant to challenge Anne about it straight away on returning, but her friend was locked in her bedroom saying she was unwell. Katherine could hear her crying but could not get Anne to speak to her. Still perplexed by this uncharacteristic behaviour, Katherine thought she ought to confide in Alexander. He was, after all, her guardian and should know what was going on at Penstroun. It made her feel better to think she could rely on the tall confident officer to help her in dealing with their troublesome kin.

Hearing a knock at her door she hoped it was him and called for the visitor to enter. With disquiet she saw it was Hugh.

'Katherine, do I disturb you?' he asked, boldly walking in.

'No,' she replied, eyeing him warily, 'there are things I want to discuss with you any way.'

Hugh stepped over to her quickly his face alighting with a ready smile. 'I'm so glad to hear you say that, for I have been longing to take you into my confidence, Katherine.'

She felt quick relief that he was about to confess what games he had been playing around the Penstroun estate. 'What is it you wish to tell me, Hugh?' she smiled at his boyish enthusiasm.

'Katherine,' he seized her hand and brought it to his lips, 'you know how fond I am of you, how utterly devoted I am to you as my mistress. I loved you from the first day you arrived at Penstroun like the noble Russian princess that you are and I have not been able to think of anything else since.'

'Please don't,' Katherine tried to pull her hand away in embarrassment, 'I don't find that amusing.'

'Do not torment me, my love,' Hugh hung on and pulled her nearer, 'you must know it to be true. Katherine I want you to marry me,' he urged. 'I may have little to offer you at this moment, but believe me things will change – are changing – and I will one day hold a position of high office.'

Katherine did not know whether to laugh or be cross. Was this one of Hugh's pranks?

'And what of dear Anne?' she demanded. 'How can you say these things to me when she lies crying in her room–' Suddenly it struck Katherine why her friend did not wish to speak to her. 'She knows you meant to propose to me, Hugh, doesn't she?'

'She finally realises that our fondness for each other is overshadowed by my greater love for you,' he lifted her chin so that she had to look into his hazel eyes.

She saw determination there – like in Alexander's – but not a glint of passion. Katherine realised she was frightened of his unpredictable emotions; despite his robust good looks and youthful vitality, she was not in the least bit in love with him. There was something unstable about him – the way he changed so quickly from smiles to petulance – and she knew she must handle this situation carefully.

'I could not hurt Anne, so,' she told him firmly. 'I am fond of you Hugh – like a brother – but nothing more.'

'I can make you love me,' Hugh said hotly, 'you will grow to love me as much as I love you.'

'I don't believe you do love me,' Katherine tried again to pull away.

'Then I'll show you,' Hugh gripped her angrily and before she could protest he snatched her face between his hands and covered her mouth in a desperate kiss.

Katherine felt suffocated by his embrace. Panic welled up inside her. Just at that moment she heard a noise at the open door. Pushing Hugh away she was aghast to see Alexander standing watching them. His face was a rigid mask, the blue eyes accusing.

'Alexander,' she forced herself to speak, 'Hugh did not mean to be so carried away, this should not have happened ...'

To her consternation he said nothing, just continued to gaze at them both in contempt. At once, Hugh regained his sunny composure and grinned at his brother.

'What Katherine means is that you should not have come spying on her. But as you have, Alexander,' Hugh gave him a challenging look, 'you can be the first to congratulate us on our betrothal.'

CHAPTER 10

Alexander stood stupefied at the chamber door wondering if he had heard correctly. He had come to tell Katherine about the priest's hole and Hugh's involvement with the Maitlands, for he felt sure she must know nothing of his brother's meddling. But instead of finding her alone, here she was in an intimate embrace with his fair-haired sibling. The pain was like a knife in his guts to see her in another man's arms and especially one he no longer trusted. Treacherous doubt returned; could Katherine be in love with Hugh?

'We are not betrothed,' Katherine was indignant. 'I have not accepted Hugh's proposal, do not look at me so.'

'Katherine and I love each other,' Hugh persisted as if she had not spoken, 'and we wish to be married soon. Do we have your blessing, brother?'

'You're mad,' Katherine turned on him in horror, 'I wish for no such thing.'

'I am not interested in your lovers' tiff,' Alexander was brusque, 'but as Katherine's guardian I wish to know your motives, Hugh.' He stepped forward switching his steely gaze to the other man.

'I need no motive but that of love,' Hugh replied defensively, taking Katherine by the arm.

'So it is nothing to do with the fortune of Penstroun, by chance?' Alexander mocked. 'Katherine is a rich heiress and you have no money.'

'That is just the sort of thing I would expect to hear from a mercenary like you,' Hugh flashed back. 'That may be the reason why *you* hurried back to Katherine's side from Muscovy, but it is not the reason I seek her hand.'

'Not even to pay back the huge debts you owe to Sir Archibald Maitland?' Alexander said angrily. 'Does your 'intended' know of that arrangement?'

Katherine saw Hugh blanch; she was dumbfounded by the bitterness between the brothers. Glancing at Alexander's furious look she knew he did not joke.

'What does he mean by that, Hugh?' she demanded, pushing him away.

'I-I have no idea.'

'Oh I think you do!' Alexander cried. 'I overheard you in league with our family's enemy. If you don't repay Maitland within the next month, half of Penstroun is forfeit, is that not so, Hugh? You don't care about

Katherine – you just care about getting your hands on her fortune. How could you be so stupid and callous?'

'Damn you!' Hugh cursed. He turned to Katherine beseechingly. 'I'm sorry. I have not been honest with you. I admit I have been a fool with money. I need your help to pay off a wadset arranged with Maitland. I wished to make some investments but I lost out heavily owing to this cursed war with France. I never for one moment thought he would need to call in his claim. I beg you to help me, dearest Katherine.'

'Half of Penstroun,' Katherine gasped, 'but it was not yours to promise – my father would never have agreed to it.'

'Your father was abroad in Muscovy,' Alexander reminded. 'Did Alastair MacQueen of Buala know of your rashness, brother?'

Hugh shook his head, his face now crimson with shame.

'Well Sir Archibald shall not have one inch of my lands,' Katherine declared, 'the MacQueens shall fight off any claim from the Maitlands.'

Alexander saw the angry glint in her green eyes and the stubborn tilt of her chin and knew she was a worthy daughter of James MacQueen.

'Now is not the time to cross Sir Archibald,' Hugh suddenly looked afraid. 'He has great influence over Captain Leighton at Fort William and could cause a lot of trouble for us. Our time for revenge will come, but please Katherine, do nothing to upset him now.'

Katherine turned on him in disgust. 'You would still crawl on your belly to this man who has humiliated you and tries to steal the lands of my forefathers? Well you are not the Ballantyne I took you for; you disgrace the Clan MacQueen with your timidity.'

Hugh flinched from her contempt.

'Don't say that,' he glared, 'don't ever say that!' In two strides he had pushed past Alexander and was at the door. 'You will see that I am no coward, Katherine!' He rushed from the room.

Suddenly alarmed by Hugh's distraught look, Katherine made to follow, but Alexander caught her by the arm.

'Let him go. He wants you to rush after him and beg him to stay; Hugh was always good at making others feel sorry for him. He will calm down and return.'

'Hugh is in deep trouble and I have insulted him when I should have offered him help,' Katherine dropped her gaze from Alexander's stern face. He pulled her round to face him.

'For pity's sake, Katherine,' he said in exasperation, 'my brother's foolish actions may ruin you and Penstroun. What could have possessed him to become involved with Maitland in the first place? It could only be greed. Your father saw that he was comfortably off here. And that's not the only way he has endangered you,' Alexander forced her to look at him. 'I have discovered a priest's hole above your tower room – Hugh and Buala must have been hiding a travelling friar there giving them mass at the very time the Maitlands were your guests. Hugh is a danger to you, can't you see that? You must send him away.'

Katherine looked at him appalled as the full realisation of what he told her sank in. 'Has Anne deceived me too, then?' she croaked.

Alexander nodded, 'She was with them when they came out of Buala's room, remember? That is the only way in to the secret chamber. It was their footsteps you heard beyond the wall.'

'Why could they not confide in me?' Katherine was indignant. 'I thought they were my friends, yet they treat me with more contempt than the wretched Maitlands.' She gave him a hurt look. 'That explains why they would not let me ride across Buala bay. This afternoon I discovered a hidden cave which showed signs of being lived in. I saw a robed man there – he could have been their priest. A ship has been lying off shore for the past few days; it must have been waiting to collect him. I thought at the time Hugh was involved in smuggling.'

'He may well be too. Did you know he receives gifts of wine from Hector?' Katherine shook her head in astonishment. 'Why did you not tell me of this cave at once?' he demanded, tightening his grip.

Katherine stiffened. 'I have not been back long and I meant to tell you. I thought in fact it was you coming to my room ...' Her lids flickered as the words died on her lips.

'But it was your lover, Hugh,' Alexander was sarcastic.

'You are impertinent, sir,' Katherine's eyes flashed. 'You know that to be untrue.'

Alexander leaned close. 'You seemed happy enough to receive his kisses until I interrupted you,' he accused. 'How do I know you wouldn't have accepted his proposal if I hadn't made such an untimely entrance? I'm sorry if my revelations have damaged your opinion of my noble brother.'

'Stop it, Alexander!' Katherine tried to lean away from him. 'Why do you torture yourself so? I am not in love with your brother.'

'Then prove it,' he challenged, 'show me you care for me in such a way.'

His mouth hovered over hers. Katherine could almost taste its warmth but she twisted away.

'You shall not treat me like a peasant now, Alexander,' she hissed. 'I shall do nothing willingly while you abuse me so. You have never offered me marriage, so why should I take your advances seriously?'

'I am your guardian,' he reminded, 'it would be wrong of me to make any such promises while you are in my care. Besides I am a landless Highlander with nothing to offer you.'

'Then you should not lead me on,' Katherine cried, feeling the hot sting of tears coming unwanted to her eyes. She pushed him away. 'You shouldn't be here alone with me now – and I don't want you here – if all you seek is quick gratification.'

Alexander felt the impotency of his position and his stomach twisted at Katherine's cooling towards him. She was right to reject his boorish treatment and yet he had been maddened by the sight of his brother kissing her.

'I want what is best for you, Katherine,' he insisted.

'Are you sure it isn't my fortune that you want,' she responded harshly, 'just like your brother?'

'Is that what you think?' He was appalled.

'I don't know,' Katherine cried, 'I don't know who to trust anymore.'

Alexander stepped back, his look desolate.

'Then what hope is there for the two of us?' his voice hardened. 'I do not want Penstroun or your charity, Katherine, I only want what is rightfully mine; Culduggan.' He turned from her, unable to bear the doubt in her beautiful eyes.

Katherine felt numb at the resignation in his voice. Why did they have to hurt one another so? She loved him and yet she must protect her feelings from being manipulated by this war-hardened Highlander. She knew his prime motive for returning to Scotland was to avenge his father and win back Culduggan. But she refused to be a pawn in any dangerous game to outwit the Maitlands. It was obvious that his desire for revenge was stronger than any wish to marry her, even if he were free to do so. Her love for him was hopeless.

She watched him walk away, unable to call him back though she longed for the comfort of his arms about her. Alexander glanced back from the door.

'I shall ride over to Culduggan tomorrow and speak with Sir Archibald. We must put a stop to his bulling of Hugh. I shall offer him a part-payment in good faith – the money left me by your father for your guardianship – and hope he will extend the time of reimbursement. If not,' he said heavily, 'we may be at war with the Maitlands sooner than

I anticipated. You would do best to make sure Hugh has that friar safely away before then.'

***

Katherine sank back into her chair as he left, jamming her fist into her mouth to stop herself weeping. She would not give in to weak emotions so easily, she determined, though her heart ached for the man who had just left her. Her new home no longer seemed a secure and happy haven, but a grim fortress that harboured too many dark secrets and intrigues. Once again she yearned for the simplicity and gaiety of her former life in Moscow.

She rose and went to a side table where she kept her writing paper and quill. By the light of the oil lamp she began a letter to her stepfather, Dr Putulo, pouring out her unhappiness to him as if he were there in front of her. Deep into the night Katherine wrote, leaving untouched the tray of food Fiona brought her. She covered sheet after sheet of paper until, exhausted by her outpourings, Katherine fell asleep in the chair, her black curls covering the bitter-sweet letter.

***

In the purple-grey dawn light Katherine saw Alexander leaving Penstroun on horseback with Baturin and mount the hill track that led over to Culduggan. Her heart was leaden to see him disappear from view. She thought with envy how pleased the flirtatious Sybilla Maitland would be to see the handsome Ballantyne come so quickly to visit. No doubt she would think his haste was on her account and perhaps, after last night's quarrel, it was.

She braced herself to confront Anne and Hugh at breakfast but found the dining-room empty and the food untouched. A flicker of unease went through her as she searched the surrounding apartments. On the point of retracing her steps upstairs, Anne burst into the drawing-room.

'He's gone,' she gasped, her face drained of all colour, 'I can't find him anywhere.'

'Alexander has ridden over to Culduggan,' Katherine answered tartly, 'and you have much to explain–'

'I don't mean him,' Anne cried, 'I mean Hugh is missing.'

'Hugh? Oh dear. We argued last night,' Katherine explained awkwardly, 'he may have been upset by my words – I rejected his proposal.

I discovered he had only asked me in order to get his hands on some Penstroun money.'

Anne showed no sign of surprise.

'I told him you would not have him,' Anne huffed, 'but that only made him more determined. He needed your help badly but his pride prevented him from asking you directly for the money. That's why he concocted this marriage idea. Needless to say, I was against it – that is why I could not speak to you, I'm sorry.'

Katherine flushed. 'You have been less than honest with me too. I also now know of your hiding a Catholic priest in my house. Was that him I saw at Buala bay, Anne?'

This time the girl's blue eyes widened in horror.

'Y-you know about the cave?' she stuttered.

Katherine nodded. 'Is Hugh involved in smuggling as well as papist rituals?' she demanded sternly. 'I have a right to know.'

Anne recovered; a tinge of pink seeping into her fair cheeks. 'Yes,' she gulped, 'Hugh is involved with Hector in breaking the English embargo on French wine.'

Katherine lost her patience and exploded, 'What a fool I have been to think you were both my friends! All the time you have taken advantage of my hospitality and risked bringing Captain Leighton's troops swarming on Penstroun with your illegal goings-on. How could your father allow such deceit?' She felt furious with Anne; yet looking at her contrite face, could not find it in her heart to dislike her.

'Do not think badly of my father. It is all in a good cause,' Anne urged, 'but, Katherine, I cannot risk telling you at this moment. I am still your friend, please believe me.' Her look was pleading.

'All in the cause of lining your own pockets to the detriment of Penstroun, you mean,' Katherine was dismissive. 'Alexander is attempting to disentangle Hugh from Maitland's net, so wherever he is skulking he should be grateful to his older brother.'

'Oh, no,' Anne looked horrified, 'he has not gone to argue with Sir Archibald?'

'And why not?' Katherine asked impatiently. 'At least one Ballantyne is prepared to stand up to him.'

'Hugh does too!' Anne cried. 'But his plans are secret. Alexander's intervention could ruin everything.'

Katherine stepped forward and took the younger girl by the arm. 'I want no more secrets; you will tell me exactly what Hugh is up to now, Anne.'

She squealed at the tight grip but knew that the mistress of Penstroun would not relent until she had an answer.

'I-I think he may have gone to the cave,' Anne gasped, 'to warn them.'

'Warn who?' Katherine shook her.

'I have promised to say nothing,' Anne winced.

'Anne, tell me!'

'I must not.'

'Then I'll go after him.'

'Please don't.'

Katherine let go. 'I shall go at once.' She hurried to the door.

'Don't leave me here,' Anne said in panic. 'I'll come with you.'

'Very well. But no delaying or tricks,' Katherine warned. 'You shall not leave my sight, do you hear?'

***

Alexander rode with Baturin into Glen Culduggan for the first time since leaving on campaign with his father; it seemed a lifetime ago. He felt the old familiar stab of expectation as they descended the thickly forested hillside to the turbulent river below, boiling cauldron-like from the recent rains. Oak and birch trees rustled and sighed in the wind as if reproaching him for his long absence.

The rich woodland scents reminded him achingly of his lost boyhood, but he was aware of a brooding gloominess about the glen. They passed several abandoned bothies on the descent, the heather-thatched roofs fallen in, their doorways like toothless gaping mouths. More shocking was that whole townships appeared empty, as if some avenging army had swept their inhabitants into the torrents below. The famine years had been cruel to his people and Alexander thought with fury that it was one-eyed Maitland who had made their plight worse; instead of giving them relief he had doubled their rents and stockpiled grain. He kicked his horse onwards to Culduggan House.

'This is my home!' Alexander shouted to Baturin over the noise of the waterfalls that thundered downriver. He gazed up at the tall tower on its mossy island with crow step gables and windows like narrowed eyes. His mother's lovingly tended herb garden was overgrown with briars and bracken, while a grotesque formal garden had been hacked out of the meadow to the south of the house, its hedges distorted into weird animals after the Continental fashion.

Alexander's face set into a grim mask as he hailed the boatman on Culduggan Island to come and collect them. He was a surely Lowlander whom the young Ballantyne had never met before and took his time coming to their bidding. Other armed men stood on the far bank staring at the unexpected visitors.

'I recognise no one here,' Alexander growled under his breath to Baturin. 'Stay here with the horses; I don't trust Maitland's men with them.'

The old Cossack remained impassive as he nodded in agreement, but his master could tell he was relishing the potential danger of their mission. He could rely on the heavily armed Russian to ward off any aggressive retainers.

Before Alexander reached the far side with the surly boatman, the plump figure of Sybilla appeared to wave and welcome him. He thought with a stab how he wished it were Katherine who came to greet him so warmly, but that was never to be. He pushed the memory of their quarrel from his mind as the saucy young Maitland daughter gave him her hand.

'I knew you would come soon, Alexander,' she said breathlessly, her broad lips parting to reveal a toothy smile, her bold brown-eyed look holding his. It occurred to him how much it would annoy the older Maitland if he made a play for Sybilla's hand. It was not such an unpleasant prospect and it might strengthen his chance of reclaiming Culduggan...

'Miss Maitland,' the tall Highlander brought her hand to his lips, 'I have been eager to renew our acquaintance and business has brought me sooner than expected to Culduggan.'

Her pretty red-cheeked face frowned at his last words. 'Business? Oh, how tedious of you, sir,' she huffed.

He swiftly took her arm in his. 'But I'm sure after I have spoken with your father, we could take the air in your charming garden,' he coaxed.

Sybilla brightened at once, pressing her bosom against his arm and gazing up from under fair lashes. 'We can do that now,' she simpered, 'I have you all to myself. You will have to wait until my father returns. Oh, what good fortune!'

Alexander's heart sank; it had not occurred to him that Sir Archibald might be away from home.

'How long will he be gone?' he tried to sound casual, though he did not want to waste time. There had been no sign of Hugh or his horse when he had left Penstroun that morning and he wanted to get back in case his brother planned some other rash ploy to prove himself to Katherine.

'Oh, he said he would be away all day,' Sybilla answered with disinterest, 'he and Captain Leighton have a job to do. It probably means they're turning some other poor peasants out of their foul hovel for not paying their rent.'

Alexander frowned, 'Is that all the people of Culduggan mean to you, Miss Maitland?'

Sybilla was taken aback by his sharpness and squeezed his arm playfully.

'I meant no offence,' she assured, 'it is just I do not take much notice of father's business with the garrison. He is for ever plaguing the dull Captain. I have no idea what they are up to except Papa said something to Hector about surprising someone.'

'Hector has gone with him?' Alexander hid the alarm he felt and kept his voice light.

'Yes,' Sybilla smiled, 'he said he would show them the way.'

Quickly, Alexander began to think through the possibilities. Hector and Hugh were involved in smuggling wine; could Hector possibly know of his brother's other illegal dealings – that of supplying Catholic priests? It wouldn't surprise him if the sly young Maitland knew about the caves at Buala – might even have used them himself for the storage of contraband coming in by sea. Alexander guessed it was to Buala that Sir Archibald and Captain Leighton were being taken.

Yet there must be more to it, he puzzled. This was overzealous action to take against some Irish friar and his scattered flock, even if the offenders were of the despised MacQueen clan. Maitland's pious Presbyterianism was only a cloak of respectability thrown over his ruthless business dealings.

Staring into the muddied torrents of Culduggan River, Alexander began to suspect that Hugh was involved in something much bigger and potentially more dangerous than covert Catholicism. Why else would he have been so afraid of Sir Archibald finding out? He must find out for himself what was going on at the Buala caves before the garrison at Fort William was alerted.

'Sir, what is wrong with having the day with me?' Sybilla pouted.

Alexander felt his blood go cold. Katherine. The last words he had flung at her were to make sure that Hugh got the priest away. It would be just like her to take the matter into her own hands; if she went to Buala herself, she might be running straight into a trap too.

'When did they leave?' he took Sybilla rather too forcefully by the arm.

'Ah, you hurt me!' she cried.

'When, Sybilla?' he repeated firmly.

'After breakfast,' she answered tersely, 'they've been gone about two hours.'

Alexander roughly calculated that they would be barely at the garrison, let alone have alerted a scouting troop. He could be at Buala before the soldiers were mustered and on the road.

'Where is your mother?' he demanded, wondering if Christina knew of the ambush.

'Taking eggs to some family, for what good it does,' Sybilla said moodily. 'She always tries to make up for my father's heavy handedness.'

'Then my business will have to wait,' he forced a smile, 'and our walk together, Miss Maitland. Please forgive me.'

He strode back to the waiting boat, leaving Sybilla squealing in annoyance.

'You are cruel, Alexander! We could have enjoyed some time alone together.'

'We shall on some other occasion,' he waved hastily and climbed aboard.

A group of men had gathered on the river bank, jostling around Baturin and the horses. The Cossack sensed their hostility but understood none of their talk, so it was with relief that he saw Alexander reappear in the bobbing open rowing boat.

Alexander greeted them in Gaelic but they did not respond as their hands hovered over their dirks.

'Stand Fast!' he murmured the MacQueen motto as he swung into the saddle and kicked his horse into a trot. Somebody picked up a stone and threw it at the retreating riders, but Alexander did not flinch as it stung the back of his neck. Ascending the steeply wooded glen, both men urged on their steads and rode hard for the coast.

***

Riding across the moorland – Katherine's favourite route with Anne over the past months – the young women did not speak. Now Katherine was impatient with its stark beauty; each bog they had to navigate and each stone the horses kicked up were just nuisances preventing her quick approach to Buala.

A nervous Anne attempted to keep apace, but was more fearful of Katherine's disapproval and losing her friendship than any protest from Hugh and her father for revealing Buala's secrets. Perhaps they had been wrong for not taking their mistress into their confidence from the start, but then they could not be sure of how deeply she felt for Penstroun and its people. She had been brought up in a quite different world and in spite of her MacQueen blood, might still be horrified by what she was about to discover.

They reached the steep deer track that wound down to the shore, a blustery wind buffeting their plaids and hair, bringing with it spots of rain. Katherine dismounted and led her pony carefully downwards. By the time they reached the beach, the rain had become quite heavy and they slithered awkwardly over the wet boulders.

'You go ahead now,' she directed Anne, 'so that any sentries will recognise we are friendly.'

The petite blonde girl did as she was told, too exhausted from the ride to argue. The sea to their right was the colour of pewter as it writhed and crashed onto the beach. Giant gulls rose at their coming and circled overhead, screeching a warning.

The nearer they drew to the secret cove, the more on edge Katherine became of the sinister surroundings. Perhaps she had been foolhardy to rush here before Alexander returned, for she did not know any more if these kinspeople were her friends. Outnumbered in this way they could extract any promise from her that they wished. She swallowed her fear and shadowed her young companion.

At last they slithered over the flat stacks of rock which hid the secret beach from the rest of Buala bay. Instead of finding it empty as Katherine had expected, it was strewn with cases on the wet sand. A chain of men were working back and forth to remove the cargo to the cave mouth. An open boat rowed away from the shore back towards the opposite islet, but she could see no sign of the mother ship.

Suddenly someone shouted from the cliff above and the men on the sand spotted the intruding women. Within moments they were surrounded and separated from their horses. Katherine was seized by the arms and led towards the cave.

'It's Lady Penstroun,' someone shouted nervously, 'don't harm her.' But they did not let go their hold on the tall noblewoman.

The opening into the cliff was only a crack in the rock and Katherine felt the panic rise as she was forced in through the narrow fissure, feeling the rock close in about her. Inside it was dark and smoky and she coughed hard, closing her eyes to the stinging smoke. She stumbled on cursing herself for her impetuousness and falling into the hands of these smugglers.

'What is the meaning of this?' Alastair of Buala barked at his daughter. Katherine opened her eyes to find they were in a lofty lamp-lit chamber of rock. It was not oppressive at all. To her amazement she recognised several of her own MacQueen tacksmen grouped around their leader.

'I forced Anne to bring me here,' Katherine intercepted quickly, 'she had no choice in the matter. I wished to see for myself what intrigues were being carried out under the protection of Penstroun.' She regarded him stonily, her poise dignified.

Alastair MacQueen blushed and dropped his gaze from hers. 'I'm sorry, Mistress Katherine,' he mumbled in Gaelic, 'this is not as it seems.'

'So you would deny that you are involved in illegal smuggling to break the government blockade?' she demanded. 'Or that you harbour a Catholic friar and endanger the peace of Penstroun? Have you so little regard for me that you could not come to me for help? Instead your laxness has allowed my foolish kinsman, Hugh, to sign away half of Penstroun in lieu of a loan he cannot repay to Sir Archibald.' She saw the old man's face look aghast at her words and he sank onto a case. Tears welled in his eyes.

'I had no idea,' his voice trembled, 'I thought the money was his.'

'Perhaps you'd better tell me what you do know,' Katherine was stern.

'Yes,' Buala sighed, 'I was foolish to think a daughter of Chief James would take no interest in her clansmen's' dealings. But once you know you will have to keep our secret whatever the cost,' he warned, 'we cannot let you go telling what you discover. It would put your people in terrible danger.'

'I will be the judge of that,' Katherine retorted.

'Please, Mistress Penstroun,' he pleaded, 'for the sake of your dear father.'

Katherine tensed. She nodded. 'Go on.'

He eyed her warily. 'That is not French wine you see stacked up on the beach, my dear – it is French arms. That is what Hugh used the money for, so his master could pay his friends for the weaponry.'

Katherine stared at him baffled. 'French weapons?'

Old Alastair nodded.

She was dumbfounded. 'What master?'

'Our Stuart monarch, King James VIII and his ally, King Louis XIV.'

Katherine gaped. Her throat dried. 'You are Jacobites?' she croaked.

'We are loyal to the King across the water,' Buala raised his chin proudly, 'as was your father.'

'You must be mistaken,' Katherine's head began to thud painfully, 'he never came out for the Stuarts and he always co-operated with the government.'

'Nevertheless, he was the driving force behind our support for the Cause,' her MacQueen cousin insisted. 'He paid for a representative from France to come to the Highlands and judge for King Louis the level of support among the clans. He must, with your help, get safely back to France.'

'A French spy is here with you now?' Katherine gasped, hardly able to take in the powder-keg of plotting she had stumbled across. 'I cannot believe it.' She looked round at Anne.

'It's true,' said her friend. 'Hugh has been guiding him around, visiting supporters after dark.'

'Where is Hugh?' Katherine demanded. 'I want to hear it from him.'

'Hugh,' Alastair of Buala called into the adjoining chamber, 'come out and speak with Mistress Katherine – and bring our French friend.'

Hugh ducked under the coarse sacking that did for a curtain, looking wary.

'We wanted to tell you – Anne and I – we didn't like keeping secrets from you. Now we don't have to lie anymore.'

Katherine stared speechless, still trying to take in the enormity of their audacious plot. Before she could find words, another man stooped to clear the doorway. In the shadowy light she saw he was bewigged and dressed in a stylishly cut frock-coat. Only when he stepped into the full glow of the lamp did her breath stop in her chest.

She knew this man.

'It cannot be,' she was stunned. Her hands flew to cover her mouth. The man stepped forward smiling and reached for her hand in greeting. Count De Maton.

CHAPTER 11

For a long moment Katherine could do nothing but stare in disbelief at the lean handsome face of the French count she had last seen on their departure from Konigsberg. From there she supposed he had made his way back to Paris and the new court at Versailles, never for one minute believing they would meet again. Yet here, incredibly, he stood before her with bent head, kissing her hand.

'I was told I would not see you, Miss MacQueen,' he spoke to her in French in his pleasant easy voice, 'but this has made my journey all the more worthwhile.'

Katherine found her voice. 'Count de Maton, how do you come to be here?' she marvelled. 'I had no idea you were at all involved with my countrymen.'

'Your father approached me in Moscow, knowing I was soon to return to France and asked me to take messages to King Louis as well as to your exiled King James at Saint-Germain.' The French count held on to her hand encouragingly as he explained. 'Chief James felt the support among the Highland clans for a restoration was strong and wished for French help.'

'Aye,' Hugh cut in heatedly, also speaking in French, 'we have suffered too much hardship and brutality under Protestant rule; your father saw it was time for change.'

'King Louis listened to your father's words and those of exiled nobles at Saint-Germain,' continued De Maton, 'and he agreed to send an envoy to judge impartially the likely support for a general rising. I volunteered to go; my respect for the late chief and your kinsman Alexander was such that I thought it worth the risk.'

Katherine drew her hand away, scrutinising his face, 'And France stands to benefit if the Scots cause trouble for Queen Anne's government?' she added dryly.

'It would be to the advantage of both our countries if King James was restored to the throne,' De Maton countered.

'We cannot win without French help,' Hugh waved a hand at the crates of arms. 'De Maton brings valuable supplies with him, but this is just a token of King Louis's confidence in us,' the younger Ballantyne said enthusiastically. 'Next year we will begin resistance in earnest.'

'Are the French serious in supporting such a movement?' Katherine frowned. 'I will not allow my clan to be dragged into unnecessary bloodshed, no matter what my gentlemen say.' She gave her tacksmen a sweeping glance, though some of them could not understand what was being said. 'Our fighting force would have to be heavily reinforced – not just with arms but with soldiers.'

'I shall return with a favourable report,' De Maton answered cautiously, 'and if enough ships and men can be spared the war with England, then we shall send help in the spring. However,' his tone was cautionary, 'the main thrust of rebellion must come from yourselves and Catholic support in England; else it will fail.'

'We shall not fail!' Hugh promised passionately. 'We have waited too long for revenge. The likes of the bully Maitland will be swept from Culduggan like a rat in a flood.'

Katherine thought suddenly of Alexander, at this very moment bargaining on Hugh's behalf to save Penstroun.

'Did Alexander know of my father's plans in Moscow?' she asked the count.

'Your father wished to take him into his confidence, that I know,' the Frenchman considered, 'he believed Alexander still had Jacobite sympathies. Unfortunately only Ballantyne himself knows what was discussed on the night your father was killed. I was not allowed to visit him in prison before I left.' He turned and regarded Hugh. 'Hugh, of course, had no idea Alexander would turn up in the middle of secret negotiations between myself and the clan chiefs here. He felt it best to leave him out of such talks, not being sure of his loyalties.'

Katherine gave Hugh a sharp look and retorted, 'How could you doubt Alexander's loyalty to the clan? Do you really believe he killed my father, in spite of your pretence otherwise?' She glared at him. 'You were wrong to exclude both your brother and myself from your dealings with De Maton; after all, I am the MacQueen heiress and he is my guardian!'

'I do not wish to doubt my own brother,' Hugh defended himself, 'but Hector said it could not have been anyone else. He told me all about Alexander's jealousy over the Russian countess.'

Katherine flushed at the reminder of the love affair between Natalya and her Scots officer. 'And you would believe the word of a Maitland before that of your own brother?' she was scornful. 'But then, of course, Hector is your partner in the smuggling of contraband.'

There was a sharp intake of breath from Alastair MacQueen, 'What does Miss Katherine mean, Hugh?'

The young Ballantyne grew agitated. 'I would not call him a partner exactly,' Hugh blustered, 'though he has made Penstroun presents of claret. He is more sympathetic than you give him credit for. Hector despises his father and does anything to defy his authority – that is why he delights in smuggling in good wine under his father's nose. He will be an ally when the time comes, Katherine,' Hugh was adamant.

Katherine stared at him astounded by his naivety. She knew Hector for a self-seeking vain young man who would sooner run away than fight for anyone's cause. A chill of foreboding spread down her back.

'For pity's sake! How much have you told Hector of your plans?'

The others looked at Hugh warily for the first time.

'He knows nothing of De Maton's mission or our meetings here,' Hugh coloured.

'And you have never used these caves for storing wine?' Katherine demanded.

'Not these ones – only the large cave on Buala bay itself,' Hugh spluttered. 'I agreed to turn a blind eye to his using the cave as Culduggan land has no access to the sea.'

'Why?' she persisted, holding his nervous look.

'He paid me for it,' Hugh's voice cracked, 'and I needed the money to repay Sir Archibald.'

Before Katherine could press him further there was a commotion at the entrance and several clansmen tussled with two angry figures. She recognised Alexander at once, his hair wet and escaping its tie, his jaw tight with annoyance. Behind him growled a furious Baturin cursing vehemently in his own language.

'Leave them be!' ordered Alastair of Buala, taking command once more. 'It appears this beach is not as remote as we thought.'

Alexander gasped, catching his breath from the fight outside. It took him several minutes to comprehend what he saw before him. Katherine stood erect and sharp-eyed; he had guessed correctly that she had come to find out for herself what was going on at Buala. Then he caught sight of De Maton. For a moment they stood and stared at one another.

'My God! De Maton?'

'Yes, friend, it is I.' The Frenchman stepped forward and they embraced with affection.

'You are kept busy by your monarch?' Alexander commented wryly. 'Or are you an envoy from Saint-Germain?'

'Both, I suppose,' De Maton grinned at him. 'I thought you would be more aware of what was going on than your kinsmen gave you credit for.'

‘But it seems they did not trust me?’ Alexander turned around and looked at the MacQueen gentry accusingly. He saw Hugh’s troubled face and wondered whether Katherine had already lectured him. ‘Not even my own brother.’ Hugh glanced away from Alexander’s intense gaze.

‘Unfortunately,’ Alexander said, ‘there is no time for me to convince you of Chief James’s trust in me, but my next message you must all believe.’ He stepped forward and met Alastair MacQueen’s questioning look. ‘The Maitlands have gone to Fort William to alert Captain Leighton. They mean to surprise someone and I believe it can only be here that they are making for. Your plans will be of little use once the government troops discover your cache of arms. De Maton must be got away at once. Does the ship still lie off shore?’

Buala nodded, ‘It came to pick up the Irish priest this morning and will return for De Maton.’

‘I don’t believe it!’ Hugh cried. ‘No one knows of this place. You alarm us unnecessarily, Alexander. Sir Archibald has never been to Buala.’

‘It is Hector who is to lead them to the quarry,’ Alexander snapped, ‘somehow he would appear to know everything.’ The two tall brothers squared up to each other.

‘Hugh,’ Anne broke in beseechingly, ‘you have not told us all you know, have you?’ She touched his arm. ‘It is important for all our safety that you do so now.’

He turned his flushed face to hers and Katherine saw the shine of tears in his eyes.

‘Hector found out about our secret holding of mass – ages ago – last year,’ Hugh’s voice was strained. ‘He said he would tell no one as long as I helped him in his smuggling exploits; he started that before the war with France. Now it is even more lucrative.’

‘Good God, you fool!’ Alexander cursed.

‘Hector the blackmailer,’ Katherine said in contempt, ‘that I can believe.’

‘But I never told him of our secret plans to support King James, I swear!’

Alexander gave an exasperated cry. ‘All he had to do was watch your movements, Hugh, can’t you see that?’

‘But he hates his father,’ Hugh tried to defend himself, ‘he would not lead him here.’

'He is Maitland's son, through and through,' Alexander retorted, 'no matter his spineless appearance. They will use people ruthlessly to advance themselves and swell their pockets, no matter what sweet words they may say. I am sure he knew of Chief James's plans to bring me back to Penstroun to fight the Stuart cause. I'm convinced he had something to do with the old chief's death.'

'Then you are in as much danger as Hugh by remaining here,' Alastair MacQueen stirred himself, 'they may be coming to arrest you as a plotter as well as your brother.' His voice grew urgent. 'There is only one course of action open to you both. You must go into hiding with De Maton until tomorrow when the boat is due to come for him, and then hope to get away to the ship at first light.' He stood and spread his hands. 'The rest of you will disperse back to your homes. If you are needed at Penstroun, Miss Katherine will give the call to arms. These cases must go in the back cave – we'll block them in with rocks, once the tide is in they will not be able to search here until tomorrow. Let us hope they find nothing suspicious and decide to abandon the quest.'

'You cannot send us into exile again,' Hugh cried in anguish, 'I will not go!' Anne looked at him unhappily and clutched his arm.

'It may not come to that,' Alexander turned to Katherine. 'You must return to the castle immediately.' He took her hand briefly and squeezed it. 'You must be brave. The troops may want to search Penstroun, but you will act as if nothing has happened.'

'Of course,' Katherine replied hoarsely, 'Anne and I will entertain the Captain and his men if necessary, although I will hate such a task knowing you are a fugitive from them.' She looked into his face, her large green eyes shining with tenderness.

She knew now that he was no fortune-seeker, but a true clansman of MacQueen, ready to risk all for his friend De Maton and even his foolish brother. Katherine was ashamed she had doubted him too.

Alexander's heart twisted with regret at the proud loving look she gave him. He wanted to take her in his arms right there and kiss away her fears. But he could not. He did not know if he would see her again in this world. All he was certain of was that never again would he run from Scotland like a hare from the government hounds, no matter what Buala said, he would stay and fight. Fate would decide if he lived after these next dangerous hours or days.

Around them, the MacQueen kinsmen rushed to stow away the crates of arms.

'Forgive me for my harsh words to you, Alexander,' she murmured.

'Go my brave Katya,' he spoke low amid the noise of departing clansmen and kissed her hand lingeringly, 'I shall always be near you.'

Katherine trembled at his touch and the softness of his tone, not wanting to take her eyes from his loving lingering look. It was the gaze of a man who was saying a final goodbye and it made her heart leaden.

'Come, my dear,' Alastair of Buala took her arm, 'we must make haste.'

***

Katherine did not look back as they struggled across the sand, heads bent into the pouring rain. A thick mist had begun to roll in off the sea with the rising tide, covering the shoreline like a blanket; they only found their horses by the faint whiny of the patient beasts. Katherine thought with a flicker of hope that the garrison troops would never find the bay in this mist, or would fall over the cliff's edge in the attempt.

It seemed an age before their small party was back in sight of Penstroun. They hurried upstairs quickly to undress from their soaking clothes and Katherine ordered them all claret to revive their bruised spirits. Later, she sat with Anne, toying with her needlework to try and occupy herself while her mind went over worrying thoughts of the others.

Had Alexander managed to find a safe hiding place for De Maton in some abandoned summer shieling? Where were Maitland and Captain Leighton? Were they at this very moment in bloody combat? It had been hours since they had all parted in the mist.

Her reveries were interrupted by Anne's aged father bursting into the drawing-room.

'They are here,' he wheezed, his face a ghastly mask, 'prepare to receive the English captain and his unwelcome companions.'

'Then they cannot have found the others if they come seeking here,' Katherine whispered hopefully to Anne as they composed themselves.

Presently a stocky young officer with a square face and broad nose entered, still clutching a dripping cape. His boots squelched as he came towards Katherine and bowed briefly.

'I am sorry to inconvenience you at this late hour, madam,' he said in a clipped voice, 'but I wish to question you on the whereabouts of your kinsmen, Alexander and Hugh Ballantyne. They do not appear to be with you?'

Katherine's heart began a rapid beat but she managed to smile at Captain Leighton and the scowling figures of Sir Archibald and Hector behind him.

'Gentlemen, this is an unexpected pleasure; you will take some claret with us?' She bade Anne pour them a goblet each. 'Indeed I am surprised to find you all abroad on such a dismal evening. Perhaps you will spend the night with us; the mountain paths can be dangerous in the dark and mist.'

Katherine sat down and the captain followed. Sir Archibald, however, remained standing, his patched face puckered in anger.

'You have not answered Captain Leighton's question, Katherine,' he barked. 'Where are the Ballantyne boys?'

'Oh, did I forget to say?' Katherine answered sweetly. 'They have ridden over to their cousins at Carranish for a few days hunting.' Turning to the officer she continued, 'Do you know the MacQueens of Carranish, sir? I have only had the occasion to meet them once, they live in such a remote glen, but I am told the sport there is excellent.'

'No,' Captain Leighton glanced nervously at Maitland, 'I do not know them or the glen of which you speak.'

'And why should you be seeking my kinsmen, Captain Leighton?' Katherine raised innocent eyebrows and gave him a wide-eyed look.

He cleared his throat. 'We have reason to believe they have been harbouring a French spy on your lands.'

Katherine felt Anne tense next to her and glimpsed Buala's horror-struck face. She let out a peal of laughter.

'Oh, sir, your imagination runs away with you. Nothing as exciting as French spies ever happens at Penstroun. Our greatest event is receiving the travelling tailor, isn't that so, Anne?'

'Indeed,' the pale girl managed to smile. She stood up and refilled their cups of wine, eager to keep herself occupied.

The English officer blushed in confusion.

'Then I am sorry to have inconvenienced you, madam,' he apologised, 'I shall leave with my men immediately.'

'Without even searching the castle?' Hector spoke up petulantly. 'These Jacobites could be hiding under your very nose.' He gave Katherine a vicious look. 'They have a priest's hole in the tower.'

She returned his offensiveness with a hurt expression, 'Cousin Hector, you are most unkind in your suspicions. You know very well Penstroun is loyal to the Crown and I wish to help the Captain in any way possible. Your accusations are unfounded and inappropriate.' She stood up and held her head high. 'If you must, Captain Leighton, your men may search my home, but I tell you now you will find nothing untoward. If there is a secret room in my tower then I have yet to find it.'

The garrison officer was impressed by this woman's dignified defiance of the Maitlands; it was something he failed at himself. They had forced him into a wild chase across these God-forsaken moors with tales of a treasonable plot and a French ship. He had suffered hours of fruitless search along a soggy coastline, Hector unable to find the supposed plotters hideaway in the mist. Now he had been forced into the embarrassing position of insulting this beautiful and kind gentlewoman in her own home. He had had enough of the scheming Maitlands for one day.

'That will not be necessary, dear lady,' he stood and drained his goblet. 'I must return with my men to Fort William. Please accept my apologies for interrupting your evening like this.'

Katherine gave him a generous smile and showed him to the door. 'It has been a pleasure to make your acquaintance, Captain Leighton. I hope you will call again for a more leisurely visit.'

'I would enjoy that,' he bowed, eager to be gone.

'Uncle Archibald,' Katherine smiled at the older man's scowling face. 'Hector,' she nodded. Both Maitlands left behind the officer without a word to any of their hosts.

From the upper windows Katherine and Anne and her father watched in silence as the men mounted under the sway of lamps in the gateway and the Captain marched his men away. Only when the shadowy figures could no longer be seen did Katherine and Anne clasp one another in a fierce hug.

'You were wonderful, Katherine,' Anne cried, 'I was too scared to speak.'

'You quite entranced that Englishman,' Alastair MacQueen gave a gruff laugh. 'You're a brave one, Mistress Katherine,' his look was admiring. 'Your kinsmen and the Frenchman have their lives to thank you for.'

'I hope they are safe,' Katherine said fervently. 'I shall go out at dawn with food for them; this will be a bleak night to spend in the heather.' She could not bear the thought of not seeing Alexander again.

'Then you shall not go alone,' Buala insisted.

***

Alexander crouched down low at the sound of hoof beats along the ridge above them. At a signal from him the others pressed themselves further into the damp foliage of bracken and heather. Then the tramp of booted men thudded by so close, he feared they would hear his ragged breathing. They sounded weary and in no mood to stop and search about them as they made back to the fort, Alexander thought with relief. After several minutes he relaxed and peered out of their narrow gully.

'They've gone,' he let out a sigh. De Maton and Hugh sat up pulling their cloaks tighter about them. Baturin crawled up the hillside a little way just to make sure they were alone. 'At first light we'll make for the beach,' Alexander instructed, 'we must be there when the boat comes in to collect you as arranged, De Maton.'

The Frenchman nodded, spraying drops of rain as he moved. 'Katherine must have convinced the soldiers that there was nothing suspicious,' he gave a tired smile. 'She is a woman of resource and spirit, my friend.'

Alexander grunted in agreement. He felt suddenly empty at the thought of her at Penstroun without them. Did she think of him at this moment too?

'I think it will be difficult for you to leave her, no?' De Maton queried gently.

'I do not intend coming with you,' Alexander answered. 'I've not been back in the country long enough for them to link me with any conspiracy. I will take my luck here but I will never leave Scotland again.'

'Then I shall not go either,' Hugh declared, 'I will stay and risk imprisonment too.'

'You must go, Hugh,' Alexander ordered, 'the Maitlands have too much evidence against you and you owe too much money. You are a danger to Katherine while you remain at Penstroun. In the meantime you will better serve our cause back in France where you have contacts.'

Hugh fell into a sullen silence and eventually they all dozed fitfully until dawn pricked the eastern mountains.

Baturin shook Alexander awake.

'It is time we made our way down to the shore,' he growled. His master sensed his unease.

'Is there something troubling you, Baturin?' he searched the grizzled face.

Baturin shrugged, 'Just a feeling, nothing more. I don't think we are alone; we must go carefully.'

Alexander nudged the others awake. Stiff with cold in their wet clothes, they stumbled through the heather and made a slippery descent to the beach. It was quite clear of mist now and the tide was out; they could make out the shape of their horses by the cave mouth from where they had emerged to find something to eat. They snorted softly in the still air at the men's approach.

Straining his eyes in the half-dark, Alexander's spirits lifted at the sight of the hunched appearance of the small rowing boat dipping on the purple-black sea towards land.

'Here she comes,' he whispered to the others and left the shelter of the cliff.

A moment later three figures detached themselves from the rocks, startling the small band of men. Alexander's hand went immediately to his pistol and he had it aimed at the first intruder in a second.

Hugh pushed his arm down in warning, recognising them. 'It's Katherine,' he hissed, 'and Anne and her father.'

Alexander's relief was followed quickly by fright that he might have harmed them.

'What in God's name are you doing here?' he demanded. 'You could have been shot just now.'

Katherine flinched from this cold greeting; she had so longed to see him again. Her night had been sleepless picturing them in discomfort and worried for their safety. Now she had come to say farewell it appeared Alexander did not want her there.

'We brought you meat and wine,' she answered. 'We wished to say goodbye before you left. But as usual I have upset you.'

Alexander bit his lip at her reproof; he had not meant to be sharp with her, but had been unnerved by how close he had come to shooting at her.

'Forgive my rudeness.' He stepped forward and took her hand, squeezing it briefly. 'That is kind of you, Katherine, you should not have risked coming.'

The men fell on the food hungrily, all the time keeping a watchful eye on the approaching boat. The sky was lightening quickly, turning the sand a pearly grey.

As the oarsmen splashed into the water to help them aboard, Hugh turned to Anne. In spite of the fact her father watched he took her in his arms and kissed her fondly.

'I shall come back for you, my love,' he whispered to her. 'Forgive me for hurting you by my thoughtless actions.'

Anne wept into his shoulder and swore she would wait for him however long he remained abroad. Then Buala gently but firmly pulled her back, concerned that they delayed too long in the parting.

'Let him go now, child,' he coaxed, 'it grows too light.'

Alexander helped De Maton into the rocking boat.

'Thank you, my friend,' the count clasped him warmly, 'and thank you, Katherine for helping us.' Katherine looked at them baffled.

'You are not going with them, Alexander?' she gulped.

He gave her an openly possessive look. 'I'm not leaving you again, Katherine.'

Her insides somersaulted at the loving expression on his ruggedly handsome face and she answered him with a trembling smile.

'Oh Alexander, it's selfish of me but I'm so happy to hear it,' she reached out and touched his hand. 'I will do all in my power to defend you from your enemies.'

Resisting the urge to kiss her, Alexander braced himself to part with his brother.

'I'm sorry we have been at odds since my homecoming, Hugh,' he said in a low voice, 'but you are my only brother and I love you still.' He smiled with affection, 'It gives me some satisfaction to think Maitland's hoarded money has been spent on weapons to use against him.'

Hugh embraced Alexander, unable to find the words he wanted to say. 'Go quickly,' the elder Ballantyne urged.

Hugh splashed into the shallow water.

'I'll come back to Culduggan, you'll see!' he shouted rashly as De Maton hauled him aboard.

The group on the shore watched in tense silence as the boat pulled away. Even at a distance they could make out Hugh still standing looking back at the shore. De Maton rose to pull him down. At that very moment a shot rang out from the cliff above them, echoing deafeningly around and ricocheted off the small craft. Katherine saw the two passengers silhouetted in the dawn, frozen in shock from the attack and then a second shot burst overhead and one of the figures went down.

Alexander pushed her to the ground and shouted at the others to make for the shelter of the rocks. He pulled out his pistol and fired in the direction of their assailant. Further above him he saw Baturin do the same. Buala crawled over to his horse and disengaged the musket from its side. He aimed it at a dark figure in an overhanging rowan tree and fired. The man tumbled from his perch and fell onto the rocks below.

'Maitland's men,' Alexander cursed as he saw the blue and green of the retainer's coat. He crept closer to the sheer cliff wall, aimed and fired. From the yelp above he knew he had wounded another. Behind he could hear answering shots ringing out from the escaping boat; one of them was putting up a resistance.

But new attacking fire came from their exposed left side and he ordered Katherine to try and make for the cave. If they reached its safety there was also enough ammunition to keep off a regiment of Maitland's ruffians. Looking up he saw dozens of crouched figures sprawled above them ready to pick them off if they moved.

Steeling himself he shifted position to protect Katherine the more. A second later a bullet bit into his raised shoulder. He doubled up with the pain and rolled over. Katherine gasped in horror as blood began to ooze through his shirt, Alexander's face creasing in pain. Still stunned by the ferocity of the attack, she knew she must do something to save her friends. She shouted up to them, 'Are you there Sir Archibald?'

'Yes,' a voice bellowed back. 'Is that you, Miss MacQueen?'

'Do you mean to kill us all?' she screamed desperately.

'You can prevent it by delivering yourself to us,' he barked, peering down from his position above. 'We shall let the others escape if you agree to come peacefully.'

Alexander clenched his jaw and rolled onto his wounded shoulder; he took aim with his good arm. Katherine grabbed onto him, hissing, 'No, he'll kill you!' She shouted up to Maitland. 'Cease your fire and I will go with you.' She got to her knees, heart drumming in fear.

'Don't Katherine,' Alexander grimaced, 'they're not to be trusted.'

'Your opposition is fruitless, Ballantyne,' Sir Archibald's voice rang down, 'I'll allow you to follow your brother out to sea. It is Katherine and Penstroun that we are determined to have. One more fugitive Jacobite is of no interest to us now.'

Katherine and Alexander exchanged desperate looks. Impulsively she bent over him and kissed the wounded Highlander on the lips. 'I love you, Alexander,' she whispered, 'please get safely away for my sake. Let Anne see to your wound.'

'I care nothing for my safety, only yours Katherine,' he said through gritted teeth. 'The clan will come to your aid.'

Sickened at having to leave him Katherine stood up, walking proudly into the open. 'Take me then,' she called out, 'on condition that the others go free.'

'Agreed,' Maitland cried, 'walk up the track towards us.'

Katherine did as he ordered. Three men grabbed her as she clambered up the pathway.

'I will go with you,' Anne cried and ran after her friend. Katherine swung round in alarm.

'Stay back and help Alexander!'

Anne hesitated.

'Fetch the other wench too,' ordered Maitland.

Anne was roughly seized.

'You promised,' Katherine was furious. But the women were bundled up the slope.

Buala knew he had used the last of his bullets. In frustration he unsheathed his sword and made a dash for his daughter's captors, charging uphill.

'Stand Fast!' he yelled.

Sir Archibald watched him coming and then shot him straight in the chest.

The old MacQueen warrior gasped in surprise but carried forward and slashed one of Maitland's men on the back of the neck. The man screamed and fell back on Buala, the two bodies tumbling back down the rocks. Katherine looked back in horror at the sprawled limp body of her father's cousin, his scarlet and green plaid spread about him like a noble banner.

Anne screamed and tried to wrestle free. Katherine tried to throw off the men who held her and go to her friend, but could not. She watched in distress as Anne grew hysterical.

'Let me comfort her,' Katherine pleaded. Maitland ignored her.

'Put them on the horses,' Sir Archibald barked.

Katherine swallowed down bile. 'You heartless devil!'

'I wish Katherine to ride with me,' Hector emerged from the gloom with a triumphant leer, 'my future bride.'

Katherine flinched in disgust. 'I'll never marry you!'

'No one ever denies a Maitland what he wishes,' Hector came close, his fat florid face gloating as he looked her up and down, 'and I wish to have you, Katherine, I always have done.'

The two women were hauled roughly onto separate beasts, Anne wailing for her dead father. Katherine went rigid as Hector swung up behind and clasped her round the waist. Surrounded by Maitland's band, they set off at a quick pace. Fighting the sickness that welled up inside, Katherine strained for a glimpse of Alexander. She was tormented to think that he lay on the beach below, slipping into unconsciousness as the lifeblood seeped from him. She screwed her eyes shut.

'Please God may he live,' she cried inwardly, tears of anguish welling up behind her closed lids. The words drummed over and over in her head as they cantered for Culduggan.

CHAPTER 12

For the rest of that nightmarish day, Katherine was incarcerated with Anne in a turret room at Culduggan, not knowing what had become of their men. Katherine paced to the window and back a score of times, torturing herself with worries over Alexander. Anne was convinced that Hugh had been shot too, though Katherine was not sure who had been wounded in the open boat.

She watched her young friend anxiously, her blue eyes dull and dark-ringed with crying for her father and Hugh, her face a pinched white mask. She had said nothing for hours now and would not be comforted, turning to the wall where she lay on her plaid staring blankly. Worn out with weeping, Anne no longer responded to her friend's words of comfort.

Towards dark, a knock startled Katherine and she braced herself as the door opened. Christina Maitland glided in quietly with a tray of drinks, her daughter Sybilla holding a lamp high to light her way. The tall dark prisoner watched them warily from her position by the window.

'You must be thirsty,' her aunt said in her usual distracted way, the frown pulling her eyebrows together, 'I am told you have taken no refreshment since arriving, my dear. I have been away visiting and only returned an hour ago. I must say I was surprised to find you both up here and not downstairs with Hector.'

Katherine felt herself tense with anger.

'The captured do not usually mix socially with their captors,' she retorted, 'and I have no wish for your son's company, Aunt Christina.'

The older woman's face fell and she put the tray down nervously on the table. 'That is hardly the gratitude I expected from my brother's daughter,' she replied rather hurt.

'Yes,' Sybilla butted in, 'after my father and brother saved you from a Jacobite plot. What those men were planning was quite treasonable and they put your life at risk.' Her brown eyes stared at Katherine and her thick lips curled in disdain, 'But you are too haughty to pay us Maitlands any thanks for saving you and your friend – and to think my brother even seeks to protect you further by offering his hand in marriage.'

Katherine's eyes stung with indignation at this distortion of the truth; she knew Sybilla merely repeated what her father had said. She turned on her cousin.

'And should I be grateful that my kinsmen Alexander and Hugh Ballantyne have been shot and may already be dead on the shores of Buala?' she shook with rage. 'They are nobler than a thousand Maitlands!'

Sybilla's look tightened. 'I know that is not true,' she answered. 'The Ballantynes scampered like crabs out to sea and left you to my father's mercy.'

Katherine looked at her astounded by the assured manner, the blinkered naivety of her young cousin. She turned to her aunt.

'And I suppose Sir Archibald told you that your cousin Alastair MacQueen also fled out to sea?' she trembled.

Christina looked uneasy. 'It must have been a painful betrayal for Anne.' There was a low moan from the huddled figure by the wall and Katherine heard her friend's tears come again.

'The betrayal has been yours,' Katherine stepped forward and gripped her Aunt's arm. 'Your so-called merciful husband shot dead your cousin Alastair at point blank range when he tried to prevent his daughter and myself from being abducted.'

'No,' Christina shuddered and tried to pull away, 'don't say such a wicked thing.'

'You know very well what kind of man your husband is,' Katherine hung on tightly. 'You try and make amends for his cruelty to the people of Culduggan with your parcels of food, but you cannot bring back the life of my loyal MacQueen of Buala. Sir Archibald did not save me from my clansmen; I gave myself as hostage for their freedom. You do not seriously think I want to marry your son after the way he has blackmailed Hugh and made sure Alexander was arrested for murder in Muscovy?'

'That's not true,' Christina gasped.

'Yes it is,' Katherine hissed. 'Hector has betrayed the trust my father showed in him when he took him to Muscovy – I believe even then he was spying on Chief James – might even have caused his death. Did you know my father was a Jacobite too, Aunt Christina?'

'Stop it!' her aunt cried, eyes wild with terror. 'I cannot believe what you say of my poor boy – you are sinful to accuse him so.'

Katherine let go her grip on the deluded woman. How could she get through to her aunt?

'Can't you see what's happening here right under your nose?' she challenged. 'Your husband intends to get his hands on Penstroun at any cost. He thought he had by marrying you – thinking my father had no heirs. But I was the fly in the ointment. So he bullied Hugh into signing over half my lands in a wadset. But this plot has dropped into his lap like a gift. With his rivals out of the way, he intends forcing me to marry his son and heir, can't you see that? But then you want Penstroun too, so perhaps you approve his violent methods?'

Her aunt stifled a whimper, her hands flying to her mouth. 'I won't listen to any more, you wicked child,' she trembled. 'My husband is a pious man. It is the MacQueens who have been foolish in their support of James Stuart; it has brought us nothing but grief.'

Katherine turned away in exasperation. Her aunt had lived too long with the scheming Maitlands to know what was right anymore. She was blind to the truth.

Sybilla spoke up. 'Is it really true that Alexander is wounded?'

Katherine spun round at the doubt in the young girl's voice; for once her expression was unsure.

'Yes,' she replied, her voice suddenly shaky, 'one of your father's men shot him in the shoulder and left him to bleed on the beach.' Her eyes stung as she remembered his blue eyes creased in pain and the agony of leaving him there.

All at once, Sybilla picked up her skirts and ran from the room, flinging an accusing look at her mother as she went. Christina Maitland seemed on the point of saying something more when footsteps sounded behind them and Sir Archibald appeared in the doorway.

'What are you doing here, wife?' he snapped. 'It is not becoming for a Maitland to be doing servant's work. You will wait for me downstairs while I talk with our niece.'

Christina pressed her lips together and hurried from the room.

'You will dine with us tonight, Katherine,' he ordered brusquely, 'and Miss Anne if she so wishes.' He waved a careless hand at the figure curled on the floor. 'Tomorrow Stevenson will conduct the marriage ceremony between yourself and Hector. When things have settled down and we can be sure of no more trouble from the MacQueens, you can return to Penstroun with your new spouse. There shall be no repercussions from your involvement in the French plot once you are married to a Maitland. The Buala girl will also be protected.'

'You call this protection?' Katherine was contemptuous. 'My people will not be cowed by you – they will come to my rescue.'

'The MacQueen gentry are either in the garrison goal or dead,' he goaded.

Katherine felt faint. She swallowed down her panic. 'Then you will have to drag me in chains to marry your son,' she said with spirit. 'I will not come willingly.'

'You *shall* marry him,' Sir Archibald said through clenched teeth, his one eye narrowed as he regarded the infuriating woman who defied him. 'And do not think my men cannot fend off any half-hearted attempts at rescue. Your peasants are in disarray without the leadership of your kinsmen – and Captain Leighton's men still comb the coastline for treasonable groups of MacQueens. If I had my way your renegade clan would be put to the sword and then we would have an end to their troublemaking for good.'

'I shall fight you, Sir Archibald, with all I have at my disposal,' Katherine flushed with anger, 'whether married to Hector or not.'

Maitland laughed harshly, 'You are as hot-headed as your foolish father and look what happened to him, thanks to his misplaced loyalties.'

Katherine looked at him sharply. 'You knew he was a Jacobite, didn't you? You arranged for Hector to go with him to spy on him, I'll warrant.'

'I did no such thing,' Maitland barked back, 'Hector needed to go for other reasons.' She noticed him colour slightly. 'However, he did discover that your father was attempting to recruit for the Stuart cause; the more fool he.'

'And was Hector instrumental in his death?' Katherine demanded, her dark eyes blazing.

'Hector does not have the guts for murder,' he replied contemptuously, 'you should know him better than that.'

'But he knows who did kill my father,' she followed him as he made for the door, 'tell me who his murderer was!'

Sir Archibald turned, giving her a cruel smile, 'The Russians arrested his murderer,' he mocked, 'but you saved his life. Supper will be served at eight o'clock.'

He banged the door behind him, leaving Katherine trembling with shock and indignation at his words.

***

Alexander sat propped against a rock in the dank cave, his shoulder numb from the tight bandage Baturin had pulled about it. He watched while his servant coaxed and tended a small fire in the entrance. Behind him De Maton stirred fitfully in a delirious sleep, the bullet that had struck his chest still lodged in the bone.

Alexander waited impatiently for Hugh to return with medical help and news of the rallying MacQueen tacksmen. Eventually he could stand the waiting no longer and got to his feet.

'God knows what has happened to Katherine by now,' he exploded, 'will they never come?'

Baturin was about to growl at his master to sit still when his ears pricked at the sound of hooves on the sand outside. For his large bulk he moved with quick stealth towards the opening and peered out.

'Your brother comes,' he answered, 'though it looks like he's alone.'

Alexander, holding his left arm awkwardly and gritting his teeth, got to his feet.

'Stay still, sir, and let him come to you,' Baturin protested. Ignoring him, Alexander hurried out to the twilit beach.

Hugh, out of breath, dismounted. 'They gather on the cliff tops above Buala. John of Carranish is bringing a doctor for De Maton and yourself.'

'I have no need,' Alexander was brusque; 'it is my friend who is gravely wounded.'

Hugh knew better than to argue with his older brother. 'Do we strike tonight, Alexander, or wait until dawn?'

The dark-haired Ballantyne frowned in thought and gazed out to sea. 'How long did the ship's captain say he could wait before setting sail?'

'Tomorrow forenoon,' Hugh replied, 'he has already delayed too long.'

Alexander nodded. 'And how long will it take for all the clan to gather?'

'It will be dark before the men from Carranish and Lochinch are rallied and they will have walked such a way, they will be in no condition for fighting tonight,' Hugh judged.

His older brother accepted his opinion. 'Then we must gather for attack at first dawn. We will shelter in the woods above Culduggan River; God knows,' he added bitterly, 'there are enough empty homes to hide in.'

'Baturin,' he swung round, wincing with pain, 'you must wait here until the doctor arrives and sees to De Maton, then I will send a scout to lead you to Culduggan.'

Baturin protested at being left behind, 'Am I a nursemaid that I am to stay here and tend the Frenchman? No Cossack shall be treated so. These arms itch to be active.'

'And they shall be,' Alexander could not help a smile at his truculent servant, 'we shall campaign together against the Maitlands soon, I promise, Baturin. Now fetch me my horse.'

The old Cossack grumblingly did as he was asked and helped his master into the saddle. Alexander clenched his teeth at the pain that shot through his shoulder as he mounted, but said nothing.

Following Hugh back up the rocky tracks, they found groups of MacQueens huddled in the dark around glowing pieces of peat, their dark plaids pulled over their heads from the rising night wind. Alexander and Hugh went among them instructing each band in the plan of attack. As the word spread they kicked out the small fires and made off towards Culduggan on horseback and foot.

The Ballantynes calculated there were four score men gathered already with more to arrive as the night wore on.

'The Maitlands will be driven from Culduggan or we'll die in the attempt,' Hugh promised Alexander as they rode at the head of the advancing clan.

'We must do nothing to endanger the lives of Katherine or Anne,' the other cautioned, though he was silently pleased at his brother's loyalty. The doubts about him that had crowded his mind in recent days dissolved with one look at the fierce reckless light shining in Hugh's hazel brown eyes.

After two hours in the saddle riding back and forth to guide the men on foot, Alexander was confident they could reach the high dense forests and catch a few hours of sleep before storming Culduggan House. He had already thought out the best way for the advance party to cross the river to the island; not by the usual calmer stretch of water, but from behind, swimming through the fast moving narrower stretch that was all but hidden by ancient overhanging rowans and birch trees. He and Hugh had braved that treacherous neck of water as boys and knew when to let the current carry them and when to strike out for gnarled branches.

For the sake of speed they had taken the main track across the moor; the turning into Culduggan glen was fast approaching. Abruptly, the MacQueen fighting strength ran straight into a garrison patrol, heading back for the fort.

Alexander signalled for the gentry to hold their fire as an officer rode up to him at the head of his small but well-armed contingent. Judging by his uniform, he must be the Captain Leighton that Katherine had spoken about.

'What the devil is going on?' Leighton demanded of the tall imposing Highlander. 'And who are you?'

'I'm Alexander Ballantyne, rightful heir to Culduggan – and these are my kinsmen,' Alexander pointed to the armed men behind him. 'We have no quarrel with you, Captain, and shall let you pass on unhindered, but we have business at Culduggan.'

'The devil you will!' the captain blustered, unnerved by this Highlander's imperious manner. 'You and your brother are wanted for harbouring a French agent. This is as far as you go, Ballantyne, I will not have you causing further trouble for the good Sir Archibald.'

At once, Alexander drew out his pistol and pointed it menacingly at the English officer; immediately Hugh, Buala and Carranish did likewise.

'You are outnumbered, Captain Leighton and it would prove a messy business if we had to fight you here. Any reinforcements from the garrison would come only in time to bury you all,' Alexander's tone was grim. 'You would do better by joining us in rescuing Mistress MacQueen of Penstroun and her kinswoman Anne MacQueen from that knave Sir Archibald. He holds them captive at Culduggan.'

'Lady Penstroun?' Captain Leighton asked incredulously, thinking of the beautiful and courteous woman he had met just a day ago. 'Impossible!'

'Not so,' broke in Hugh hotly, 'he holds them both against their will. They only agreed to be taken to save our lives at Buala–'

'That's enough,' Alexander silenced him; his brother's reckless tongue would be their undoing.

'So you *were* involved in some plot,' Captain Leighton said uneasily, 'you have admitted as much.'

As a soldier, Alexander itched to do battle with the captain now – fight these men who delayed their rescue of Katherine and take the consequences. But instinct told him Leighton was an honourable officer – he had shown instant concern for Katherine and Anne – so he would have to trust him. Better for Katherine and Penstroun to get this man on their side. Quickly he pulled his horse alongside the officer's.

'A word with you alone?' Alexander asked. The captain nodded and they trotted off a short distance. 'I am only concerned for the safety of

Katherine MacQueen and her friend,' he spoke low, 'I am the Lady of Penstroun's guardian. Maitland is a brutal man and I fear he means to force her into a union with his son to gain the lands of Penstroun.'

'Why should I believe a Jacobite?' Captain Leighton replied stiffly, his look wary as he searched the other's face.

Alexander controlled his temper, he thought briefly of De Maton lying in pain in the dark cave and the risks he had taken for them. He mission must not have been in vain. 'You have my word that I will deliver myself up to you for questioning over this so-called plot if you will help in the freeing of Mistress Katherine and her cousin.'

'Let me go and talk to Sir Archibald,' Leighton countered. 'Make him see sense.'

'No,' Alexander was resolute, 'we must take him by surprise. There is no knowing what he will do to the women if he thinks his plan may be thwarted. Also,' he bargained, 'there must be no retaliation taken against either Mistress Katherine or members of her clan. Do we have an agreement, sir?'

Captain Leighton looked into the strong resolute face of his adversary with a twinge of envy. He was struck by the man's fearless loyalty to the young MacQueen heiress. It was useless at this point to challenge the strength of this martial clan, but he might be able to make some political capital out of the situation if he could hand Ballantyne over as a Jacobite plotter.

'And afterwards you will come peaceably?' Leighton asked.

'You have my word,' Alexander said.

'Then I agree,' the officer said curtly, swinging his horse back towards the others, 'but there must be as little bloodshed as possible – no settling of old scores,' he added nervously.

Alexander ignored this. 'With your aid we'll go in tonight rather than wait for the morning,' he smiled grimly, 'I know the layout and shall give the orders.' Before the English officer could argue, the young nobleman rode off to relay the message to his men.

***

Dinner at Culduggan was a strained affair, with Katherine and Anne silently mutinous, hardly touching the food before them. Christina was also subdued and Sybilla excused herself early from the table saying she felt unwell.

Sir Archibald and Hector drank heavily, the latter leering over his stoup of claret at the distant disapproving face of his bride-to-be. He thought she looked bewitching in a plain satin gown of his mother's which bit in at the neckline to show her more ample bosom. Her hair curled in long dark tendrils from her high forehead to her creamy shoulders.

'We shall hold the wedding ceremony tomorrow noon,' Sir Archibald belched slightly over his port and rose to his feet, 'it shall be performed in here with the household present to witness the proceedings.'

'I shall not go through with it,' Katherine spoke up at last and she saw her aunt flinch at her defiant words.

The older Maitland glowered at her, his brown eye bloodshot. 'You will do as you're told if you wish no harm to befall your clansmen. I have only to say the word to the Captain at Fort William and they shall be rounded up like sheep for the slaughter – those that remain on Scottish soil that is,' he laughed spitefully.

'Surely you will not force this union on my niece, sir?' Christina was goaded by the injustice out of her timidity. 'I do not like to see her unhappy,' she mumbled, aware of Hector's piqued look. Her only boy had been so manipulated by his father, she no longer recognised him. His face wore the same petulant cruel look as her husband's and she shrank from his hostile stare.

'Be quiet, woman,' Maitland shouted at his wife, 'what do you know of such things? Just be content that you will soon be living at Penstroun again, though why you feel such attachment to the place I cannot imagine.'

'Perhaps because my aunt was happy when she lived there,' Katherine flashed back, 'and not in terror of her life as she is here.'

She saw Christina flush at her words, but she did not contradict her. Sir Archibald steadied himself against the table, glowering at them both.

'I care little for your opinion,' he slurred, 'marriage is a matter of duty and not happiness. Why can't you women ever see that?'

Unnerved by Katherine's mutinous look he walked unsteadily to the window and looked out. The moonlight came and went behind racing clouds.

Suddenly a shadowy movement caught his attention below. It was as if one of the shaped hedges moved forward and then hunched into a different form. He stared harder and then saw another figure move.

Throwing open the casement window he leaned out and bellowed to his guards. No answering call came back.

'There's something amiss,' he sobered up sharply, 'I'm going below. See that no one enters or leaves this room, Hector,' he commanded and strode from the dining-hall.

Katherine rushed immediately to the open window her heart racing at the thought of deliverance. On the chill wind she caught the sound of shouts and the clash of swords rang out in the dark.

'They have come for us, Anne!' she cried exultantly. 'Up here!' she shouted into the wind. 'We are here!'

A moment later Hector grabbed her arm viciously and pulled her away from the window, banging the casement shut. With a sick dread she felt the press of a cold blade against her throat.

'You shall stay with me, my beauty,' he hissed in her ear, 'do not think of trying to escape.'

Katherine looked about her wildly, but saw there were other guards at the door outnumbering the women.

'Leave her be,' cried Anne, shocked out of numbness.

'Sit down both of you,' Hector hissed at Anne and his mother, 'and no one will be harmed.'

***

MacQueen men lay dead from the first fierce clash with Maitlands' retainers on the far bank of Culduggan River. But the paid mercenaries did not fight with the same fire as the attacking clansmen and many had fled into the woods above. Throwing off his plaid, Alexander had led his force into the icy waters. He had not realised how weak the wound in his shoulder had left him until the current tore his pistol away and he nearly drowned. But Hugh had come swiftly to his aid, carrying him with his own broad frame. Captain Leighton's troops stood waiting on the far side to cut off any escaping Maitlands.

As Alexander had judged, the guards on the island had been completely surprised by the MacQueen men emerging like a pack of wet and baying hounds from the treacherous stretch of river north of the tower.

With Hugh fighting ferociously at his side, Alexander fought his way round to the back entrance. For a tantalisingly brief moment he thought he heard Katherine's voice calling to him from a window far above, the contrary moon catching the gleam of a woman's face and then it was gone. Whether or not he hallucinated, Alexander knew it spurred him on the more despite the fire of pain that consumed him.

He prayed that the old door leading from his mother's kitchen garden had not been walled up. While the men from Lochinch made an assault on the front entrance, he planned to lead the elite swordsmen of Buala and Carranish in at the back.

'It's still here!' he cried and beckoned to his sturdy Cossack, thankful that the bear-like Baturin had caught up with them in time. 'Put your shoulder against this,' he ordered, slashing at the brambles which hid it.

But the thick door would not budge. Hugh, in desperation, took several men with him to lift a wind-fallen tree and carry it back to the door. With Herculean effort they threw themselves behind the trunk and battered the old door. After two attempts it splintered and they broke in.

Up the back stairs they pounded meeting only startled kitchen servants who screamed and fled before them. At the top, where the old stairway joined the entrance to the great hall a group of armed men stood in their way, protecting the squat bullish figure of Sir Archibald. As the raiders emerged out of the dark, Alexander saw the shock on Maitland's ravaged face.

'I, Culduggan, have returned at last!' the young Ballantyne heir crowed and went on the attack, knocking Maitland's raised pistol from his hand.

There was an ear-splitting din as the gun went off and the bullet struck the floor. Maitland dodged behind one of his guards and unsheathed his sword. The two bands clashed in combat, engaging each other at close quarters with swords and dirks. Alexander beat his enemy back into the lofty hall, left unused since his father's day except by the hounds that fouled its corners. Soon the chamber was ringing with the clang of blade on blade as the Ballantyne brothers took the advantage, spurred on by the thought of their warrior ancestors. Carranish and his men had the upper hand in the entrance way. Maitland's men were dropping their arms in fright at the sight of an enraged Cossack hacking his way into the hall.

Suddenly Maitland slipped and fell to the floor, his face grey and sweating from the exertions, hardly able to breathe.

'Where is she?' Alexander panted, his sword to the other's throat.

'Upstairs in the dining-room with Hector,' he gasped, 'please spare me – I'll bargain with you.'

The young Highlander looked at him in disgust, thinking how little mercy this man had shown to any of his family. 'You'll bargain with no man,' he replied through gritted teeth, his scar livid against his cheek, 'get up and fight me for Culduggan.'

'Look out, Alexander!' Hugh cried from behind and half turning the older brother glimpsed one of Maitland's men lunging. A swiping blow to his wounded shoulder sent him reeling in agony to the floor. In a flash, Maitland scrambled up and reached for his discarded sword to finish off the nobleman while he lay sprawled and unarmed.

On the point of plunging his sword, Sir Archibald was rammed out of the way by Baturin's huge bulk. The blade swung down and stuck in the wooden floor. Maitland howled in fury and tugged at the weapon to free it. But Alexander, with one last effort, got to his knees, pulled back his right fist and swung at his enemy, catching him full on the jaw.

Sir Archibald's head snapped back. A look of surprise rippled across face and then it froze into a ghastly grimace as he toppled forward onto the half prone Highlander. As he hit the floor his eye patch sprung off his face revealing the scarred hollow. He lay still; the eye socket puckered as if in a grisly wink. He was out cold.

Baturin drew out his dagger to finish him off.

'No,' Alexander panted, 'leave him. Let him rot in Leighton's gaol.'

Hugh came breathlessly to Alexander, 'It's over, brother; the others are defeated or throwing down their arms.'

'Katherine,' Alexander rasped, his mind fighting off the faintness that threatened to envelope him, 'she's still in Hector's hands.'

Hugh and Baturin helped him to his feet and supported him to the door. As they reached the entrance again a tall figure emerged on the stairwell in a rustle of satin. Alexander saw Katherine standing before him, her dark hair loose about her neck and shoulders, her eyes wide with shock.

'You are alive?' she whispered, her throat tense with anxiety, staring at the wounded man before her, held up by his Cossack comrade.

Alexander gave a ghost of a smile and nodded. Then his face clouded. 'Where is Hector?'

Katherine came forward, a glint of triumph in her eyes. 'We have him bound upstairs with linen cloths,' she announced. 'Sybilla tricked him into thinking she would help guard us and then kicked him between the legs, so he was good for nothing but yelping. She has some brave MacQueen blood in her after all. My men have Hector now.'

'My brave Katya,' Alexander gasped in admiration.

Hugh laughed, euphoric at their success. Timid steps sounded beyond and Anne appeared in the dim torchlight.

'Hugh,' she gasped in shock, 'I thought you were dead.' She ran to him and buried her head in his chest, bursting into tears.

'Thank God you are safe,' he stroked her fair hair and kissed her forehead, bringing his arms about her. Katherine flushed to see their open demonstration of love and slid Alexander a look.

'We shall deliver Hector and his father into Captain Leighton's hands,' Alexander said, light-headed with pain, 'he waits patiently on the riverbank.'

'Captain Leighton?' Katherine asked incredulously. 'Have you not taken a great risk by involving him? He wanted to arrest you ...'

Her words died as she saw Alexander's grim exhausted look, his handsome eyes glancing away from hers.

'Hugh,' he touched his brother's arm, 'you must make your way immediately to the ship. We shall keep the garrison troops occupied here tonight, but it is too risky for you to remain. De Maton might not live to see France again and you must be our envoy to the French.'

'Not now that Maitland is defeated,' protested Hugh, 'I cannot leave Culduggan.'

'You put Katherine's life in danger if you stay,' Alexander said hardening himself to his young brother's appeal, 'you are still branded as a Jacobite.'

'Then I shall go with you,' Anne declared and fixed him with steady blue eyes. 'Now father is dead, I would rather go into exile with you, Hugh, than live in the fear of never seeing you again.' Hugh stared back at her, too overcome to speak his thanks.

'Then go now, the two of you,' Alexander urged, the last of his strength ebbing away, 'and God speed.'

'And you, Alexander?' Katherine fretted.

'If I am not there by the turn of the tide tomorrow,' he told Hugh, 'you must sail without me, do you understand?'

Hugh clasped his tall brother in a swift embrace, knowing that he did not intend going with them. Anne and Katherine hugged one another tight in farewell; the older girl's heart weighed heavy at the thought of losing another close friend so soon.

'I pray for your safe passage to France,' Katherine kissed the young girl and pushed her gently away. Numbly she watched the two figures disappear down the stairs and out of sight.

'Katherine,' Alexander spoke her name gently and looking at him she saw the vivid shining of his eyes. 'Let us waste no more time denying our feelings for each other. Come to me, my heart's love.' He held out his good arm to her, the left one limp and bloodied by his side. She came to him and slipped her arms around his neck, clinging to him fiercely.

'Oh Alexander, I was so afraid for you,' she whispered and kissed his scarred jaw.

He tilted her chin up and gazed into her green eyes, brushing away the brimming tears with his fingers.

'And I for you,' he answered, barely audible. Crooking her head in his hand he bent and kissed her tenderly on the lips, feeling strength flowing from her into his limbs. 'Whatever happens, Katherine,' his voice made hoarse with the throbbing pain in his shoulder, 'always be assured of my love for you. I am at peace knowing the Maitlands cannot harm you anymore. What I must do now I also do to ensure Penstroun remains yours.'

'I don't understand,' Katherine's heart froze at the warning in his voice, 'do you plan to follow Hugh and Anne? I can't bear the thought of you not being with me. I love you so much, Alexander.'

Below, a loud hammering began on the main door which the MacQueens had bolted to stop any escape attempt by Hector Maitland. Katherine whipped round as the huge oak door was freed and saw the red coats of Captain Leighton's men stream onto the stairs.

'You bargained with him, didn't you?' Katherine whispered in distress.

Alexander pulled her to him and kissed her once more with a desperate passion that confirmed the awful truth. She clung to him, her body convulsed in dry sob, knowing he was about to be taken from her again. How could she bear it? His vivid blue eyes held hers proudly as he gently pushed her towards his servant.

'Take care of my beloved Katya,' he told Baturin. Kissing her hand, he said, 'my brave, Katherine, your love gives me the courage to face them.' Then he turned abruptly from her stricken face.

'Tell them the truth,' Katherine sobbed after him, 'that you had nothing to do with any plot. Promise me!'

The broad-shouldered Highlander did not glance back or reply to her plea as he descended to meet Captain Leighton. Yet her words echoed after him, dream-like in his light-headed state and warmed his heavy heart.

'I'll wait for you always,' Katherine called in a strong voice, 'Stand Fast, Alexander!'

EPILOGUE

Edinburgh
March 10th 1703

My dear Katherine,

I have at last reached Scotland having wintered with Elspeth in Konigsberg. I left Moscow as quickly as we could on hearing the grave news of Alexander's uncertain fate and your terrible ordeals. Dearest child; would that I could be at Penstroun to comfort you now, but it is important that I remain to press for Ballantyne's release. My brother-in-law, Sir John, is a privy councillor and advocate here in Edinburgh and having heard of the young Culduggan's bravery on your behalf is determined to represent him.

Such strange revelations came to light before leaving Muscovy concerning your cousin Hector Maitland; it leaves me in little doubt of his blighted character. These things I cannot reveal to you in a letter, but look forward to your imminent arrival in Edinburgh for Hector's trial. The cowardly Sir Archibald has disappeared to the Low Countries and left his son to his fate.

I am impatient to embrace you again. May God bless you.

Ewen Putulo

***

Penstroun
May 1st 1703

My dearest Alexander,

It grieves me that I was unable to visit you when in Edinburgh last month, though my thoughts are with you constantly. As you may have heard, Hector was found guilty of abducting me and of a variety of smuggling offences. But the most despicable act of all was connected with my father's death.

Natalya Matrapov had been plagued by doubt over your guilt in the murder, knowing that Hector had indeed left her house briefly on that fateful night. He must have overheard your plan to meet with my father – I had a strong feeling of someone else being in the room that night and wish I had acted upon it. After making certain enquiries, the coun-

tess discovered that Hector's sly friend, Rupert Crocker, had also been seen at the Scottish Hostelry and my father had talked to him after leaving your room. Witnesses were found who heard Crocker's threats and heard a gun go off shortly afterwards.

After interrogation by the Russians, Crocker confessed to the chief's murder, saying that he had been a spy in the pay of the British government and was trying to prevent my father from bringing you home to Scotland. He rightly suspected my father was the figurehead for a Jacobite rising in the Highlands. It appears Crocker was blackmailing Hector for information on Chief James's movements and paying him richly too. Hector was an easy target because he had boasted to Crocker that he had been sent abroad by Sir Archibald after assaulting the former boatman's daughter at Culduggan. The poor girl gave evidence against him too. What a despicable pair those Maitlands are!

My father, of course, had no inkling of Hector's blackguardly behaviour and believed his nephew sympathetic to the cause so dear to his heart – that of the Stuart restoration.

Dearest Alexander, I'm sure you suspected Hector's involvement all along, didn't you? Was it to protect your brother and my Jacobite clansmen at home that you would not speak to save yourself in Moscow? How proud my father would have been of you, Culduggan. Whatever your feelings towards the Countess Natalya, you must be grateful for her intervention. She has indeed proved a friend to us all.

My dear stepfather is with me now and we await news of your trial daily. My aunt and cousin Sybilla are staying with us for the moment – it would amuse you to see how Aunt Christina blossoms under the attention of the good doctor. We all pray for your deliverance.

Adieu, my dearest heart.

Your Katya.

***

Penstroun
May 30th 1703

From the cliff path, Katherine gazed down at the empty shingle beach where the loch met the sea and breathed in the salty freshness as the spray fizzed on the rocks. The sun burst through the clouds at intervals to warm her face and neck, her hair whipped back in the breeze against the soft woollen plaid of scarlet and moss green.

In the distance along the shore she could see the beaches at Buala glinting like pale gold, washed clean long ago of the blood and treachery that had stained its pure sands the previous terrible autumn. As always when she took this path, her spirits rose with the buffeting wind and she felt strong enough to face the uncertain future.

Wheeling her horse round, her breath caught in her chest at the sight of a rider drumming towards her across the moor, swerving the white patches of bog cotton. Was this news of Alexander at last? Katherine tensed, hardly daring to hope. She gripped the reins of her stout pony and waited, straining to make out the advancing figure.

When the horseman was a hundred paces away, something in the powerful frame and the glint of auburn in his dark hair, made her heart jump painfully in her breast.

'Alexander?' she gulped and kicked her horse into a trot. Moments later he had reached her, the strong chiselled face pale and gaunt, but the wry smile unmistakeably his.

He slipped from his horse and came to her, grasping Katherine around the waist and pulling her down to him. For a moment she clung to him in choked silence, hardly able to believe she held the flesh so dear to her.

Katherine looked up into his eyes, more startlingly blue than the sky above. 'You are free?' she whispered tearfully.

Alexander nodded. 'Thanks to your step-father and Sir John,' he smiled. 'There was insufficient evidence to convict me of treason. No one believed a word the prisoner Maitland said.'

Katherine hugged him again, 'I am so happy, so very happy,' and the tears of relief coursed down her cheeks.

Alexander took her arm and they walked back towards the point, too overcome to speak. After their initial exultation at seeing each other, Katherine agonised that what she had to say might force him abroad again. She braced herself.

'Hugh and Anne are safe in France,' Katherine tried to control her trembling. 'They are to be married this summer.'

'That is good news indeed.' He scrutinised her. 'But there is something else – what is wrong? Tell me, Katherine.'

Tears stung her eyes. 'I'm afraid your dear friend De Maton did not survive the voyage home.'

She saw his face tense with sadness; he turned away and did not speak for several minutes. Katherine forced herself to go on. 'Hugh says there will be no invasion plan this summer.'

'So he must remain in exile once again?' Alexander sounded full of despair.

Katherine nodded unhappily. 'But he wants you to join him in France and be brothers in arms.'

He gave her a sharp look.

'Is that what you want, Alexander?' Katherine questioned. When he did not reply, her heart plunged. 'It appears your fighting skills are in demand,' she tried to make light of her misery. 'My stepfather tells me Tsar Peter has granted you a full pardon and wishes you to return to serve him in Muscovy.'

'Yes, I have the pardon with me.'

Katherine glanced at him from under heavy lids. Was there excitement in his look? Perhaps he would always be a mercenary at heart, thirsting for adventure and would never be content to live peaceably in his homeland.

'I am of age now,' she spoke with dignity, 'and you are no longer tied to me as my guardian. You are free to leave Penstroun if that is what you wish.' She held his look.

Alexander saw the down turn of her full lips that belied her defiant look. 'I'm thankful to be released from my duties as guardian,' he admitted.

Katherine blushed and turned away. 'Then I will not stand in your way of going to join Hugh or returning to serve Tsar Peter. Though I cannot deny that I will miss you sorely, Alexander.'

'I'm pleased to hear it.' He gave a half-smile as he placed his hands on her shoulders and pulled her around.

'Listen Katherine; with Sir Archibald fled and Hector in prison, the lands of Culduggan will be restored to the Ballantynes. It was generous of you to give Christina and Sybilla a home at Penstroun,' he said, tracing a finger down Katherine's cheek. It was the image of her beautiful face that had kept him from despair at his incarceration in an Edinburgh goal. 'As Ballantyne of Culduggan my wish is to remain here, close to you,' he smiled at her tenderly. 'How could you doubt it?'

Katherine searched his face. 'So you honestly have no wish to join Hugh in France or continue soldiering and making your fortune in Muscovy?' She held her breath.

'My fortune was made the night I met Katya, the dancing peasant girl,' he murmured as he pulled her to him and bent his face to hers. 'And my happiness would be complete if she would agree to marry me.'

'Marry?' Katherine gasped.

'I wanted to ask you long ago in Moscow – that fateful evening at your house I was about to propose – but my intentions were thwarted by tragedy.'

Katherine's heart pounded at the words she had longed to hear, a joyful laugh escaping her lips. 'Oh, I agree, Alexander!' she cried and threw her arms about his neck, kissing him roundly on the lips.

He gave a cry of exultation.

They came together in a fierce embrace, holding onto each other as if they would never let go again. Katherine wept with happiness, her insides melting at his loving robust kisses. She was home and Alexander had come back to her.

Above, the gulls circled and called over the cliffs of Penstroun as the sun bathed them in golden light, like a blessing from the ancestors. Never again would they be parted. Katherine was never so sure of anything in her life. She would love this handsome, fierce and tender Highlander till the end of time.

The End

If you have enjoyed HIGHLANDER IN MUSCOVY, you might like to read another of The Scottish Romance Collection -
THE JACOBITE LASS: A stirring and passionate story inspired by Scottish heroine Flora MacDonald

Scotland, 1722: on a remote and windswept Scottish island an enigmatic poetess foretells tragedy for the proud MacDonalds of Clanranald and the birth of an extraordinary child. That child is the passionate and free-spirited Flora, daughter of Marion. Flora's early years are spent roaming around her father's cattle farm, running wild and free with her brother and his friends. From early on she adores fair Neil MacEachen. But when her father dies suddenly, Flora and her mother are plunged into poverty and it seems beautiful Flora is destined to skivvy in the kitchen and dairy for her harsh aunt. Until one night dashing soldier, One-eyed Hugh, her mother's former lover, kidnaps mother and daughter and takes them to Skye.

Back on the Outer Isles, Flora is groomed as companion to the chief's daughter. She is still in love with childhood sweetheart, elusive Jacobite, Neil, yet finds herself irresistibly drawn to dark-haired, teasing and passionate Allan of Kingsburgh, one of the mighty Skye MacDonalds, who makes no secret of his desire for her.

Before affairs of the heart can be resolved, the exiled Prince Charles Stuart lands on the Outer Isles in his bid to win back the crown and his arrival ignites the Jacobite Rising of 1745. Scotland is plunged into bloody civil war; families and clans are torn apart in their loyalties and Flora's life is changed forever. The fate of a fugitive prince is in her hands. Will she risk everything for the sake of those she loves?

Deeply emotional and uplifting, THE JACOBITE LASS is set in the turbulent times of 18th century Scotland and is based on the true story of Scottish heroine, Flora MacDonald.

Extract from the beginning of THE JACOBITE LASS

Chapter 1
Benbecula, Outer Isles of Scotland, 1722

'Tell me,' Marion urged, watching Mairi's expression like a hawk. 'Is it to be another son?'

The girl's silence was infuriating, unsettling. She sucked on her plump lower lip as she stared at the dregs in the delicate china teacup. But the bard's daughter would not be hurried.

Marion glanced out of the parlour window, anxious that her husband Milton would not catch her dabbling in such superstition; the men were cutting the hay. No doubt her eldest boy Ranald would be running around getting in the way, grabbing at their scythes. His hair was the colour of ripened corn and words flew out of his mouth like swifts; her darling boy. Her younger son Angus followed Ranald about like his small dark shadow.

'No,' Mairi finally said, giving Marion a bold look, 'you are carrying a lass.'

Marion sank back in her chair. Why did she feel sudden disappointment? A girl would be a companion for her in later years and her elderly husband would be overjoyed; a daughter to wipe away his grief at losing his first wife and baby girl so long ago.

'She will be bonny and brave,' Mairi continued in her low mesmerising voice. 'This lass will bring you joy and heartache in equal measure. She will be known for her courage and beauty far beyond the Long Isle – even far beyond the mainland of Scotland.'

'Oh enough!' Marion gave a nervous laugh and stood up. 'You are just trying to flatter me. I can't believe in such nonsense. Tea leaves tell us nothing except the strength of the tea.'

Mairi kept staring at her – the girl had the most extraordinary eyes – one pale blue, one hazel brown.

'I don't need the leaves to see what is to come. It is there in my mind's eye. Sometimes I wish it wasn't.'

Marion was unnerved by the girl's intense look and strange words. She wanted her gone. It was her lively cook Janet who had brought her in for Marion's amusement, distracting her from a dozen housekeeping chores.

'If you go to the kitchen, Janet will give you cheese to take home to your father.'

She crossed the bedroom that doubled as her parlour, already thinking ahead to tomorrow's butter churning and the supplies that needed taking up to the summer pastures. Perhaps the boys could go too; their fizzing energy and the pregnancy were tiring her out.

'You will have other sons,' Mairi said, following her across to the window. 'And daughters too.'

'That's hardly likely–' Marion checked herself. Her husband Milton still came eagerly to her bed, yet he was growing old and already had heirs. But that was none of the girl's business.

Abruptly, Mairi reached out and placed a hand firmly around Marion's swelling belly beneath the loose gown. The baby fluttered under her touch. 'But this one you carry now will be the brightest star, outshining them all.'

Startled, Marion flinched away, slapping at the girl's hand. 'You impertinent child; you have no right to touch me.'

Mairi's look turned insolent. 'I'm no child,' she smirked, with a toss of red ringlets. 'And we MacVurichs have just as much royal blood in our veins as you MacDonalds.'

Marion snorted. 'The blood of tinkers more likely.'

Mairi gasped in offence.

The remark was out before Marion could stop herself, but it was the girl's fault for goading her. Marion was proud of her heritage and would not be compared to the family of their lowly tenants. She was descended from the Lord of the Isles through her minister father and from Robert the Bruce, King of Scots, through her mother's family. That was why, eight years ago, a powerful man of the Clanranald clan, Ranald MacDonald of Balivanich and Milton – known by all as Milton – had taken her for his second wife, despite her shameful condition.

Thinking of Milton now made Marion's stomach lurch. Her husband would have no truck with superstitious tea-readings and it did not take much to ignite his temper. He might be as old as her father but he had the energy and impatience of a man half his years.

'I'm sorry if I offended you,' Marion said, 'but you must go now.'

MacVurich's daughter narrowed her eyes. 'You may think you are better than me, Mistress Milton, but for all your boasting of being the kin of the high and mighty MacDonalds, you are as fearful as a mouse.'

'How dare you!'

'I dare,' Mairi hissed, 'because I will be a famous bardess and powerful men will fall under the spell of my words, while you will always be frightened of losing the men you love.' She gave a cold smile. 'Keep a watch on your husband, Mistress Milton.'

'Get out!' Marion gasped. 'My husband will make sure you never set foot in this house again.'

Mairi pulled her homespun plaid over her wavy hair in a gesture of contempt for her hostess. 'No one insults a MacVurich.' She stalked to the door and flung it open. Turning, she jabbed a finger in fury. 'I curse your two boys!' she cried. 'May the salt waters of the Minch be their cold grave!'

Marion stood stunned, gulping for breath. The sound of the girl's bare feet stamping on the wooden staircase died away. She pulled back quickly from the casement window in case Mairi MacVurich should look up with her evil stare as she left Balivanich House. As she hid in the shadows, shaking with fear and anger, Marion felt her unborn stir.

She placed a swift hand over her belly. '*Please* be a boy,' she whispered, 'and prove that witch wrong.'

Back came a defiant kick and Marion let go a sigh of relief.

***

Janet welcomes comments and feedback on her stories. If you would like to do so, you can contact her through her website:

www.janetmacleodtrotter.com

Printed in Great Britain
by Amazon

20285309R00119